TONIGHT the brilliant .... tion of this fascinating foreign city, all combined to keep Nathaniel wakeful. And being wakeful, he began to think rather too obsessively of the enigmatic young woman already residing under his roof as governess.

She was an urchin, a wanderer, a self-willed, probably amoral creature. He had been aware of her sexuality the moment he had met her. In spite of her youth she possessed wiles of which he was sure she was perfectly aware, the sudden awakening of those large sulky eyes into brilliance, the secret half smile, the transformation from torpidity into animation. Her complexion was so different from Amelia, who was pure *famille rose*. Perhaps that was what he was going to find intriguing about the situation, this serene wife on one hand, and on the other this strange girl with her childishly bony shoulders, her gaucheness, her apparent anxiety to please, and then the surprise of her swift knowledgeable gaze.

It was wrong, but he could not stop thinking about her. . . .

Dorothy Eden

The Time
of the
Dragon

A FAWCETT CREST BOOK

Fawcett Publications, Inc., Greenwich, Connecticut

THE TIME OF THE DRAGON

THIS BOOK CONTAINS THE COMPLETE TEXT OF THE
ORIGINAL HARDCOVER EDITION.

A Fawcett Crest Book reprinted by arrangement with Coward-
McCann & Geoghegan

ISBN 0–449–23059–7

Alternate Selection of the Literary Guild

Printed in the United States of America

First printing: January 1977

10 9 8 7 6 5 4 3 2 1

Dragon House, Peking

November, 1899

Chapter 1

Amelia, usually so certain of clothes, and not having too much personal vanity anyway, changed her mind twice about what to wear to the ladies' tea party at the Winter Palace.

Neither she nor Nathaniel had set foot within the sacred precincts of the Forbidden City. The stories that reached them about that formidable figure, the Empress Dowager of China, the great Tz'u-Hsi, the Dragon Empress, were sufficient to make the boldest foreigner a little nervous of being actually admitted to that awesome presence. It was said that the Empress watched unmoved when the death sentence on any unfortunate subject who had offended her was carried out. A powerful eunuch beheaded the crouching, trembling offender with one stroke of his axe, and the courtyard, one of the innumerable courtyards of the Imperial City, ran with blood.

As the white doves fluttered overhead, and the cool breezes stirred the almond blossom, the audience stood with impeccably folded hands, until the Empress rose and made her stately return indoors. Justice was done. The spirit of the criminal had gone to its ancestors a little more prematurely than had been intended, that was all.

It was the French Revolution and the grisly spectators around the guillotine all over again. All the Empress Tz'u-Hsi lacked was a pair of knitting needles and a piece of knitting. But her exaggeratedly long fingernails were encased in turquoise and jade shields. She could never have accomplished anything so homely as a piece of knitting. It was said that she didn't even feed herself, but was fed by kneeling servants.

"Human nature," said Amelia, speaking half to herself, "can be so frightening. It can have depths. You must just hope never to stir them up."

"Are you speaking of the natives, madam?" asked Cassidy, her elderly maid. Cassidy was British to the bone marrow, and always referred to the inhabitants of any foreign country as natives. It seemed to her a suitably derogatory expression.

"The Chinese, Cassidy. My husband says the Oriental mind is the most unfathomable of all. They are a delightful people, but one must accept their sudden outbursts of cruelty. It's simply their nature."

"All those bound feet," muttered Cassidy. "Tottering like cripples."

"Not the Manchus. The Empress Dowager hasn't got bound feet. And I do agree, it's a barbarous custom. My brother-in-law is campaigning against it in Shansi. But reforms take time, and there's always the point that Western civilization isn't perfect either."

"If you'll just make up your mind about what you're going to wear, madam," Cassidy said patiently. "You said the green silk, but now you tell me to put it away."

"Yes, I've suddenly realised that the throne room, or wherever it is we are taking tea, will be full of colour. You know how the Chinese love red lacquer and brilliant things. If I wear the dark blue taffeta at least I won't clash with anything. And my pearls."

"I've put your pearls out, madam. And your gloves and fan and handkerchief and bead bag. Or would you prefer the silver bag?"

"No, the bead will do nicely. I expect the ladies of all the legations will be there. Imagine. Eleven languages! I can cope with French and a little German, but otherwise we will just have to bow and smile at one another. Next week I intend to begin learning Manchu, otherwise how can I ever talk to the servants? I'm sure the cook is cheating me. We couldn't have used seventy eggs last week, even though Ching says Chinese eggs are 'welly small.'"

Cassidy sniffed, her dour face expressing no surprise.

"It's a game with them, madam. They think the foreign devil is here to be cheated."

"But they do it so charmingly. And they adore the children."

"Crafty," said Cassidy. "I wouldn't trust them an inch. Those yellow faces hide secrets, you believe me."

"I'm quite prepared to believe that the Empress Dowager's does. After all, we're uninvited guests in her country. She couldn't possibly have wanted eleven foreign legations crouched round the gates of the Celestial City like a lot of watchdogs."

"If they can make you pay for seventy eggs a week, they'll be happy enough to keep you here," Cassidy said shrewdly.

"My husband says it's important not to let my cook lose face. I have to learn that essential art. After all, we've only been here six weeks. Do you think the children are happy?"

Cassidy sniffed. "They're being spoiled rotten by that Chinese amah. Master Georgie loves being called Small Master, and Miss Henrietta and Miss Lucy giggle every time they're called Missy. They're beginning to give orders, if you please."

"Are they, indeed? I know we should have brought a governess out. But my husband assured me we would find a satisfactory one here. There are always legation staff sending their children home to school or going home themselves, and leaving the odd unattached female who wants to stay in Peking. But so far we haven't found the right one. I may hear of someone this afternoon. Anyway, it isn't doing the children any harm to have a holiday from lessons. Let them get acclimatized. And speaking of that, Cassidy, how are you getting acclimatized yourself?"

"Peking isn't Henley on Thames, madam."

"But don't you find it rather refreshing?"

"All those faces like lemons," Cassidy said. "Looks as if they all have yellow jaundice."

"I expect they think we're pretty colourless."

"We're British, madam, and they'd better not have the cheek. I don't know what you're going to do when your perfume is used up," Cassidy added, sprinkling some drops on a lacy white handkerchief. "You'll never buy this kind here."

"Then I'll have to educate my husband to like another kind. Or I can send to Paris for some more. Don't dwell on trivialities, Cassidy."

Nathaniel had bought her that particular scent on their honeymoon in Paris ten years ago. She had kept it, and, associating it with happiness, had used it ever since. It was foolish of her not to have brought a larger bottle. But she hadn't been able to think of everything in the haste of departure. It had happened so suddenly. Nathaniel's father, James Carrington, who had lived in this house, with its fascinating series of rooms and courtyards, had died unexpectedly, leaving the Peking end of his business vacant. He had been one of the great authorities on Chinese ceramics, jades and ivories, and had exported them judiciously to Europe where Nathaniel in London and his brother Edmund in Brussels looked after an imposing list of rich customers.

Mr. Carrington had said he was only scratching the surface of the market. China was bursting with the art of centuries. For instance, there were numberless royal tombs near the Great Wall that would one day yield up their treasures.

In the meantime numerous commercially-minded merchants were anxious to sell their T'ang tomb horses and their jade carvings of water buffalo or carp or little short-legged Mongol ponies to the Western world. Haggling over prices was a subtle art in itself, and one which they much enjoyed.

Nathaniel wanted to buy for museums as well as for private customers. His laudable reasons were that he was making Europe and America aware of the endless subtleties and beauties of Chinese culture. Making money in the process was something to be regarded as a bonus. It enabled him to buy his wife French perfume and the sort of clothes necessary for a royal reception. He wanted nothing less than the best for Amelia and his children. They provided the right decorative background for him, and naturally he loved them as well. He thought that Amelia had the delicate colouring of Ch'ien Lung *famille rose*. One day he meant to have his whole family painted by one of the best Chinese artists. Fine brush strokes on silk was the way he saw them. He would never have dreamed of coming on the long journey to China and leaving them at home. He wouldn't have cared to live alone, anyway. He liked the comforts of home life. Perhaps they would stay here for several years, if they settled down happily. He was finding the buying end of the market, the endless treasure hunt, much more absorbing than the selling one.

It was late in the year 1899, and one felt, although it was only a different figure on a calendar, that the new century, the twentieth, must bring changes. But not to British supremacy in the world. That was unlikely and unthinkable.

Amelia, in any case, would have refused to be left at home. Apart from keeping together as a family, which she thought intensely important, her only sister Lilian was married to an English missionary, Thomas Beddow, who ran a Protestant mission in the province of Shansi. After the winter was over—and winters were bitterly cold in that part of China—Amelia and Nathaniel intended to make the long journey by train, "the firecart" as the Chinese nervously called it, to visit Lilian and her husband. Thomas was a devout, almost fanatical Christian whom Amelia privately thought would like to have been one of the old Christian martyrs. She had never understood why Lilian had fallen in love with him. He loved the whole world so much that one fancied his far-off gaze never rested consciously on individuals. One hoped this was not so, both for Lilian's and their child's sake. They had one small daughter named Angel. Thomas thought this a beautiful and entirely appropriate name. Amelia wondered how the child could live up to it. Henrietta and Lucy had their own conviction that the as yet unmet Angel must be awful, and Georgie was sure she had wings. He couldn't wait to view such a wondrous sight.

Any thought of Georgie, her only son, made Amelia's lips soften with tenderness and amusement. He was such an original little boy, gap-toothed, naughty, eager, funny. He looked adorable in the padded Chinese coat she had bought him for the colder weather. She could never resist spoiling him a little, although she dearly loved her daughters, too, Henrietta who, as the eldest, took herself so seriously, and shy, blond Lucy.

She was a very fortunate woman, even if she wondered at times how much Nathaniel loved her. She had reason to suspect it was not as much as she loved him, although a man apparently lived by different rules. She tried to accept that and dismiss an old unhappiness from her mind. Not so old, really. Only last year. Not long enough ago for the shock to have entirely worn off.

She had welcomed the trip to Peking as an escape from the house which, for a while, would hold unhappy associations. She would have forgotten them by the time they returned. She and Nathaniel would be closer than ever.

Anyway, she much preferred her lively, passionate husband to the intense dedicated man her sister had married. Imagine never to wear a Paris gown and sprinkle herself with expensive perfume. Imagine always singing hymns and saying prayers. How did the Chinese, with their love of beauty, like the dour missionaries? Not that the peasants' desperately poor world held much beauty, but they would probably deny that. They had the sky, the wind, the water, the willow trees, the egrets returning in the spring, the fluttering doves and hoopoes, the distant golden roof of a Buddhist temple, the incredible green of the paddy fields.

Already, after only six weeks in Peking, Amelia was certain she was going to love both this vast strange country and its inhabitants. She had been reading poetry written a thousand years ago. *There are shadows in the blue pavilion of the dancers. And music rising and falling. . . .*

And the legends were fascinating. The children were particularly interested in the story that the willow tree was a wizard. He must come alive at night, Georgie said, pointing wonderingly to the willow hanging over the pool in the courtyard, and go stumping about on wooden legs, casting his spells.

It was an old willow, gnarled, crooked, its yellowing leaves dropping into the dark water. When its long drooping strands shivered in the wind, sensitive, imaginative Lucy shivered, too, so Amelia refrained from telling another legend that the beautiful shaggy white and gold chrysanthemums were the ghosts of dead children. Anyway, that was not a story for children. But to her it was poignant and beautiful. While Nathaniel searched dedicatedly for his Ming and Sung vases and ancient pottery figures, she was becoming absorbed in stories and words and phrases. *Sleep with the lily hands.* . . . She didn't sleep well. She was not very strong. Phrases like these comforted her during the long nights.

Living in Peking, she thought, was going to be an exciting and beautiful experience.

This afternoon the Empress Dowager's tea party would be one of its highlights and how fortunate she was to be invited. The little square-figured Manchu queen gave few receptions to foreigners nowadays. It was rumoured that, encouraged by her nephew Prince Tuan, and her government, the Tsungli Yamen, she was developing a hostile attitude towards the "barbarians" who, ever since the notorious Opium Wars, had taken up uninvited residence in her country, all of them with their own private interests which had nothing to do with the good of the Chinese people.

The members of the eleven legations called themselves the Corps Diplomatique, Nathaniel informed Amelia. After the tea party today the American minister and his wife, the Congers, were giving a reception at the American legation. She would be meeting the husbands of the women who had been honoured by the royal tea party. The German minister, Baron von Ketteler, the Russian, de Giers, the Frenchman, Pichon, the American, Mr. Conger, who, although he denied territorial ambitions for America, was unwilling to have his country excluded from commercial interests. Amelia had already met Sir Claude MacDonald, the British minister, a handsome Scotsman with exaggerated, waxed moustaches, and his wife, Lady MacDonald, mother of two small children. She and Nathaniel had been cordially welcomed at the British Legation. It was so good to have more people of one's own kind in Peking, Lady MacDonald had confided to Amelia. There were always shady businessmen looking for a sharp deal in opium or guns. But James Carrington had been a friend, and it was good to have his son and his family here. Perhaps they could share picnics and visits to their summer residence at Waiheiwai where they took the children in the heat of June and July. Peking was quite unbearable when the summer was at its height.

This was all so utterly different from her previous quiet life in the Thames valley, twenty miles from London, that Amelia could still scarcely believe it. She certainly could not believe that this afternoon she would curtsey to the Empress of China. Did one curtsey or prostrate oneself? She must ask Nathaniel. She couldn't risk getting her head slashed off for irreverence or impropriety.

Nathaniel came in as Cassidy was fastening her pearls. He nodded to Cassidy who, like the well-trained servant she was, withdrew.

"Stand up and let me look at you," he said. His critical eyes went over Amelia as she stood obediently. He gave her skirt an expert twitch. He liked to think he was a connoisseur of women's clothes.

"That's nice," he said. "But you always look just the thing."

"Do I? I've changed my mind half a dozen times about what to wear. But I did think one shouldn't try to outshine the royal apartments, or indeed the Empress herself."

"Now that would be impossible. She'll be wearing one of those fantastically embroidered Chinese robes that nobody could compete with. And you will look like a princess among, I predict, a lot of badly dressed Europeans."

Amelia felt the delight course through her veins. Since last year she had needed this kind of assurance.

"Really, Nathaniel. You'll make me vain."

"Quite right. A beautiful woman should have vanity."

He was in one of his soft and charming moods when the ambitious light was quiet in his eyes and his long, hollow-cheeked face had its rare gentleness. Amelia knew the afternoon and evening were going to be a success. She suddenly wanted to rush to the children and tell them to share her happiness.

Nathaniel saw the look in her eyes and said, "Now calm down, my love. This is all probably going to be deadly dull. You'll find yourself eating bowls of rice, and talking nostalgically about the food back home with Mrs. Howard Gebbler from Missouri."

"Who is she, for goodness sake?"

"I just invented her. But there'll be someone of that kind there, for sure. I've told Li to have a sedan chair waiting at four thirty. I'll walk to the Tien An Men gate with you, but that's as far as I'll be allowed. Do notice everything so you can tell me about it. I believe the Empress has a wonderful collection of clocks. It began a century ago when the Jesuit priests used to bring Louis XV enamelled watches and other baubles to please the Manchu emperors and convert them to the Christian faith. I think you may find quite a lot of French furniture inside the palace. But above all, look at the porcelain."

"You know I can never tell Ming from Sung. And

really, I think those little gray bowls very uninteresting."

"Barbarian." Nathaniel kissed her brow. "Go straight to the American legation when the party's over. I'll meet you there. And don't get drunk on jasmine tea."

Chapter 2

The legation district, surrounded by the immensely high and thick Tartar wall, had a European look. The legations were large houses set in vast walled precincts, the French on the corner of the Street of the Legations and Marco Polo Street, and near to one of the great gateways in the wall. This gateway, flanked by red stone lions (which Georgie loved), led out to the Chinese city and the Mongol market. The real China, Amelia thought, colourful, crowded, noisy, odorous, alive.

Inside the compound the atmosphere was much more decorous. The German and the American legations stood further down the street, and on the opposite side, set in seven acres, was the great rambling building of the British legation and chancery. In some parkland in the distance, a Chinese prince, Prince Su, had a palace, with all the courtyards and pavilions and dwarf trees and flowers that the Chinese loved. A French grocery, Père

Nicolas, was conveniently near the French legation and farther down the street was the popular Peking hotel, a favourite place for dinners and banquets.

The Italians, the Belgians, the Russians, the Japanese and the rest of this polyglot representation of the Western world, were situated at various points, and there were also rows of houses, such as the one the Carringtons lived in, mostly occupied by Europeans. It was a world within a world, and completely overshadowed by the dreamlike sight of the Imperial City, with its rosy red walls and yellow-tiled roofs, stretching away into the distance. Amelia was about to enter this forbidden wonderland for the first time.

Not through the great Tien An Men gate, for that entrance was reserved for royal personages alone, when their coming was announced by the beating of gongs and blaring of trumpets, and trappings of great magnificence. Foreigners were expected to use the little side gates, and slip quietly from one world into another.

Here, Amelia found that she had to change her hired sedan chair for a Palace one, upholstered in red satin, and carried by two broad-shouldered eunuchs.

Now her heart began to beat nervously. She wished Nathaniel were with her, as she went through the gates into a world of marble courtyards guarded by marble tigers, one leading into another, of dwarf trees and lily-covered pools, and cooing doves, and endless small palaces like dolls' houses, which one presumed was where the Emperor's concubines lived, for sometimes one caught a glimpse of a rouged face at a window, or the flutter of silk. Up marble steps and through more doorways until at last one stepped out of the chair at the doorway of the Winter Palace itself.

All the ladies were arriving, and descending from their chairs, chattering in low excited voices. The predominant language was English, Amelia was glad to hear. She moved to greet Lady MacDonald, and Alice Conger.

Then the little group was bidden by a large imposing eunuch to follow him through numerous small highly decorated rooms until, with a flourish, he threw open the door of the room where the Empress Dowager waited.

She sat just within the door, a little square figure dressed in a stiff yellow silk robe sumptuously embroidered with rioting dragons and flowers. As the European ladies came in she held out her hand, indicating that she would shake hands with each of them. This eliminated the necessity of making an obeisance, Amelia thought thankfully. The little soft hand laid in hers was surprising. She would have expected a hard imperious grip, for there was no softness in the face of this strange powerful woman. Rather an intense watchfulness, and barely veiled hostility. Or did one imagine that? Her mouth was set in a firm unsmiling line, her eyes were piercing bright ebony slits. Her sleek hair was pulled into a knot on the top of her head, and skewered there with a long jade pin. She was sitting on a divan covered in the same imperial yellow as her robe. Her legs were short, her unbound Manchu feet encased in painted square-toed shoes scarcely touching the floor.

Each of the guests, to her surprise and delight, was given a small jeweller's box which contained an identical ring, a large pearl in a heavy gold setting. There were cries of appreciation. The Empress watched without expression as the ladies slid the rings on to appropriate fingers. Amelia was sure that this gesture of goodwill was pure hypocrisy and wondered if it would be very rude to refuse her gift. She decided it would be, but it was galling to have to pretend pleasure. She slid the little box into her handbag, and stood back out of the way as the Empress signalled for her carrying chair. Amelia counted in wonder as no less than twelve eunuchs came forward to deferentially assist the royal personage into the chair, which also was draped in yellow silk. She was then carried from the room across a courtyard and into the banqueting hall, her guests following on foot. Some of the younger women were stifling nervous giggles. Amelia was thinking that, from the back view, the Empress was amazingly like Queen Victoria, short and dumpy, but of immense regality. One would surely never dare to oppose her, any more than any of her subjects would oppose Queen Victoria sitting in Windsor Castle.

She was trying to remember everything so that she could tell it in detail to Nathaniel and the children. There were bowls of superb chrysanthemums, some spectacular jewelled clocks ticking quietly in the background, and many obviously priceless porcelain bowls and ornaments, and lacquered tables. The tea bowls out of which they drank weak, fragrant tea were decorated with green dragons, the fine porcelain transparent. The Empress who was reputed never to eat in public, nevertheless out of courtesy ate rice from an Imperial yellow bowl, fed by kneeling attendants.

"Isn't it just fabulous," whispered a young American girl to Amelia. "But, my, I'm scared to clatter a spoon in case I get my head chopped off."

"S-s-sh, don't make remarks like that," Mrs. Conger, the American minister's wife, hissed reprovingly. "Mrs. Carrington, let me introduce Miss Medora Deacon who is visiting Peking. The naughty child missed her ship from Tientsin, so she has to wait a few weeks for another."

"You seem quite happy about it, Miss Deacon," Amelia said, looking with interest at the girl. She had an unusual face, rather plain with its sallow skin and high cheekbones, but redeemed by gleaming dark eyes.

"Oh, yes, I am happy." She leaned towards Amelia, whispering, "Actually, I missed the ship deliberately."

"Really! Didn't that upset the people you were travelling with? You surely weren't alone? You don't look much older than my eldest daughter."

"I'm twenty, which is quite old enough. And I was travelling with an aunt who—well, you understand."

"I can hardly understand without you telling me," Amelia said, smiling pleasantly. "And I'm afraid this isn't the place to do that. The Empress is watching us. I don't know how much English she understands, but I have a feeling she will sense exactly what we are saying. And thinking, too."

She said this, still smiling, knowing they were out of earshot of the Empress, but conscious of a feeling of uneasiness. Those watchful ebony eyes in the lemon-coloured face were not friendly. This unusual tea party had definite and disturbing undercurrents.

But hadn't everything in China undercurrents and sub-tleties not understood by the Western mind! Nathaniel found that every day in his business. The elaborate po-lite rituals, the surface amiability, the inscrutability be-neath the polite smiles. Ching, the cook, bowing, and swearing he was not cheating her, he did his uttermost best for Big Missy. The boys in their blue coolie coats working industriously, sweeping the courtyards, hurrying hither and thither, whenever she appeared, but, she was sure, sinking into lethargy the moment her back was turned. Li pretending that her interests and her comfort were of paramount importance to him. The amah, Ah Wan, breaking into wide smiles at the naughtiness of Georgie, or the cleverness of the girls. What were their secret thoughts? How genuine was their desire to please these palefaced foreigners?

Well, it was no use worrying about that now, when she was supposed to be enjoying herself. The servants, anyway, were comparatively innocuous. But the Empress Dowager was another matter altogether. One felt she could wave a wand and turn them all into grinning stone lions, or some other extraordinary thing. Her power was palpable.

A Chinese attendant bowed before Amelia, breaking

into her thoughts, and indicated that the Empress would like to speak to her. "Me!" Amelia murmured in astonishment.

Nervously, she approached and involuntarily curtseyed to the little imperious figure. As she straightened she was aware of the intense black stare on her.

The Empress said something rapidly in Manchu, and an interpreter addressed Amelia.

"Miss Callington, Great Lady wish to know if you take many things out of China."

"Many things?" Amelia was puzzled.

"Great Lady says your husband's ancestors did so."

"Oh, you mean trading in antiques. But merchants wish to sell these things. Tell Great Lady that they like to make money. Many taels."

The interpreter rapidly translated this, and Amelia, watching the impassive yellow face of the Empress, wondered again if she imagined the hidden but intense hostility and anger.

She was addressed again.

"Great Lady say these treasures belong to the Chinese people. Unimportant things may go, yes, but she hear about a tomb horse—it belongs to Chinese people's ancestors. It stay here."

Amelia remembered Nathaniel's excitement shortly after their arrival, when a merchant had brought to him a glazed pottery horse with a funny toy-like rider holding a bird on his clenched fist. It was a most exciting find, but it was wiser not to enquire from the merchant who had offered it to him where it had come from. Tomb mounds in China were sacred. Ancestors must not be disturbed.

"Tell Great Lady that I will inform my husband of what she says."

She waited uneasily while this was being translated, fearing a royal edict that would have to be obeyed. She knew that Nathaniel had already despatched the T'ang horse, packed in immense wrappings, by ship to England.

However, the Empress seemed to remember that this was a social occasion and Amelia was her guest, for she gave a slight but gracious inclination of her head, and the interview was at an end.

Soon afterwards she rose, indicating that the party was over. Voluble with relief like children out of school, the ladies hurried out to their waiting chairs, and set off for the American legation. At least there, there would be something more palatable to eat and drink than rice and sticky sweetmeats and scented tea.

It was growing distinctly chilly in the evenings. The bleak Peking winter was on its way. The last caravan of camels loaded with merchandise had arrived from Mongolia, and now the route across the Gobi desert was closed until the spring. The sand-laden wind blowing straight from the desolate wastes would shortly be sweeping the city, the earth would be brown, the trees bare, the many ornamental pools and lakes (the Chinese always included water in their landscapes) would be still and black, scarcely reflecting the tattered reeds at their edges. There would be no picnics or race meetings or expeditions to temples in the surrounding countryside. Entertainments would take place indoors, which was a pity, for in the summer one sat outdoors on the little terraces or in the courtyards which were lighted by the gay Chinese lanterns swinging in the trees.

Indoors, said Alice Conger regretfully, tonight's affair was just another party, although she had hired a Chinese band which would play Oriental music. And there was rice wine, if Amelia wanted to be adventurous.

Amelia decided to have a conventional dry sherry, and gratefully espied Nathaniel in the crowd.

She made her way immediately towards him, and took his arm, partly because the little act of possession pleased her and partly because she had detected the bright greedy look in his eye. He enjoyed meeting people at parties, collecting them like he did his treasures, discarding most, because he was highly critical but cultivating the ones who attracted him with his skilled and deliberate charm. She wanted to keep him at her side for as long as possible.

He patted her hand absently and said, "I'm glad to see you are quite intact, my love. May I present Colonel Manners. This is my wife, Colonel. She's just been drinking tea with the Empress Dowager, and there was the little matter that she might say something out of turn and lose her head."

The Colonel, an elderly man with a thatch of white hair, magnificent white moustaches, and fierce blue eyes, looked at Amelia with interest and obvious admiration.

"It would have been a tragedy to have lost such a charming head. How did you find the old dragon, Mrs. Carrington?"

"I thought her a most fascinating person, though rather awesome. We were each given a rather expensive gift, a pearl and gold ring. You'll see most of them being worn tonight. I'm sure that was a diplomatic rather than a generous gift. And she sent a message for you, Nathaniel."

"For me! How thoughtful of her."

"Not the sort of thoughtfulness you will appreciate, I'm afraid. She was giving a delicate warning about taking ancestral treasures out of China. She's heard of your tomb horses."

The Colonel nodded, unsurprised.

"The old lady has her spies. But this country is stuffed with tomb horses and whatever you may call it. The Chinese were glad enough in the past to trade them for opium. Your father knew that, my boy. Although he never traded in opium."

"I'm sure he didn't," Nathaniel said. "He paid in good English guineas, and so do I. That horse the Empress is referring to has gone, anyway. Nothing I can do about it. It was shipped from Tientsin last week on the *Eastern Star*."

"Why, that's the ship the American girl missed," Amelia said.

"What girl is that?"

"I met her at the tea party. She's here tonight. You're bound to meet her."

The elderly Colonel's eyes twinkled with youthful zest. Clearly, young women aroused his interest more than T'ang horses.

"I think you must be speaking of Miss Deacon. A bit of a rebel, I believe. We get 'em here, you know. They land like flying fish, running away from parents or convention or an unwanted marriage, or any of the problems that beset high-spirited young women. Think they can solve 'em in the romantic East. Did you find youth a repressive time, Mrs. Carrington?"

"Not necessarily. I suppose I was a conformer. Anyway, I married young."

"Deuced young, if you've got a girl of ten. You don't look more than a girl yourself."

"I was nineteen then."

"And married happily, may I ask? No, I don't need to. I can see it in your face."

Nathaniel laughed.

"Beware of Colonel Manners, Amelia. He has a terrible reputation for flirting."

"Well, dammit, the runaway American isn't the only person who came to Peking for some amusement. I did myself."

Amelia liked the old man with his poker back and his intelligent alive eyes.

"Do you enjoy living here, Colonel?"

"Naturally, or I wouldn't stay. Though I think we may be in for a little trouble. However, it'll blow over."

"What sort of trouble?" Nathaniel asked.

"Well, this thing of the Empress mentioning your T'ang horse. A few years ago she wouldn't have known about it or been interested in such a trifling thing.

There's a burst of nationalism going on, fostered chiefly by her rather rum nephew Prince Tuan. And there's talk of rebellion in the provinces. Scraps of news drift in. Sir Claude has his ear to the ground."

"Rebellion against whom?" Nathaniel asked.

"The missionaries, chiefly. Foreign devils. The peasants have decided they don't care much for Christian beliefs, or more likely don't want them forced on them. Even the converts are getting into trouble, and being called secondary devils. And it seems they object to the churches the missionaries build. Something about the spires interfering with the spirits of wind and water. But they say the same about the telegraph poles we've built along the railway. The wires humming scare them. They think they're evil spirits. They're a superstitious lot, like all natives."

"But they have centuries of culture behind them," Amelia said.

"The fortunate few. The mandarins and the scholars. If you're born in the top lot, you're all right. If you're not, you're an ignorant peasant with an unpleasant streak of barbarity. They're directing their hatred against the missionaries at the moment, but it could be only the peak of the iceberg. I have an uncomfortable feeling that they'd like to get rid of all foreigners."

"All the legations?" Nathaniel asked disbelievingly.

"Who knows. There's some plotting going on in the Imperial Palace."

Amelia caught Nathaniel's arm.

"Do you think Lilian and Thomas are all right? My sister is married to a missionary, Colonel."

"Where are they?"

"In Shansi."

"That's a big province. They'll be all right, Mrs. Carrington. This will blow over. Forgive me. I shouldn't have brought up the subject. Don't let it spoil your party. Let me see who I can introduce you to. What about Madame Leonora Vavasour, our opera singer? She has a splendid voice. She's to favour us with a number later, I believe. Must say I've never been able to take to that twanging Chinese music. Give me a full-blooded Wagnerian soprano any day."

"Who is the lady sitting on the couch?" Amelia asked. She had been looking curiously at the doll-like figure of an elderly lady, with high-piled snowy hair and delicately painted cheeks. She wore a Chinese silk dress and was as gaily coloured as a tropical bird, her bosom and hands glittering with diamonds.

"Oh, that's another confirmed exile, the Marchioness of Comerford. Her husband died here of typhoid, fifty years ago. She could never bring herself to go home. She couldn't desert his grave, she said, and the house at home would be too empty. She couldn't face it fifty years ago, and now it's much too late to do so. Odd. Human dilemmas. We all behave in different ways."

"And you, Colonel?" Amelia asked.

"Oh, I'm just an older soldier. Took part in the Opium Wars, then I sold my commission because I wanted to stay in the country. Got attached to it. But let me introduce you to Lady Comerford. She loves a new face."

Amelia was invited to sit on the couch beside the little Marchioness. She realised that the rouge and powder, not too expertly applied (those wide still beautiful eyes must be rather blind) failed to hide the wrinkles and pouches of at least eighty years. What an indomitable old lady this must be, with her carefully arranged silk skirts, her ringladen fingers, her proud head. She was as impressive in her way as the Empress Dowager, though those lavendercoloured eyes could never have held cruelty or ruthlessness.

"You must tell me all about yourself, Mrs. Carrington. So nice to see new faces."

"Surely a great many people come and go here, Lady Comerford."

"Oh, indeed. However, they don't all have faces one cares to linger with. Have you children?"

"Yes, three."

"Charming. And a good amah, I hope."

"She seems very good as far as one understands what goes on in the Oriental mind. The children like her. I have still to find a governess, though. My two daughters need to study, and Georgie is getting out of hand."

"I remember my governess used to pinch me, but on the upper arms so that the bruises wouldn't show. A frustrated type of woman, governesses, I doubt if the perfect specimen exists. If she's too old she's sour, and if she's too young her head is full of dangerous romance. You might have done better to bring one with you."

Fleetingly, the name of Gertrude passed through Amelia's mind. She repressed it quickly. "My husband was finding the expense of transporting a wife and three children and a maid on such a long journey rather heavy, without a governess as well."

"Your husband is an interesting-looking man. He makes one think of a young and happier Abraham Lincoln. All that bony strength, but not the dourness. Is he easy to live with?"

"Not entirely," Amelia admitted.

Lady Comerford nodded. "But who wants a dull husband?"

Amelia, feeling that she had been disloyal to Nathaniel, quickly added, "He can be terribly strong-willed, he takes what he wants, like that tomb horse the Empress Dowager was talking about, but he's such a good man. You should hear the principles he instills in the children. A slogan every morning at breakfast, like 'Today I won't tell a lie' or 'Today I will be kind to everyone.' Things like that. It makes the children respect him."

Lady Comerford's delicately painted eyebrows were raised with the merest suspicion of irony.

"What our Queen inflicted on the women of England

when she created her idea—or ideal—of an obedient husband, because I'm sure poor Albert never lived up to her fancies. What man could? You must understand, my dear, I'm not talking of any man, but the sort of man you or I would marry. We want some strength and character, and—what's the word—recklessness, perhaps. Am I offending you? I know I have this habit of plain-speaking. It's almost the only privilege one has left when one is old."

Amelia protested that the old lady was not offending her in the least, on the contrary she had spoken the absolute truth.

Especially since at this moment Nathaniel, on the other side of the room, was bending his handsome dark head over a young woman dressed in green. She couldn't identify the girl from her slender back, but Nathaniel found her interesting enough to be listening to her, rather than talking himself. A significant phenomenon, Amelia thought. Or was she just being ultra-sensitive? And was she to be so for the rest of her life?

She only knew for certain that Lady Comerford's outspoken remarks had been made because she, too, had noticed the absorption of the couple.

"Yes, an interesting man," Lady Comerford was murmuring. "A distinct asset to our small colony. You must both visit me."

"You live in the compound?"

"In a doll's house, with a tiny courtyard full of caged birds. We sing to each other." The old lady spread her fan and closed it, like a bird preening its feathers. Then she tapped Amelia on the arm. "But not in the way that Madame Leonora is about to sing. How tiresome. Now we must all be quiet and listen to that female bull bellowing. If there are these strange rebels called Boxers threatening us, she will be enough to frighten them off."

Amelia laughed, forgetting Nathaniel for a moment, and Lady Comerford whispered naughtily from behind her fan, "They say she was the mistress of the former Russian minister. He was recalled to Moscow. He had a wife with a face like a potato, poor fellow. Ah, I have many amusing things to tell you. But first we are condemned to listen to, if I may hazard a guess, the Jewel Song from *Faust*."

Lady Comerford's description of Madame Leonora's voice was scarcely exaggerated. It filled the room, and would easily have filled a large concert hall. It was a truly magnificent voice with a fine range. Surely, in Europe, she could have had a very successful career as a coloratura soprano. What had brought her to Peking and kept her there? The banished Russian minister? She was a big-breasted handsome woman with flashing eyes and large white teeth which the intensity of her singing displayed fully. Amelia wished Nathaniel had been sitting beside her. They could have exchanged amused glances. They had similar reactions to so many things. She would have enjoyed Madame Leonora's performance so much more if she had been able to link her little finger with Nathaniel's in their private form of communication.

But he was sitting on the other side of the room beside the slim lady in green. And Amelia saw now who she was. Medora Deacon, the runaway American. She had changed her dress since the tea party. She looked much older and much more sophisticated, as no doubt had been her aim. One could see she was the sort of girl who would find a chaperone irksome. It was very possible that the unknown aunt, aboard the *Eastern Star* that was steadily steaming away across the China sea, was equally relieved to be rid of her troublesome charge.

The song ended to a burst of applause. The static scene became fluid again. The waiters, in their immaculate white jackets, began carrying round refreshments. Amelia stood up, knowing that she was going to make her way across to Nathaniel, whether or not she was rude in so abruptly leaving the Marchioness, and whether or not Nathaniel would welcome her breaking in to his tête-à-tête with Medora Deacon.

He did welcome her warmly. His eyes were sparkling with their particular look of triumph, indicating that something pleased him. He wanted to tell her about it.

"Amelia, I was just about to find you. I believe you and Miss Deacon have met. But do you know what the marvellous thing is? She has agreed to come and be governess to the children."

Amelia's guess that the American girl could look attractive was true. A becoming flush disguised her sallowness. The long jaw and high cheekbones that had looked downright plain at the Empress Dowager's party were now unusual and almost remarkable. Her low-cut dress showed off her narrow shoulders and slim figure. Although a dress like that was much too sophisticated for someone so young. She was at the age for white tulle, and a single row of pearls, instead of this clinging jade green silk, so cleverly simple and unadorned.

"Oh, wait a minute, Nathaniel," Amelia said quickly, "I don't think we can engage a governess so impulsively. I mean, references, and—"

"I really can read and write, Mrs. Carrington," Medora Deacon said, an undercurrent of amusement in her voice. "And I'm moderately respectable. I guess my aunt wouldn't say so, but truly I am." Her dark eyes were glowing with curious, lambent light. Half of Amelia's mind wondered if she always looked like this when in conversation with a handsome man, while the other half wondered anxiously to what extent Nathaniel had committed himself. How unfortunate that Miss Deacon wasn't a nice plump prim girl whom one would have engaged without any qualms.

But one had the feeling that here was a firecracker, one of those noisy Chinese things that burst unexpectedly, and kept one on tenterhooks.

"Don't you think, Nathaniel, that Miss Deacon ought

to come and see us in the morning? We can't talk seriously in all this noise. I would want to ask a lot of questions. Forgive me, Miss Deacon"—Amelia smiled as charmingly as she found possible considering her uneasiness—"but I am one of those creatures my husband finds irritating, a worrying mother."

"Then may I call in the morning, Mrs. Carrington? Honestly, it's rather important, because the Congers don't want to keep me forever, and I haven't much money."

"Shouldn't you have thought of that before you missed your ship?"

The girl gave her small smile.

"Not necessarily. I knew something would turn up."

"There's no harm in giving her a trial, at least," Nathaniel said on the way home. His voice was abrupt. He felt Amelia had been discourteous.

She was too tired to defend herself. The walk down Legation Street seemed very long. A cold wind whipped across the empty spaces and sand stung her eyes. The towering Tartar wall was gloomy and prisonlike and immense. All the excitement of the day had gone.

And she could never bring herself to mention the name Gertrude. That was a story that had been finished absolutely. Hadn't Nathaniel sworn to it?

Why should she imagine there could be a repetition because Nathaniel had looked kindly at Medora Deacon? He always looked kindly at young ladies. Gertrude, that fair-haired, insipid, shy creature, had been the first with whom he had dared to go farther. (Or the first Amelia had discovered?) That was a suspicion she couldn't live with. She had dismissed it as violently as Nathaniel had rejected it, and had believed his protestations of love, and had forgiven him. A man could slip once or twice in his life. A man lived by different rules.

Amelia knew that she was subject to sudden dejections when she was overtired. Comparatively simple problems became heavy and unfaceable. In the morning, when she was rested, she might not find Nathaniel's decision about the American girl so upsetting. She knew that if she discussed it now they would quarrel. After all, it had always been understood that she managed the household while he managed the business.

"We've got to find out more about her background," she said at last.

"Goodness me, you're not still worrying about that nice girl." He knew she was. She detected the too hearty note in his voice.

"Colonel Manners said that people landed on these shores like flying fish." She didn't add old Lady Comerford's remark that governesses were a frustrated breed. Medora Deacon didn't look frustrated. But then she wasn't yet a governess. Which made Nathaniel's action all the more exasperating.

"I don't think Miss Deacon looks in the least like a flying fish. More like a mermaid. Slim and slippery and rather cold. Dearest, if you don't approve of her we won't have her. But be fair. Interview her first. Ask all the questions you want to. If she doesn't come up to your standards then there's no harm done. I thought she was young and lively and the children would like her."

"Oh, I'm sure they would."

"Isn't that important?"

"Of course. Only she doesn't seem much older than Henrietta. And you know how susceptible ten-year-olds are."

"You're afraid she'll have a bad influence on the girls because she's struck out for independence. Is that a wrong attitude for a girl to have? I certainly know I want our daughters to have spirit."

"As long as it's only a question of independence," Amelia said. "I'd be happier if we could hear from her aunt, or some other member of her family."

"So we can, but not by tomorrow. You must use your famous intuition instead."

She had already done that, Amelia wanted to say. She refrained, however, because as Nathaniel had said it wasn't fair to form an opinion of Miss Deacon on such slight acquaintance. She must do as her husband asked and talk to her quietly in the morning. She thought she would know if the girl were lying. In any case, if she were a failure, she could be dismissed. Amelia decided that she really was making heavy weather of the problem. After all, why not let the children judge Miss Deacon? They would be the ones who would be most involved.

She was ashamed of herself for being so obsessed with the matter of employing a governess when she should be thinking about more disturbing things, the Empress' delicate warning to Nathaniel, for instance, and the possible danger that Thomas and Lilian and their little girl Angel might be in, with those bandits roaming the countryside.

This was an alien country, and they were very much foreigners. All Westerners should keep together. The runaways must be harboured.

Even if already she was jealous of Nathaniel's championship of this particular runaway. For that, if she were honest with herself, was at the bottom of her prejudice.

Chapter 3

Henrietta had quickly discovered what was in the wind.
She was an inquisitive child and took her position as the
eldest in the family seriously. The two younger ones had
to be protected, for Lucy was hopelessly shy and sensitive, and Georgie lived in a dream. He was at present
obsessed by dragons. In England, where they had lived
a normal life (nothing here was normal, Henrietta had
decided, it was all very odd indeed, including the way
Ah Wan giggled when nothing funny happened), it had
been imaginary highwaymen on the river towpath that
had been Georgie's passionate interest. He said now, in
a lordly manner, that dragons were much more dangerous, but the girls needn't be afraid. He would slay them
with his sword.

"You haven't got a sword," said Henrietta.

"What is slay?" asked Lucy apprehensively.

"Kill," said Georgie, with relish. "Stick their eyes out.

And their grinning teeth. And their long wet tongues. Papa will get me a sword if I ask him."

"The bandits use swords," Henrietta said. "The Empress Dowager's guards do, too. They chop off people's heads. Papa says they call us barbarians because we're British, but I think it's they who are barbarians. Lucy, why are you looking so scared?"

"You're saying ugly words," whispered Lucy.

"Oh, don't be such a coward. Listen, can you both keep quiet? Mamma's got some woman coming to interview to see if she'll be our governess. We might listen outside the door if you promise not to sneeze or giggle or anything."

"Is she here now?" Lucy asked.

"She's expected at eleven o'clock. I heard Mamma telling Papa. She said the first test would be her punctuality. Shall we watch out of the window?"

So it was that a little later the children saw Medora Deacon come across the first courtyard. She looked very neat in a white blouse and a long dark skirt, with a prim little straw boater tipped forward over her eyes, the part of her face that was visible long-jawed and plain. Henrietta had imagined someone exotic, in long Oriental robes, perhaps. Everyone in China was so different, how could Miss Deacon look like this!

"She's ugly!" she said incredulously.

Lucy, however, was reassured, and said that Miss Deacon looked just like Miss Gertrude Wimpole, whom they had left in London, and who had been dull but kind and had suddenly begun bursting into tears for no reason. Kindness was the most important thing, in Lucy's opinion. Georgie was the one with the wild imagination. He perceived at once that Miss Deacon would believe in dragons. He just knew.

"Her face is wild," he said.

"But we couldn't see her face. She had it bent," Henrietta said reasonably.

"I could," said Georgie. "I hope Mamma keeps her. We can play fighting the Boxers."

"Oh, you are a silly little boy. She's here to teach you lessons. Anyway, what do you know about Boxers?"

"Plenty," said Georgie. "They wear red sashes and they're magic. You can't kill them with swords or guns or anything."

"Don't talk like that," Henrietta said sternly. "You're frightening Lucy."

But Georgie was carried away on his flight of fancy.

"They live in the hills and they're probably going to kill Uncle Thomas and Aunt Lilian. But Angel will be able to fly away on her wings."

"Georgie, whoever told you this?"

"Ah Wan did, and Li showed me how to use a sword. So Lucy doesn't need to be frightened. I'll protect her."

"You're a silly little boy," Lucy said bravely.

"I am not."

"Be quiet," hissed Henrietta. "Mamma has taken Miss Deacon into the drawing room. Let's listen. After all," she added righteously, "this is a matter that concerns us."

Amelia was relieved and yet irrationally disappointed that Medora Deacon looked so respectable this morning. What possible grounds could she have for not engaging this demure and obviously intelligent young woman who sat opposite her and talked of her past life.

There was so little of it, of course. She had only been out for two years. Before that there was the kind of girls' school to which prosperous Philadelphian bankers sent their daughters. There was no fault to be found with her education, or her family background. So why the world cruise with the aunt instead of the pleasant social life a girl in her position would lead until she married?

"Aunt Agatha wanted a companion," Miss Deacon explained. "She'd persuaded Mother and Father to let me

travel with her, and I thought it would be wonderful to
see the East."

"So wonderful that you stayed?"

"I guess so, though there was the point that Aunt Agatha and I didn't get on so well."

"Whose fault was that?"

"If I said it was hers you wouldn't believe me, and
anyway it would sound kind of mean. It was probably
just that our natures clashed."

"But you didn't think you owed her something for taking you on this trip?"

"Oh, I'd repaid that long before we got to Shanghai.
All that fetching and carrying and never being allowed
out of her sight. I was almost ready to jump overboard."

"Could it have been that she didn't trust you out of
her sight?" Amelia said quietly, and was startled at the
way indignation made the girl's long sallow face come
alive. At one moment she was a plain little creature, at
the next those huge eyes were flashing with deeply felt
emotions. A dual personality? Interesting, of course, but
was this what she wanted for the children?

Without meeting the aunt, one wouldn't know who was
to blame for the incompatibility. Or even why the aunt
had been persuaded to take an obviously not-too-well-
loved niece on such a long trip. Had there been some
scandal at home? Had the prosperous father made it
worthwhile for his sister to saddle herself with his difficult daughter?

Amelia was essentially fair, and realised that she was
allowing herself to be biased, simply because she, personally, did not find Medora Deacon very attractive.
Nathaniel had told her to follow her intuition. If she did
so she would have decided by now to politely show Miss
Deacon the door.

But common sense prevailed. The children badly
needed a governess and there was no one else in sight,
nor was there likely to be now with the winter setting in

and no travellers arriving. There was no harm in giving Miss Deacon a month's trial. Nathaniel would be pleased, and, with regular lessons, the children would settle down. Henrietta was getting bossy, Lucy was homesick, and Georgie was finding he could twist the servants round his little finger. Besides, Alice Conger would be grateful to have the future of her uninvited guest arranged for.

"Aunt Agatha and I didn't get on," the girl was saying frankly. "But do aunts and nieces always have to? Or mothers and daughters, for that matter. Everyone has to be herself."

"And you think you can be more yourself in Peking?"

"Away from my family I can. Oh, I don't mean that to sound bad, Mrs. Carrington. It's just that older people can be so stuffy and old-fashioned. My parents have never understood me. I think maybe I'm a changeling. I simply didn't want to spend all my youth going to co- tillions and sewing bees. I want to see things and learn things, and have my senses ravished, as they are in this heavenly place. The Winter Palace yesterday; that was really something. But if Aunt Agatha had been there she'd simply have spent the time complaining that her feet hurt."

Her eyes flashed up to meet Amelia's, suddenly afraid that she had given away too much, that in spite of Mrs. Carrington looking so young, she was the mother of three children and therefore might be stuffy, like the older gen- eration.

She need not have been anxious for, for the first time, Amelia was regarding her with some sympathy. She was a romantic, impractical, rebellious, a dreamer. Georgie had his own brand of make-believe which kept him su- premely happy, but perhaps a touch of Miss Deacon's intense response to beauty (if that was what it really was) wouldn't hurt the girls. Henrietta was a little plodding, and Lucy needed more spirit.

"Well, then," she said pleasantly, having made an

abrupt decision, "since we're both strangers here, we can learn about China together. I suggest you come for a month and see how we all get on. But I will want to write to your parents, so I would be obliged if you would give me their address."

"Of course. They'll be so pleased. They'll think I'm settling down."

Amelia lifted her brows.

"And you're not?"

The strange dark eyes, kindled with enthusiasm, looked at Amelia with an honesty she had to appreciate.

"I'll do my best to teach your children, Mrs. Carrington. I really love children. But I'm kind of wild. That's always been the trouble at home. After the winter, who knows what I might do?"

"They tell me that a Peking spring is something that must be seen. So don't plan to fly off before you see that. On the other hand there are so many rumours going about, as you must have heard, that none of us may be able to stay here."

"You think the Chinese will kick us out?"

"I don't know. My husband tells me that foreigners haven't been popular here since the Opium Wars. And if anyone has influence over her people it's the Empress Dowager. I got the feeling yesterday that she hated us all, secretly and rather viciously. Did you feel that?"

"I thought she was a marvellous but rather ghastly old woman. Anyway, they say she smokes opium herself, so why be angry with the foreigners for bringing it?"

"Does she really? I didn't know women did."

"Mrs. Carrington, you're in the wicked East."

Medora Deacon's gently teasing voice made Amelia laugh. Suddenly she felt the less sophisticated of the two, a pampered protected woman, while this girl had already acquired a great deal of worldly wisdom. She was still not entirely easy about what she had done, but she did know that the new governess was going to liven up the house.

"It's for a month's trial only," she emphasised to Nathaniel. "If she doesn't suit, she must go. But the children seem to like her, particularly Georgie. I'm afraid they might aid and abet one another in imagining things."

"What sort of things?"

"Well, dragons on the roof, lion dogs in the willow tree."

Nathaniel laughed heartily. Now that he had got his way he thanked Amelia in his softest manner. Was he just a little too pleased that Medora Deacon was going to be part of the household? Was she always going to be suspicious of her husband? The little worm of jealousy curled inside her, and she made herself remember the long sallow face beneath the straw boater. That was the face one hoped Nathaniel would see. Not the suddenly alive and luminous one.

She was a bit of a witch, really, that girl. But not in the least like the other one who had temporarily bewitched him with her flyaway blond hair, and her soft silky face. Anyway, the fact remained that the children had to have a governess.

"I will write to her parents in Philadelphia. I found out very little about her except that she's a rebel. I don't suppose that will do Henrietta or Lucy any harm."

"Good gracious, no. They just need someone intelligent to occupy their time."

"Did you think she was intelligent?"

"Very."

"I think she has her head in the clouds. And she's really quite plain. You'd be surprised. She isn't a siren in a long green dress all the time."

Nathaniel was smiling, his quizzical gaze telling her that he knew the thought in her mind. He kissed her lightly.

"Don't tell me you're jealous of another woman's looks, my love. You can't be. I've never seen a more beautiful woman than you, and how often have I told you so?"

"I believe you'd like to put me in a glass case with your Sung and Ming bowls," she said.

"I would, but I wouldn't leave you there long. By the way, the Empress' warning to you last night wasn't made lightly. She's issued an edict today."

"What does it say?" Amelia asked in alarm.

Nathaniel took a piece of paper from his pocket, and read aloud, " 'Let each strive to preserve from destruction and spoilation at the ruthless hands of the invader his ancestral home and graves.' Wouldn't you know that would happen just as I have planned a trip to the Ming tombs?"

"Where are they?"

"Near the Great Wall."

"Nathaniel, don't go!"

"I'm not going to rob the tombs. This is a purely innocent expedition."

"But will the Empress believe that? And there are all these bandits roaming about."

"I'm not afraid of bandits. Now Miss Deacon is joining our household, she can keep you and the children company. Rupert Fortescue from the Chancery is coming with me."

Amelia clasped her hands.

"I wish you wouldn't go."

"Darling, you are a nervous creature."

"I know I am. But there were those rumours we heard last night about rebels, and also the Empress is a sinister woman, not to be trusted."

"My dear foolish wife, the Empress isn't going to interest herself in a small journey made by two Englishmen to admire her country's antiquities. And the business won't prosper if I just sit and wait for things to be brought to me. I want to go and look for treasures.

Don't you remember my father's story of Mongolians eating out of Han dynasty bowls in an inn near the frontier? I'm just going to keep my eyes open. And I want to see some temples. In the spring we'll all go on an expedition, but the weather's getting too cold to take the children now."

"How long will you be gone?"

"Seven or eight days. Rupert's done this trip. He knows the way. He's a nice fellow, and an authority on the invasion of the Great Khans. I've asked him to come in this evening. When does Miss Deacon arrive?"

"Later."

"Splendid. We'll have a jolly evening. She and Rupert should get along famously."

They did, too. And Amelia succeeded in putting fears and conjectures out of her mind as Rupert talked about Kublai Khan and his famous pleasure dome, so near to this very place where they were sitting. She succumbed again to the mystery and fascination of this ancient country. Miss Deacon did, also, judging by the rapt look on her face. She was a slim figure with folded hands and large still eyes. She listens with her eyes, Amelia thought, and knew that Nathaniel was watching her, too, although he seemed to be paying complete attention to Rupert Fortescue.

Rupert was an extremely English type, fair-haired and blue-eyed, with a look of frailty that was almost certainly deceptive. He reminded Amelia of her brother who had been killed in India a year ago. He had been the youngest officer in his regiment and, in spite of his look of delicacy, had been decorated twice for gallantry, once in one of the first engagements of a small frontier war, and once posthumously. Rupert Fortescue said he had accepted his posting to Peking because he wanted some adventure. He was pretty expert at riding a mule and he was a fair shot, too.

"Guns?" said Amelia apprehensively.

"We may have to shoot wild duck for our supper."

"As long as it's only duck."

"We promise it won't be a Boxer," Nathaniel said lightly.

"Why do they call themselves Boxers?" Medora asked. "I think of that as something to do with fists."

"So it is," Rupert answered. "The Fists of Righteous Harmony is one of the interpretations. It's the missionaries who have nicknamed them the Boxers. They're a secret society who pander to the superstitious in the peasants. They boast that they're the spirits of heroes and can't be injured by guns or drowned by water or damaged in any way at all."

"Lucky for them," said Medora.

"They'll be a formidable enemy if they start fighting," Nathaniel said. "That sort of confidence probably will make them indestructible."

"And we have about one field gun and four rifles in the whole of the legation compound," Rupert said. "But if the enemy's unkillable, even they won't be of much use, will they?"

Amelia listened, and suddenly gave a deep shiver. This was a very long way from the green Thames valley. A very long way. . . .

At midnight the wind, that dry gritty icy blast from the Gobi desert, had dropped and the moon shone brilliantly in a clear frosty sky.

Georgie, Henrietta, and Lucy Carrington slept profoundly, in spite of the day's excitements and alarms. Miss Deacon had unexpectedly come into their bedrooms after Ah Wan had tidied up their clothes, and after Mamma had kissed them good night. She had stood at the foot of Henrietta's and Lucy's beds and had said in her strange slightly harsh American voice, "You'd better sleep well, because lessons start tomorrow, and I might look soft but I'm not."

Henrietta didn't think she looked soft at all. Neither

did Lucy. In the dimness of the night light she looked as tall and thin as a broomstick. Georgie, when she stood at his bedside, thought the same about her witchlike appearance. Unlike the girls, however, this excited him. He foresaw that they would have marvellous eerie stories and wild games. Miss Deacon wasn't too old, that was the best thing about her. Georgie didn't object to old people, but there were too many of them. Even Henrietta was getting bigger and bossier every day. He and Miss Deacon would ride tigers and fly on dragons. He had a suspicion, he didn't know why, that Papa felt the same about her supernatural powers. However, Papa was old and his flying days were certainly over.

In her large, airy room, the only decent-sized bedroom in the house, Amelia watched Cassidy hanging up her clothes and wished she would hurry. But one couldn't hurry Cassidy. All her movements were slow and meticulous. Just as Medora Deacon had seemed to listen with her eyes, Cassidy exhibited her feelings in the deliberate way she folded clothes, the way she held a pursed prim look on her face. Something wasn't to her liking. The American girl coming to the household? Naturally Cassidy wouldn't approve of engaging a young lady without references. But this wasn't orderly England. The cook cheated, the houseboys' impassive faces were unreadable, Miss Deacon was, so far, an enigma. One must just take chances. At least Amelia was relieved that the governess question was settled, the children liked Miss Deacon and Nathaniel was pleased.

Cassidy would never have ventured an opinion on Miss Deacon, but Amelia knew well enough, by her stiff silence, that she was disappointed not to be asked. One could only hope she would not be actively unpleasant to the girl. Whose side did one then take?

Amelia lay watching the hard bright moon, surely not the same one that shone gently over England's peaceful green valleys and hills, and wondered if Nathaniel would come to her room. She was a poor sleeper, and some time ago they had decided on separate rooms, each thinking of the other's comfort. This did not mean that Nathaniel did not frequently stay with her until morning. Although his visits had been less regular since Georgie's birth. She had taken a long time to recover from that, and although the doctors did not forbid another pregnancy they were frank in not encouraging it. She was subject to headaches and always looked fragile. Sometimes she enjoyed the way Nathaniel treated her like precious porcelain, but just occasionally a strange hot longing rose in her to be handled roughly and passionately, as she sensed he would any woman other than his delicate wife. But perhaps she was wrong.

It was selfish to be having these thoughts when there were so many other things to concern her, Lilian's and Thomas' safety, the hostile elements in this vast country, Nathaniel's proposed expedition to the Ming tombs, almost certainly watched by the Empress' spies. . . . She turned restlessly. This was going to be one of her sleepless nights.

Nathaniel had slept immediately his head was on the pillow, but the moon shining on his face wakened him two hours later, and then he couldn't sleep again. It occurred to him to go in and talk to his wife. But if she were asleep it would be a pity to wake her. She never succeeded in getting enough rest. Her look of fragility had always pleased him aesthetically, she was his show window so to speak, and immensely treasured. He would not have had her different in any way. If it meant practising more celibacy than he cared for, that was a mild price to pay. Although there were times when the price became beyond him. To be absolutely honest with himself, he was the kind of man who found certain women irresistible.

Tonight the brilliant moonlight, the thought of the expedition at the end of the week, the stimulation of this fascinating foreign city, all combined to keep him wakeful. And being wakeful he began to think rather too obsessively of that enigmatic young woman already residing under his roof.

She was an urchin, a wanderer, a self-willed, probably amoral creature. He had been aware of her sexuality the moment he had met her. In spite of her youth she possessed wiles of which he was sure she was perfectly aware, the sudden awakening of those large sulky eyes into brilliance, the secret half smile, the transformation from torpidity into animation. Her sallowness was so different from Amelia, who was pure *famille rose*. Perhaps that was what he was going to find intriguing about the situation, his serene wife on one hand and on the other this strange girl with her childishly bony shoulders, her gaucheness, her apparent anxiety to please, and then the surprise of her swift knowledgeable gaze.

This was an entirely different situation from the one precipitated by his behaviour with Gertrude, which he deeply regretted, wondering still how he could have been taken in by her. What he had thought a delightful innocence was insipidity, and even before Amelia had found out about their liaison (innocent enough, confined only to kisses and embraces) her devotion had become embarrassing. He had determined never again to get into such a contretemps. For a man of the world it had been clumsy and ridiculous, and that silly over-emotional young woman not worth the trouble she had caused. Besides, he had hated hurting Amelia. Even more, it had wounded his vanity that she should have temporarily lost her trust in him. Any future extramarital affair he indulged in (what man didn't?) would be conducted with the most absolute discretion. Yet, although he recognised that Medora Deacon was an altogether different matter from Gertrude, here he was bringing another source of temptation into the house. He told himself he was thinking of the children's welfare. They must have someone, they couldn't remain ignorant and uneducated, and until the spring it was unlikely that any other unattached female would drift into Peking. Medora was only a waif, a rather naughty child who may have to be disciplined with the children. He was capable of that. He wondered why he found such a prospect so exciting.

Medora wore a simple long-sleeved cotton nightgown and did her hair in slender dark snakes over her shoulders. She looked like a schoolgirl. Her thoughts, however, were completely adult. She knew that this was going to be one of the nights when she scarcely knew how to contain the strange excitement that consumed her. She adored that feeling. It was so different from the times of black depression and rebellion. She usually hovered between the two extremes. There seemed to be no neutral ground for her, although she was learning from expediency to hide her feelings. On her sad days she was quiet and contained. These moments of burning excitement were more difficult to conceal, and, with the right person, she didn't conceal them at all. According to her elders she experienced joy from the wrong things, forbidden things such as indiscreet flirtations with other women's husbands. They had never understood that to her the forbidden was the irresistible, such as her escape from dull repressive Aunt Agatha, her journey alone to Peking, the excitement of entering the Forbidden City and encountering the formidable old woman on the Dragon Throne, and now the meeting with Nathaniel Carrington, who with those brilliant hungry black eyes and hollow cheeks must be the most attractive older man she had ever met. Of course he was married, but that fact gave Medora the challenge she enjoyed, the fierce glowing excitement, the touch of wickedness that made her come fully alive.

She liked the children, too. The girls were as quiet and obedient as their pretty mother could have wished. The little boy was a kindred spirit in that he saw things larger than life.

Medora Deacon, the rebel, the problem child, the despair of her parents, had no intention of telling the gentle and good Mrs. Carrington of her elopement which had come to nothing, because Father had not only had spies, but faster horses. They overtook Neville and herself before they were ten miles from home. Neville, confronted by Father's grim anger, had turned craven and sworn that he had never touched her (which was true), that she could go back home and be returned, pure and unsullied, to the marriage market.

She had thought herself passionately in love with Neville. He was dark with whippy good looks, ten years older than herself, and something in the financial world where it was rumoured that he was much too clever to be trusted. She was the daughter of a rich man whom he was not prepared to stand up to when the crucial moment came. Slick money deals were one thing, a charge of abduction was another. Anyway, he saw that Medora completely lost her looks when she was frustrated or unhappy.

From then on she had felt that her life, which she longed to live to the full, was being senselessly wasted.

Until coming to Peking, until the Empress' party, until meeting Nathaniel Carrington. She was sure that the immediate future would hold all the excitement she craved. It was no wonder that the hard bright Chinese moon kept her awake.

Although, twisting the Empress' ring on her finger, thinking that it was going to be her talisman, she did hope to behave well enough not to disappoint Mrs. Carrington. And badly enough, the treacherous side of herself whispered, to please Mr. Carrington.

In their spacious bedroom on the first floor of that large rambling house, the British legation, both Sir Claude and Lady MacDonald were awake.

Lady MacDonald never slept when she knew her husband was worried, as he was now by the rumours of a Boxer uprising in the spring. In a harassed way he was wondering whether to write to Lord Salisbury in London for more troops. But the other legation ministers had decided to let things ride at present, and he did not wish to seem an alarmist. He had friendly Chinese converts coming in from the provinces with messages rolled into quills and hidden in their long plaits. The last message had said that the Boxers' latest vow was that they must protect the Ch'ing dynasty and exterminate the foreigner.

Not expel. Exterminate. A nasty word. As if they were dealing with rats.

But it couldn't come to war. The Empress Dowager, her scheming nephew Prince Tuan, the Tsungli Yamen itself, would surely not encourage a rebellion against eleven powerful nations, all with resources at their command—if sent for in time. The actual resources on hand were pitiful. But the rebellion hadn't begun, and most likely it never would.

Sir Claude threshed over on his side and began to breathe deeply. Lady MacDonald recognized the signs and knew thankfully that he would soon be asleep. She allowed herself a short period of homesickness, longing for the tranquillity of England's green countryside and the pure air of Scotland's highlands, then briskly told herself that she had chosen this life when she had married, so there was no excuse to complain. She must do what she could to help that nice young Mrs. Carrington enjoy her stay. That would be a pleasant task.

In his bungalow, Colonel Manners woke from a vivid dream of being engulfed by screaming yellow hordes, as had happened to him once, in a narrow street in Shanghai during the last year of the Opium Wars. What a barbarous race the Chinese could be. They hid so much ancient evil behind their bland faces, their love of pretty things, doves, wind-bells, peach blossom, children. They were altogether too devious. He wouldn't trust a boy in his house if the Boxers broke in. Give him a good old-fashioned European any day, French, German, Austrian, anybody. Even the Boers in South Africa, with their stubborn relentlessly religious strength, were preferable to the narrow-eyed Asians.

Slit throats would be the order of the day, if this band of rebels began to rampage through the country. He believed that all the Legation ministers were being too complacent.

Yet, like the old war horse he was, the thought of battle stirred his blood. . . .

Lady Comerford was afraid of the long winter nights. She had never been afraid in England. But that had been a long time ago. Humphrey had died at five minutes past midnight, and for years afterwards she regarded that as the hour of death, and stayed awake tensely until it was past. Even though she was now old and tired and drowsed a lot, the habit of wakefulness at midnight persisted. She was telling herself again what a silly old fool she was for still being unable to leave her beloved's body in alien soil. Such a handful of unaware bones he was now. She could have had a comfortable old age in England, one without the alarms and excursions of an unpredictable people, of an autocratic ruthless Empress, of bandits and war lords, and now these mysterious Boxers who tied red sashes round their waists and pretended to be fiery dragons.

However, it was too late to do anything about it. She would have to go on presenting her gay face at parties, dressing up in the bright colours she loved, chattering vivaciously, never admitting her midnight fears. And at last being laid beside that handful of bones in the Westerners' cemetery outside the city.

She would see it through to the end with panache, she hoped. But she was a very fearful person, and apprehensive of showing her cowardice.

One by one the lights went out of all the legations. Before falling asleep Alice Conger's last words to her husband were "Thank goodness we've got rid of that odd creature Medora Deacon, but I don't know what I've let Amelia Carrington in for."

"She did it of her own free will," said her husband.

"Or her husband's. It seems to have been his idea."

"Really? Not the sort of young woman I would want around, I admit. Too moody. If the Boxers attack us, Alice, we're in a vulnerable position. We might find we have to move into the British legation in the care of that Scotsman with his stiff whiskers. I've never really understood the English, even less the Scots. Perhaps that sulky little b—hum—Miss Deacon is the kind of woman they secretly admire."

Alice gave her husband a little push.

"Now, my love, I didn't ask you to indulge in fantasies. It must be the moon. Look how bright it is over the Imperial City. Shall I draw the curtains?"

"I'm not looking at the moon," said the American minister, taking his wife's hands off his shoulders and guiding them inside his pyjama jacket.

Deep in her opium dream, the Empress Dowager had still not quite been able to forget the hated foreigners grouped like insolent watchdogs round her palace gates. She was wearing loose robes. Her little parchment hands with the two grotesquely long nails encased in their jewelled sheaths lay quietly on her breast. Her eyes were dulled slits in her blank face. She didn't hear the ticking of the pretty enamelled clocks or the whisper of silk as one of her attendants, cramped from long stillness, moved cautiously. Vague memories of her son, Prince Tung-Chih, as a little boy came to her. It had been best when he had been a child and she could pamper and scold him. Later he had disappointed her, he had been petulant, self-indulgent, delicate, and had died before he reached the age of twenty so the power had become hers once more. Or was it now Prince Tuan's, her nephew's? He hated the foreigners even more fiercely than she did.

She thought of the ladies from the foreign legations with their ugly clothes, their rice-pale faces, the greed in their eyes when they had seen the gift of the rings, creamy pearls set in gold, not of the highest quality. But what did those drab women know of jewellery, the perfection of cool jade, of ropes of black pearls, of rubies and emeralds? The white foreigners were apparently not sexually potent enough to have more than one wife, which made her despise them even more.

However, the ancestors of these same foreigners had brought the magic pipe that held her nightly pleasant dreams. It had seemed miraculous at first. It still seemed good to her, an old lady. But it was not good for the young and vigorous whose strength was sapped by the insidious fumes, whose mental processes were damaged, whose eyes became dulled and lifeless, like the dead poisonous centre of the poppy flower itself.

No, the meddling greedy foreigners, not only wanting to possess strategic portions of her country but also attempting to persuade her people to abandon their ancient religious beliefs, must go. Before the spring was over, before the heat began and she spent the long days drowsing in her summer palace. . . .

Dragon House, England
January, 1975

Chapter 4

Although the house in the Thames valley had a Chinese name, and a clipped yew dragon fashioned out of the hedge, it was completely Victorian English. Set back from the river, with long sloping lawns, a terrace and a pergola, it looked dark and gloomy in the winter. Even in the summer when the roses were out and the trees alive with birds the house had a chilly, secretive look. One needed sunny weather so that one could be outdoors. In winter, when the garden was dank and leafless and the river ebony-dark it was too melancholy.

Hugh inevitably made a fuss when Georgina broke the news that another weekend at Dragon House was expected of them.

"Your family." Hugh referred to the Carringtons with tolerance and boredom, and always with impatience. At least that had been how he referred to them until Georgina's father had died. Now it was "your aunts," since there were no male members (unless one counted the feeble and crippled Charles) left alive.

However, Hugh was polite to the aunts, especially now that there were only two of them left. Aunt Lucy, more fey than senile, a little ivory bone of a woman with a puff of white hair and innocent blue eyes that had never lost their lifelong shyness, and Aunt Suzie, nine years younger than Aunt Lucy and still immensely virile, with sleek black hair and a jetty brilliance in her hooded eyes.

Aunt Henrietta, the eldest sister, had died two years ago, leaving Lucy shattered and bereft. Neither had married. As children they had lived through the Boxer Rebellion in Peking, a far-off, almost forgotten episode in the annals of British history. It had been a fearful traumatic experience from which neither of them had really recovered. Henrietta and Lucy had lived together in a Sussex village, withdrawn from the world, looked after by a faithful maid, Bessie, who fortunately still took care of Lucy and shielded her from the terrors of the modern world, hooligans throwing stones at the windows, for instance, which took Lucy right back to the fanatical yelling and screaming of the Boxers outside the great Tartar wall.

George, their younger brother, Georgina's father, had similarly lived a scholarly and secluded life, not marrying until he was in his forties, and much later regretting his dilatoriness, for he had realised that he wasn't going to see his beloved grandson, Benjamin, reach more than the age of five years. Seven, he had said, was the ideal age for a boy. He had been seven in Peking and filled with the wonder of everything. Ben was seven now, but his grandfather had lain for two years under a mellow Cotswold stone in a peaceful country graveyard. Aunt Lucy said that, with his innocent eager face and comical fancies, Ben was exactly as his grandfather had been.

Since his grandfather was not there to indulge him in

his fancies, Aunt Suzie did so, instead, but a little too wildly. She was inclined to give Ben nightmares.

Aunt Suzie was the one who had escaped the trauma of the siege because she had not been born until it was over. Nevertheless, the long shadow of Peking touched her, too, for of all the family she was the one who had an obsessive interest in everything Chinese. It might be said that she had inherited this from her father, Nathaniel Carrington (Georgina's grandfather), who had been a dealer in Chinese ceramics and other antiquities. But her love of lacquer screens and chests, of ivory and jade carvings and faded bowls and jars of the Han and Ming dynasty was tied up with her interest in the rebellion, which she considered herself so unlucky to have missed, her love of drama, and her admiration for the late Empress Dowager of China, the great Tz'u-Hsi. She was uncannily like the Empress herself, short and squat, black-haired, black-eyed, with a formidable presence. She chose to wear yellow, the Chinese imperial yellow, a great deal. She skewered her thin black hair into a knot on top of her head, blackened her eyebrows, and let the little fingernail on each hand grow monstrously long. She was an actress who had so grown into her character that now she genuinely imagined herself to be the Empress Dowager of China reincarnated and living in a quiet English country house surrounded by her small court.

At least that was Georgina's belief. She did not, as Hugh did, think Aunt Suzie an absurd old fraud. To tell the truth, from childhood she had been nervous of Dragon House, its dark rooms filled with plundered Oriental splendour, and particularly of its mistress, the strong-minded inscrutable Aunt Suzie.

Ben, on the other hand, adored everything about it. Nothing pleased him more than an invitation to spend a weekend or a longer holiday at Dragon House. He provided a mesmerised audience for Aunt Suzie's more bloodcurdling tales, and then whooped about the garden, slashing at things with willow wands, letting out his pent-up excitement which more often than not ended in nightmares. He was particularly fond of the willow tree at the bottom of the garden, its gnarled branches hanging over the dark sluggish water of the river. Grandfather had told him that the Chinese believe the willow tree to be a wizard, but he personally had never, even in Peking, been able to discover whether it was a good wizard or a bad one. Aunt Suzie maintained that all wizards were bad. Whatever sort of an impression would a good wizard make? Meek mealy goodness got nobody anywhere.

Hugh hadn't much patience with all this make-believe, and thought Ben might become a figure of fun with his less imaginative schoolmates. But Georgina, remembering her father with deep devotion, said that if he had not been harmed by fancy, Ben would not be, either. It was in anticipation of Ben's pleasure that she decided they must accept Aunt Suzie's command, for that was what it amounted to, to come down for the last weekend of January. Aunt Suzie wanted to give a dinner party. She had a charming new friend, an actor, and he must be kept amused. Winter was so deadly dull, wasn't it? One must enliven it as much as possible. There would be Georgina and Hugh, and Ben, of course, and Charles, and Hal Jessel, the actor, and a girl friend of Hal's as house guests, and some of the less virulently dull of the locals would be asked to dinner.

"Will you drive down," Aunt Suzie wrote, "or let me know which train you are arriving on so that Smythe can meet it?"

Aunt Suzie was one of the few people in the Thames valley, or indeed the whole of England, who could still afford to keep servants. She had married twice, both husbands were dead, and both had left her comfortable fortunes. Her only son, Charles, had been a spendthrift, a small querulous man who had once managed to get his hands on a considerable part of her investments, and then had frittered them away in gambling clubs and on race courses. When his mother had discovered what was happening she had furiously put a stop to it, leaving Charles virtually penniless. He had lived on friends for a while, drunk too much, and finally had had a road accident which had left him partially paralysed and permanently doomed to a wheelchair. The sad thing was that it had meant a return to Dragon House to become the prisoner of his mother, a succession of nurses, and his own useless limbs. He had withdrawn into himself, scarcely speaking, his skin taking on a yellow tinge, his eyes bitter and watchful. He was the crown prince without followers or influence, and with no hope of issue.

From all the Carrington children, Henrietta, Lucy, Georgie and Suzie, there was such meagre issue. Only Georgina and Charles and now Ben.

It was as if that terrible terrifying eight weeks in Peking in their childhood had dried up some life force, and the family was in danger of dying out, like a diseased branch of that symbolic tree, the willow.

Georgina longed to have another baby. Hugh was not the easiest of husbands, he was a complex person, clever, impatient, restless, who could never hide his contempt for people who bored him. But in his moments of tenderness he was irresistible, and her whole body ached with love for him. She belonged utterly to him and would always do so. She knew his ability to hurt her, although he never failed to be deeply sorry afterwards. She considered this the price she had to pay for being married to someone so much more brilliant and effective than herself. They got along better than most couples because beneath their day-to-day differences and irritations there was that deep enduring love. At least, Georgina hopefully believed that this was so.

She firmly maintained her right to make all domestic

decisions. She would accept Aunt Suzie's invitation to Dragon House whether Hugh liked it or not. It was for Ben's pleasure, she said, not for her own. She disliked that rather spooky house, and would prefer listening to Aunt Lucy's wandering memories in her cosy Sussex cottage rather than watch Aunt Suzie doing her Empress of China act. Also, poor Charles was so pathetic and so impossible to reach. Hal Jessel sounded like another of the witty amusing brittle young men whose company Aunt Suzie enjoyed. Privately she called them her eunuchs, her black eyes sparkling with malice. But if Hal Jessel were bringing a girl friend, he must be rather more masculine than Aunt Suzie's previous favourites had been.

Poor Hugh. It wasn't his favourite sort of company. But if they went this time they needn't go again until the summer.

Ben couldn't wait to see how the dragon Smythe was cutting in the yew hedge had developed. Smythe called Ben young master, which pleased him immensely.

"It takes years to make a living animal, young master," Smythe said, when Ben transparently showed his disappointment that the dragon was still rather shapeless.

"Is it going to be alive? Is it going to breathe fire?"

"It's alive, so to speak, because it's made out of growing yew. I have to keep clipping and shaping it or its tail would turn into a bush and its wings would fall sideways when they should be pointed upwards. As you, being well informed about dragons, should know. It takes time and patience, but by the time you're grown this will be the best dragon in the country."

"But you won't be alive then," said Ben, looking critically at Smythe's grey head. "Neither will Aunt Suzie."

"That won't matter because it's your dragon, young master."

Ben went hurtling indoors to report this conversation

to Aunt Suzie. He found her in the drawing room, a dumpy little figure sitting on a yellow silk couch, dispensing jasmine tea to her guests.

There was Father sitting in the window seat beside a girl with red hair cut short, Mother talking to a good-looking man in a brown corduroy velvet suit, and, of course, Uncle Charles looking pinched and peevish in his wheelchair in his usual corner by the fire. There were never any other children at Dragon House, but Ben didn't mind this as he considered it uniquely his territory.

Aunt Suzie was beckoning him to come and take one of the little sticky cakes she always served for tea. She was wearing the ring set with a large baroque pearl that had come from the real Empress of China. It had been given to her mother at a tea party in the Imperial Palace in Peking when the Empress had been in a generous mood, and had been pretending to like the foreign white women from the legations. She had given each one of them at the party an identical ring. At least, that was the story Aunt Suzie told. The heavy ring hung like a rock on her bony third finger. She was also wearing turquoise-encrusted shields on her little fingers to protect their long nails, and she had on one of her long stiff robes embroidered with chrysanthemums and rioting dragons. She was wonderful, Ben thought. And he wasn't in the least afraid of her. Well, only slightly.

"So you've been out to see your dragon already," she said in her deep harsh voice. (Like the croaking of a Peking crow, Father said.) "What did you think of it?"

"It's coming on nicely, Smythe says. It's to have a long curly tongue."

"Which will spout smoke and flames to frighten off evil spirits," Aunt Suzie said, and Ben could have sworn, by the look in her eyes, that she believed this would really happen. "You haven't spoken to the dogs yet."

Ben obediently stooped to pat the two fat pugs snoring on cushions at Aunt Suzie's feet. He didn't truthfully care

much for them. He wanted a little tough Jack Russell
terrier, but if he had one, Mother said, he would never
be able to bring it to Dragon House because it would
frighten the life out of those fat lazy pugs. Aunt Suzie
kept pugs because they had been the favourite dogs of
the late Empress. They were not exactly lion dogs, but
they slightly resembled them.

"Ben," came his mother's voice, "you haven't spoken
to anyone else yet. Come and say hullo to Uncle Charles.
And this is Mr. Jessel." The good-looking man with the
crinkly golden hair put out a long fine hand, like a
woman's. "And Miss Russell."

"Amy," said the young woman who had been talking
to Father. She smiled in a friendly way. She wasn't exactly pretty. She had freckles, and her hair was gingerish,
rather than red. Her eyes were like green glass. Ben decided that he quite liked her and suspected she mightn't
be bad at games. Aunt Suzie always wanted to play Boxers in the dark shrubbery, a rather nerve-tingling game,
since she didn't seem to think it at all ridiculous that an
old woman should tie a red scarf round her head and
leap out shouting, *"Sha! Sha!"* in her croaking crow's
voice. In this game Ben always had to be one of the
foreign devils without enough guns or ammunition. But
he thought that if Miss Russell would join in the game,
she could be a foreign devil, too, and reinforce his ranks.

In the meantime, instead of eating the sticky cake,
which he didn't like, he wanted to hold the cool jade
Mongolian pony that was always on the side table in his
hands. Next to Smythe's dragon it was his favourite thing
in Dragon House, although there were many other familiar treasures to be admired.

He loved the wild golden horsemen, curved swords
upraised, galloping round the lacquer screen. And the
twin carp, made of silky white jade, very rare. And
the golden chrysanthemums and peonies painted on the
lamps, and the red lacquer writing desk with its myriad

drawers within drawers. And the several enamelled clocks, ticking busily. And the grinning long-fanged lion dogs on either side of the hearth, and the little horned dragon with its splayed paws, which had come from the Imperial Palace in Peking. Or so the story went.

Every time she came here, Georgina realised how Aunt Suzie had looted Grandfather Nathaniel Carrington's house when he had died.

Looted was the word because that was exactly what Grandfather was supposed to have done in the Imperial Palace after the siege of Peking had ended. A lot of people had done it, he had defended himself. A kind of madness had seized the embattled legations after their weeks of terror and the brutality they had witnessed. If the newly arrived relief forces, soldiers and marines of all nationalities, who had no appreciation at all of Chinese craftsmanship, could fill their knapsacks with loot, then it was his duty to secure and preserve the best of the marvellous antiquities. He had intended giving them to a museum, or even back to the Chinese government, but when he had arrived in England he hadn't been able to part with them. He had hoarded them jealously and guiltily, and in his will they had been bequeathed to whichever of his children wanted them.

He would have expected Georgie, his only son, to have chosen the finest pieces, since he had been an Oriental scholar himself, but strangely enough Georgie hadn't wanted anything. Neither had Aunt Henrietta or Aunt Lucy. After fifty years, they still shuddered at the associations the pieces had for them. Also, being scrupulously honest, they didn't like the thought of being in possession of loot.

No such aversion touched Aunt Suzie. But she hadn't lived through the horror of the Boxer Rebellion, and therefore had nothing but a fascinated interest in it. She decided to move into the old Carrington house on the Thames, renaming it Dragon House, and leave its treasures undisturbed. She had always been deeply interested in the character of the last Empress of China, but it was only after she had moved back into her childhood home that she herself became, in her mind, the unrepentant Tz'u-Hsi returning from exile, with all the panoply of a great and loved ruler.

Aunt Suzie was a little mad, Georgina suspected. But not dangerously so. One must only watch that she didn't over-excite Ben.

Hugh had been talking to Amy Russell because he shirked trying to engage Charles in conversation; Hal Jessel was as predictable as all the previous young men, stagestruck and on the make, and the old woman was, if anything, more outrageous than ever. What a household, and why did Georgina have this obligation to come here? Georgina had such a tiresome conscience about her family.

She sat beside Aunt Suzie now, her head tilted slightly on her long slender neck, her eyes filled with the gentle dreaminess Hugh knew so well. It meant that she wasn't listening to a syllable of that croaking autocratic voice. She was thinking of something else entirely, as she frequently did when he talked to her. She suffered from a chronic lack of concentration, which was both infuriating and endearing. Where had she been, he would sometimes ask, and only to be told that she had been imagining them all flying to New York and shopping in Tiffany's.

"Tiffany's! Do you have a secret desire for diamonds?"

"Of course I don't, but it's fun imagining things that will never actually happen."

"Why will it never happen?" Now Hugh was needled by her apparent lack of confidence in him.

"Darling, you know why not. You're a hardworking barrister, and barristers don't make fortunes. By the time we've paid off the mortgage and got a new car and educated Ben, we're not going to be able to afford expensive trifles from Tiffany's." Her face, not formally pretty, but soft, expressive and enormously vulnerable, affected him as it always did, his irritation dissolving into a protective love. Arguing with Georgina was like fencing with a will-o'-the-wisp. She simply escaped from solid fact and usually lost the thread of the discussion. He didn't always give in to her. But he was miserable when he didn't.

All the same, she was a maddening person and he sometimes wondered why he, Hugh Morley, reputed to have one of the most lucid and brilliant minds of the younger members at the bar, had married a woman like this. All Georgina's family were a bit odd, her father had been as vague and dreamy as his daughter, the two surviving aunts were definitely senile or a little mad. He hadn't known Georgina's mother, who had died tragically at the birth of a stillborn child. Georgina had scarcely known her mother, either, and for this reason was inclined to cherish and overprotect Ben, as if she were compensating herself for her own lack of maternal love.

It was secretly disappointing to Hugh that Ben, a rather delicate and under-sized little boy, with an owlish face, prominent ears, and spectacles, had inherited so little of his father's lucidity and so much of the Carrington dreaminess.

There had to be a good many arguments about him, Hugh insisting on the need to toughen him up, to make him face the world, but Georgina simply smiling quietly and saying, "Let him grow up in his own way, Hugh. Let him be himself."

"A little owl with a head full of fantasy?"

"What's wrong with that? He can be so happy. Leave him. I like it when he talks to himself. If he isn't the sort of son you wanted, you shouldn't have married me."

There she was again, hitting below the belt. But unintentionally. Completely ingenuous, she sometimes made a factual statement which was unanswerable.

If he hadn't married Georgina he might have married a girl of his own kind, with practical common sense, and an incisive mind, and had the sort of sensible conforming children which such a union would have produced. Instead of his dreamy Georgina and his odd little owl of a son.

How much did he regret, or not regret, what he had done? This afternoon, in this crazy house, he was expecting to be thoroughly bored. That was why he was talking to the girl, Amy Russell, who, although she was apparently the pretty young man's friend, seemed to be down-to-earth and sensible. She had candid lively green eyes that gave her thin freckled face its only beauty. He found her interesting, and without affectation.

She said she was an interior decorator, and had worked mostly abroad, in Geneva and Paris. Now, with Hal Jessel's help, both financial and with contacts, she was opening a business in Chelsea. Her prices were modest. She didn't go in for high-flown stuff. Did he and his wife want their house, or even one room, done? She had some fabulous new wallpapers. She could make dark interiors light or, if you were an obsessional night lover, light interiors dark.

"But you don't look like one of those," she said.

"Can't afford to be. I have to work in the daytime."

"You wouldn't be anyway," said Amy. "Hal is. It comes from being on the stage, I suppose. He keeps all his curtains drawn until midday and we are just as likely to have dinner at six A.M."

"We?"

"Hal and me. And others. If you have a spare room in Chelsea someone will occupy it." Amy sighed and stretched. "It doesn't leave me in much shape for work."

Hugh's eyes went over the boyish body, the long legs.

A stirring excitement, which caution told him to repress, began in him.

"Will you come and see my shop, Hugh?"

"Be delighted to."

"I'll give you my card. It's just called by my own name. Amy Russell. I don't like hiding behind trendy pseudonyms."

"How did you come to be called Amy? It's so prim and Victorian."

"I know. I don't fit it. I believe it was my grandmother's idea. She was supposed to have been a character although in quite a different way to Mrs. Blenheim. Isn't she marvellous?"

"She decorates a room, I grant you. I suppose that's how you see her. But she's a damned old hypocrite. All that dressing up is just a pose to intimidate people and get her own way."

"Like judges on the bench putting on authority with their wigs?" said Amy slyly.

"But in the cause of justice. Not to indulge private whims."

"Oh, Hugh, you're pompous! How sweet!"

He had never before been called pompous. He found he disliked it very much. And it wasn't true. Surely? If he were square and pompous he would never agree to spend weekends in this eccentric house. Although perhaps this weekend was not going to be as deadly as usual, with Miss Amy Russell probing him with delicate scorn.

Did she sleep with that beautiful young man? He didn't look the kind.

Aunt Suzie, with an audience of Georgina, Ben, and Hal Jessel, was becoming eloquent on her favourite subject, her Chinese possessions. Hal was handling the jade pony, his long womanish fingers stroking its serene curves.

"I'll leave you that, dear boy, if you like it so much," said Aunt Suzie.

"You'll do nothing of the kind. It's far too valuable. You'll have me accused of coveting your treasures."

"Well, of course you are, dear boy. Anyone who is human covets what they admire."

"I admire them in their correct setting, which is here, with you as their owner." Hal balanced the jade pony in his hand, as Ben had done earlier. "This adorable creature would be lost in the abysmal clutter of my house. It would probably be pinched by one of my dishonest friends."

"Nobody would steal the pony from me, Aunt Suzie," Ben said earnestly and anxiously. "If you give it to me I'll keep it beside my bed."

"Ben!" Georgina admonished.

"Let him say what he thinks," Aunt Suzie said in her harsh voice. Her heavy face was almost tender. She loved Ben, Georgina knew, and wondered why she resented this, wondered why she had always had that lurking feeling that Aunt Suzie was not to be trusted, that under her deliberately inscrutable demeanour she was a malicious, unscrupulous, even evil old woman whose chief amusement was manipulating people. She only knew that Aunt Henrietta and Aunt Lucy had never approved of their younger sister. But Aunt Henrietta and Aunt Lucy were delightful old-fashioned Victorian ladies, where Aunt Suzie seemed to belong to no age at all. She was uniquely herself, making her own rules of behaviour.

"You shall all have a memento of Dragon House," Aunt Suzie went on, with her air of issuing an edict. "Ben obviously wants the jade pony, so it must be his. When I'm dead, naturally. Hal, dear boy, what would you like?"

"Is that a bribe, Highness?" asked Hal. He gave the radiant smile that endeared him to television and theatre audiences. "You crazy old woman."

"I'm seventy-four, which is old enough, but I'm not crazy. And I am serious. After all, I can't take my treasures with me. Even the last Empress of China couldn't do that, and she was one of the most powerful women in the world. Look at all those dear little clocks that ticked for her. She had them everywhere in her bedroom. Now they're ticking for me. Time's nearly up, Suzie, they say."

"Don't be silly, Aunt Suzie," said Georgina. "You're going to live forever."

"Am I, my love. How very reassuring. But I still adore making my will. It's the last game an old woman can play. That's why I'm apt to change it frequently. Last year I bequeathed all my Ming and Tang pieces to a charming deceitful young man called Peter. But I revoked that will when he disappointed me. I expect good behaviour from my protégés."

"You scare me to death, Highness," said Hal.

Aunt Suzie liked that. She gave one of her infrequent smiles. Her heavily blackened eyebrows lifted, making her long face clownish. It should have been funny, but it wasn't. It was curiously chilling.

"Splendid. I like to be taken seriously. You see, my problem is that when my father brought these pieces from Peking they were relatively modest acquisitions. Loot, if you like. But now their value has gone up immensely. Don't think I don't know that. I will look after my family, of course. But I also like to reward friendship. Especially friends who amuse me and are loyal." Her old hand with the macabre nail shields came out to lie on Hal's. "I value loyalty most of all. I can't tolerate traitors. If I were the great Tz'u-Hsi, I would have their heads off and the courtyard running with blood."

"She's playacting," Georgina said to Hal. "She makes these bribes, or whatever you may call them."

Hal Jessel's blue eyes were sunny, his smile full of charm.

"Don't worry, I don't want bequests. Gruesome things that smell of the grave. If you really insist on giving me something, Highness, give me something modest to remember you by."

"Really, dear boy, I might take you at your word."

"So might I you," said Hal. "But couldn't we change the subject? I thought this was going to be a party."

"It is a party," said Aunt Suzie. "And I'm neglecting my other guests. I must go and talk to the young lady you brought. I haven't decided yet whether I like her." Her eyes slitted maliciously. "You've surprised me. I thought you were one of my eunuchs. You and poor Charles. He from necessity, you, I imagine, from preference. Was I wrong?"

Hal smiled amiably. Only Georgina saw his knuckles whiten with suppressed anger. "I'm an actor, Highness. I can be whatever you wish. If you don't like Amy, then I'm sorry I brought her."

"You know I prefer men to women," Aunt Suzie said. "Tell me, why are girls so skinny nowadays? Worse than Chinese peasants in a famine."

"You must take her seriously when she talks about her will," Georgina told Hal. "It's her favourite subject. She thinks it ties people to her. I expect she always distrusts their motives."

"I imagine all rich old women do that. It's an inbuilt risk, having valuables. But some can use that particular power to better advantage than others. Your aunt is quite an entrepreneur."

"She's a bit mad," Georgina admitted. "More than a bit. But she's my father's youngest sister, so I feel bound to come here when she asks me to. Not that I want her treasures. I feel they're stained with blood. So did my father and my other aunts. But Aunt Suzie is the most unfeeling and unscrupulous old woman I know."

"As well as being mad?"

"As well as."

"You're certainly honest."

"But she's pathetic, too. She's almost as lonely as poor Charles. That's why I feel we must come when she asks us. Thank goodness Ben adores coming."

"And your husband?"

"He hates it. Although he's happier right now, talking to your girl friend. She is your girl friend, isn't she?"

Hal shrugged. "We're business associates. I'm helping her get established in London as an interior decorator. I thought she'd be wild about this place."

And privately assess the value of everything, Georgina wondered, and hated herself for her suspicious mind. There had been too many Hals in the past, but fortunately their friendship had not outlived Aunt Suzie. Hal's might, if only for the reason that Aunt Suzie was getting older every day.

Ben slept in the old nursery where his grandfather and his two aunts had been children. Georgie, Henrietta and Lucy, and their governess, Miss Deacon. No, Miss Deacon had only been with them in Peking. Before leaving England they had had an English nanny. Ben wondered about them a great deal. They had never been the old people he knew. They were forever children, lively, naughty, noisy, defiant or obedient, as the mood took them. He sometimes thought he heard them talking. Henrietta, the eldest, was bossy, Lucy timid, Georgie living in his world of fancies.

They are all inside me, thought Ben, but refrained from saying so to his mother who had come in to kiss him good-night. But they *were* all inside him, as he knew from his feelings when he played the Boxer Rebellion with Aunt Suzie. He could always hear the children crying, even Georgie who pretended to be brave.

Once he had opened a cupboard and found a lot of toys, dusty, the paint faded on them, but utterly enchanting. The cavalrymen wore red and gold uniforms, the train had a chimney and funny carriages, there was a governess cart drawn by a donkey, and some dolls with china faces and real hair. He liked the toys almost as much as he liked Aunt Suzie's jade pony, and the little horned dragon. Tonight the jade pony was on the table beside his bed. He had asked permission to have it beside him. He was afraid that tall man with the yellow hair would steal it. He knew that man had come to steal.

"Benny, love, you're too acquisitive," said his mother, standing over him. "Don't get to be a miser with your things."

With his glasses off, Ben found the slight figure at his bedside agreeably blurred.

"Did the other children's mother come and say goodnight to them?" he asked.

"Grandmother Amelia? Yes, I expect she did. She was very beautiful, they said. She had red hair. It was said that Grandfather thought she was like one of those curly bronze chrysanthemums that the Chinese are so clever with."

Ben knew all this, of course, but he never tired of hearing it again. "Can I look at the picture of the family again?"

"Oh, darling, it's on the mantelpiece in the dining room. Well, very well, if it's so important to you."

Georgina went downstairs, and presently came back with the faded brown photograph.

"It was taken soon after they all got back from China. Grandmother was ill. She never really recovered from the dreadful experience they had gone through. That's why she isn't in the picture and the nurse is holding the baby."

"The baby is Aunt Suzie?"

"You know perfectly well."

Ben studied every detail of the children in the photograph, Henrietta tall and solemn, Lucy wide-eyed, seemingly apprehensive of the photographer. Both of them wore pinafore dresses, and had their hair in braids.

Their brother, Georgie, was sporting a kilt, and grinning cheerfully. He looked a cheerful little boy. Grandfather Carrington stood very upright and looked stern and rather miserable. Probably, Ben suggested, he was unhappy about Grandmother Amelia, who wasn't well enough to be in the picture. The baby's face was a blur.

Ben was endlessly curious about the group. He could never find out enough about them and the Boxer Rebellion. Aunt Lucy was too old and forgetful and anyway had deliberately buried memories of the siege in her mind. Aunt Suzie, although she knew a great deal from hearsay, had been unlucky enough not to be born.

So Ben made up his own stories. After his mother had kissed him good-night, saying he could keep the photograph on the table by his bed if he so much wanted to, he lay in the dark repeating the lines of a poem by a Chinese poet which his mother sometimes read to him.

And in my dreams I see
The little ghosts of Maytime waving farewell to me . . .

He thought he could hear the children whispering in the quiet room. But it was probably only Aunt Suzie's pugs, sniffling at the door.

Chapter 5

Aunt Suzie always gave Georgina and Hugh the room that had been Nathaniel and Amelia Carrington's. It had a wide old-fashioned bed with a high bolster and snowy white bedspread. The wardrobe was enormous, the dressing table a black and gold lacquered piece too good to put modern cosmetic jars and bottles on. The pictures were Chinese paintings on glass in gilt frames. A faded washed blue Chinese carpet covered the floor.

One could never escape the Chinese influence in any room in this house. Georgina knew that Hugh found it oppressive. She usually comforted him by pointing out that he could appreciate all the more the spare comfortable furnishings of their mews house in South Kensington when they returned home.

This evening, however, she ignored him when he swore because he had, once again, knocked over the rickety bamboo table beside the bed. This was a frequent occurrence and she believed he did it deliberately. She felt neither amused and tender, nor irritated, tonight. She was engaged in thinking of something else entirely.

"How did you like Hal Jessel's girl? You had a long conversation with her. I must say she looks an unlikely person to be a friend of Hal's. Surely he's just another of Aunt Suzie's eunuchs? She won't take kindly to Hal paying more attention to a girl than to her."

"It's easy to see what that young man is, and what he's here for."

"Pickings?" Georgina shrugged. "He'll have to learn, like his predecessors. That famous will is changed pretty often. Anyway, Hal protests charmingly that he doesn't want a thing."

"I've seen his kind in the dock," Hugh said cynically.

"Oh, I know. Aunt Suzie will take these foolish risks. But I was asking you how you liked Amy Russell."

"She thought I was pompous."

Georgina smiled, and put her hands on his cheek in a caress.

"You can be sometimes, but I happen to like it."

He was far from pompous when he responded to her affection. He had a young and vulnerable look, not unlike Ben's, and she got that ache of love in her throat.

"Why do girls think it's attractive to be so skinny?" he said. "That kid looked about fifteen years old and starved."

"She's twenty-six if she's a day. And she looks to me like one of those restless women who are never placid enough to put on weight."

"Darling, you're being bitchy."

"No, just factual. You always tell me to be factual."

"So I do. But I think that remark was a little of each. It may interest you to know that Miss Russell would like to decorate our drawing room or our kitchen or even our bathroom. She isn't ambitious."

Georgina brushed her hair vigorously, looking at herself in the blurred glass of the old mirror. How different her face was from the thin clever one of Amy Russell. It was dreamy, soft, even a little stupid. Or was guileless a better word? Though actually she was neither stupid nor guileless. Beneath the cynicism in Hugh's voice she had detected something else. For all his pretended indignation, being called pompous had seemed to give some pleasure. It had depended entirely on who used the word, of course. Perhaps anything Amy Russell said would intrigue him.

"Neither our drawing room nor our kitchen nor bathroom needs redecorating. When it does I'll do it myself. Do make that clear to the unambitious Amy, Hugh. Politely, of course. I wouldn't want to criticise her work since I haven't seen it. Does she share Aunt Suzie's mania for chinoiserie?"

"I gather that's partly why she's here. Hal had told her so much about it. I'd have thought she was an Andy Warhol, Francis Bacon, Picasso girl."

"If she is she won't get invited here again."

"I shouldn't think she'd want to be. She'd have much more fun in her own haunts."

"What are they? Did she tell you?"

"Wine bars. Italian trattorias. I'm only guessing."

"Then she'll enjoy her dinner tonight. And she may get a VSOP cognac afterwards. She looks to me as if she exists from weekend to weekend."

"Georgina, you *are* being bitchy."

"If ever I saw a pair of opportunists—well, perhaps I am being unfair. Prejudging. Hugh, do talk to Charles tonight. He looks so miserable. There he is stuck in that chair with a dragon of a nurse, and he can't play his mother's game of making wills and wielding power. She's quite capable of leaving everything to her current favourite, and leaving him stranded. Besides, I would like Ben to get some of the Chinese things. I believe he's inherited Grandfather Carrington's passion for the Orient. Do you mind?"

Since this was his familiar Georgina, mixing up the thread of her arguments, Hugh smiled and said, "Not if that is what he wants to do. It might even be a good thing. China's getting to be a power in the world again. But he's got to look forward, not backwards to old wars, and imperial oppression."

"Yes, I know that. When I'm in this house I look backwards, too. I keep thinking of Amelia sitting at this mirror."

"Amelia?"

"My grandmother. She died long before I was born, but I was always told that she was beautiful. The weird thing is that I think I see her in this mirror with tears in her eyes. I suspect Grandfather Carrington was cruel to her with that special kind of righteous Victorian cruelty. I wonder if he had other women."

"I thought Victorian men were made of iron."

"They were sexy and sadistic, and very often, quite undeservedly, their wives adored them. I'm perfectly sure Amelia sat at this mirror wondering if her dress and her coiffure would please her husband."

"Well, yours pleases me, if that was angling for a compliment. I like that blue thing. Have I seen it before?"

"You know you've seen it twenty times at least." Georgina frowned. "That must make it very unremarkable."

"Don't be so touchy, darling."

"Yes, I am being, aren't I? I was only wondering what the little interior decorator will be wearing. She follows the way-out designers, I'll make a bet. She'll have spiky eyelashes and red spots on her cheekbones, and I'll feel horribly old-fashioned."

"I believe you're jealous." Hugh was half exasperated, half pleased. He paused from doing up his shirt, as if he were going to take it off again.

Watching him, Georgina was half pleased, too, desire stirring slowly and sweetly in her. But it wasn't the right time to make love when Hugh was titillated by another woman and she had been unable to resist provoking him about it.

It wasn't like her to behave like this. Poor Amelia had probably had to keep her mouth shut, if her husband erred.

Really, why was her mind so much on Amelia tonight? It was this house. It had the same effect on Ben. They both had the strong feeling that the people who had lived in it had never left it.

And looking back over the times they had spent here, Georgina realised, with a vaguely disturbing shock, that she and Hugh had never made love in that wide Victorian bed. And were not going to do so now.

* * *

Mrs. Suzie Blenheim, Aunt Suzie, or privately to herself Tz'u-Hsi, had little to do to dress for dinner. She merely substituted one stiff silk robe for another. This time she chose a rich crimson which she had been told was the colour of the Imperial Palace in Peking. These loose garments made the whole business of dressing simple, for no restricting girdles were necessary, a comfort to her rotund body, and she had never had her feet bound.

Her feet bound indeed! Whatever was she thinking? Sometimes she really did confuse herself with the Empress Dowager who had good square unbound Manchu feet.

She had to remind herself more and more frequently that this was only a game she played, for it often became astonishingly real. She liked deferential, even servile behaviour from her servants and guests. She had a penchant for actors because she believed she was an outstanding actress herself, and could have made her career on the stage if she hadn't belonged to a stiff, starchy middle-class family who believed only in marriage and domesticity for young women. This meant that she had suffered intensely from frustration, which made her an unsuccessful wife who was accused of killing off her husbands by neglect.

The new young man, Hal Jessel, whom she had seen in a play on television, and immediately obtained his address from the BBC was perfectly charming. He pleased her in every way, except on this visit when he had asked permission to bring a girl friend. She would soon put a stop to that sort of thing. He had only been to Dragon House twice before. It really was a bit presumptuous to ask favours so soon. But she had been afraid he wouldn't come if she had said Amy Russell was not welcome. So she had permitted it, for once.

Hal really was the most handsome of all her young men, and the most amusing and endearing. She couldn't bear to lose him yet. She might even have to weaken and give him an early reward. It was important, however, not to break her rule about giving things. Once people had their greedy hands on some cherished object they, and the object, disappeared forever. She had learned that lesson when she had playfully offered a T'ang horse to a clever young man who wrote totally obscure poetry. He had taken her at her word, packed it in his luggage, and gone. She had contemplated reporting the matter to the police as a theft, then had had second and wiser thoughts. In future she wouldn't give things away, she would only promise them in her will. Wills could be changed. But the promise could buy her amusing and desirable friendships for a long time to come.

Could she be blamed, a lonely widow, whose only company was an invalid son who hated her? And if there were a slight element of danger in this game, it made it more enjoyable. She was not a coward. The great Empress Dowager of China had never been a coward.

To be sure, she would never want to deprive Ben, her great-nephew, who was the only person she loved faithfully. The young men came and went. Hugh, Ben's father, put her on her guard, the upholding of law was his profession and he looked as if he always wanted to cross-examine her. Georgina, Georgie's girl, was nice enough, but too much like Suzie's elder sisters, Henrietta and Lucy, who had always patronised her because she had been an unwanted fourth child, and her mother hadn't loved her as much as the others. Apart from her birth being unwanted and doing disastrous things to her mother's health, the delicate and lovely Amelia couldn't believe she had a plain child.

Well, the plain child was now not only in possession of the family home, bought fairly on the winding up of Nathaniel Carrington's estate, but also of the Chinese collection which none of the others had wanted.

To be sure, that was forty years ago, and it hadn't had a tenth of its present value. They may well have regretted their decision later. However, it all proved that she was the real Carrington, the true daughter of old Nathaniel. And the next Carrington was not Charles, her son, or Georgina, but her great-nephew Ben. One saw that in his appreciation of her treasures. He would inherit the jade pony and the twin carp and the Ming bowl depicting the Three Friends of bamboo, pine and Prunus, and the little bronze horned dragon, whose only known counterpart was in a famous American museum.

Unless she got careless, of course, and Hal Jessel or one of his successors looted the treasures of Dragon House, piece by piece. But she would never allow that to happen. She was far too strong-minded and observant, and not the sort of person to grow senile like poor silly Lucy.

She looked round her room, seeing the high narrow bed, reached by a footstool, the black and gold lacquered furniture, the statue of Kuan-Yin, the Goddess of Mercy, on her bedside table, the elaborately carved mirrors, the wind-bells on the windowsill so sensitively made that they tinkled with a ghostly sound in the slightest draught. Above all she saw the reflection of herself in the pier glass, a squat but regal figure, impressively clad in the crimson embroidered robe, her head held high in a majestic pose, long jade earrings hanging from her ears, her folded hands with the grotesque little fingernails two inches long. When she put on the turquoise-studded protectors she liked to think she was sheathing her dragon's claws.

Last of all she slid the heavy pearl ring, the Empress Dowager's personal gift to her mother, onto the fourth finger of her left hand, where for years it had taken the place of wedding rings, or other gifts of fidelity. She never considered herself dressed without that ring. It made her feel imperial.

She smiled secretly to herself as she waited for the brazen clash of the gong, an instrument that had once heralded the comings and goings of royal personages in the Forbidden City. It was a pity, she thought, that it now only announced dinner. What could be done about such an anticlimax? One day she would think of an effective answer to that: something to startle her tame English guests.

Amy Russell heard the gong, and jumped convulsively. She was ridiculously nervous. Hal had said no need to be, Mrs. Blenheim was a crazy old woman who played slightly macabre games. But the atmosphere of Dragon House was more than she had bargained for. The place was fantastic. She could swear that rather clumsy bowl in the hall holding umbrellas was a wine jar made in the thirteenth or fourteenth century. If it was, its value was unguessable. She longed to get it to London to an expert. She knew a good deal herself but not that much.

The other disturbing element was Hugh Morley. He was just the sort of well-educated, fantastically good-mannered Englishman who excited her. Hal would hoot with laughter if he knew. Or would he? Sometimes there was something chilling about Hal. His charm hid a cool, calculating, greedy nature. She recognised it because she had the same nature herself. Which didn't mean that she had to admire it, or have no other quality but an obsessive desire for money and objects of value. Her greed extended to emotional things. Hal's didn't. That was the difference between them.

Georgina Morley was the sort of woman who made Amy angry, partly because she was so vague and genuinely nice and unself-conscious, more because she was Hugh's wife. She had her gentle grasp on something Amy would like for a while, anyway.

The old woman beneath all that ridiculous splendour could be a sham, and one wasn't really afraid of her. Poor Charles in his invalid chair was part of the furniture.

But Hugh Morley absorbed most of her thoughts. It had been fun to put on her long white-frilled romantic dress that made her look like a demure Victorian bride. She knew it would be the last thing Hugh expected her to wear. She anticipated his surprise. Sometimes she wished she didn't think so much about sex. Not love. That was old-fashioned, and a fraud. But sex could impede work and get her into unnecessarily awkward situations. Nevertheless, it was the vital part of life. She hoped it wouldn't affect her judgement. Perhaps Hal was lucky after all, to be unimpeded by emotions.

* * *

Charles insisted on propelling his wheelchair himself because, in spite of his paralysis, he remained fiercely independent. He hated his present nurse, a placid bovine creature. In his frustration he made all nurses the object of his hate. He knew that he was mean, querulous,

unfair, but by being so the hot knot of rage inside him
eased slightly. Live with your disability, come to terms
with it, remember you have the advantages of wealth and
every comfort. Succeeding doctors and psychiatrists and
the everlasting nurses had preached the familiar sermon.

But let them try this death in life, they with their
strong tireless legs, their freedom. Just let them try it.
And let them try accepting financial dependence on a
woman like his mother, and living in this Oriental museum. Mother had put a Buddha in his room, on the
mantelpiece, out of his reach, otherwise he would have
smashed the fat grinning creature. She had thought a
study of Buddhism might help him. But he had no sense
of the mystical. Even if he could have smoked an opium
pipe every evening, he doubted if he would have pene-
trated any veils. And where could you now get opium in
this damned dull country?

His life was over. It had only existed for those few
years between leaving school and having his accident.
He had been a thin, small, neurotically brilliant young
man, oddly enough attractive to women. He had gam-
bled, drank, dabbled a little in drugs, grass mostly, and
the odd opium pipe smoked in a dingy room behind a
Chinese laundry in Camden Town, been seen at all the
smart places, helped himself, justly he considered, to some
of his mother's money, and then pfft! He was a rag
doll in a wheelchair.

The only tolerable thing now was watching from the
sidelines as his silly mother made herself more and more
ridiculous.

He had a curved Chinese sword, the kind the Boxers
had used, on the wall in his bedroom. Sometimes he
indulged in fantasies of using it on himself or on the
more abhorrent of his mother's guests, or on the grand
matriarch herself.

Certainly not on his cousin Georgina who was the only
person he could communicate with, even though that

was to a limited extent. Just occasionally she could dig beneath his bitterness and find his trembling spirit.

She had the idea that he should begin a garden in the spring.

"You could, Charles. There are all sorts of gardening tools for the handicapped. I thought of that sheltered corner that gets so much sun. You could have a border of pansies for me, because I adore them. And stock that smells so marvellous at night. And a sundial or a bird-bath or both. Old Smythe is so absorbed in making his yew dragon, he's neglecting the flower garden. Ben would fetch and carry for you. He'd probably want to plant a willow tree. And chrysanthemums in the autumn. Those big shaggy ones." She saw his lack of enthusiasm and said, "I'm talking like this because I've only got a patio and plants in tubs, and I long for a real garden."

"Don't you think the matriarch gets madder?" said Charles.

"She's seventy-four. And she always was a bit mad. But haven't you been listening to me?"

Charles nodded reluctantly. "I just find it hard to be anything but bloody-minded. Gardens don't go with that condition. I might deliberately cultivate weeds. But what about that?" He couldn't resist drawing Georgina's attention to Hugh, who was once again absorbed in conversation with Amy Russell. Not surprising, perhaps, since Amy had unexpectedly turned into a picture of femininity. No spiky eyelashes, no gimmicky makeup. Just a demure child in white muslin, and Hugh was falling for that carefully calculated image. Well, never mind, it would make his weekend more bearable, and she was not going to be drawn by Charles' malicious insinuations.

"That girl puzzles me," she said.

"She's a tramp."

"Do you think that's all she is? I've a funny feeling there's more to it. Oh, I don't know. I seem to get things out of perspective in this house. I think it's the influence of your mother. She projects her fantasies and they're rather violent ones. Or so they seem to me. She broods over the place."

"Then don't come down. No, I don't mean that. You must come."

Georgina looked at him with her gentle luminous gaze. "You know I will."

The winter wind was beginning to moan about the house. Georgina thought she could hear the willow branches thrashing above the black water of the river. She remembered suddenly how Father had talked of the bitter wind from the Gobi desert blowing over Peking. One had imagined it was always summer there, but it was not. Amelia had shivered in her long feather boa, and Nathaniel had bought furs from the Mongolian traders who drove their camel trains through the gates of the city.

Thinking aloud, Georgina said for the second time that evening, "They said she was like a bronze chrysanthemum."

"Who?"

"Our grandmother. I wish we had a portrait of her. It's sad for someone lovely to absolutely disappear from the earth."

"Unlovely people disappear, too."

"Thank goodness. But I don't know why I always think of Amelia when I'm in this house. And Ben thinks of the children."

"Georgina," came Aunt Suzie's harsh voice. "Hal has been asking me about this tomb horse. It came from the Ming tombs, you know. Not when my father first visited them, they were unopened then, and sacred. But much later. It was still desecration, however."

"Then aren't you superstitious about giving it house room?" Hal asked in his teasing voice.

"That was partly what the Boxer Rebellion was about," Aunt Suzie went on. "The spoilation of the country's treasures by the barbarians. No, I'm not superstitious, dear boy. I regard myself as the rightful guardian of these treasures."

Hal gave his charming smile. "Then you must arrange a Ming tomb for yourself, Highness."

"And bury all these things with me? What a perfectly brilliant idea." The glitter of Aunt Suzie's eyes showed beneath her heavy eyelids. "Then everyone would be foiled, wouldn't they?"

"And you'd be deprived of your favourite game, Mother," said Charles with his cold lucidity. "No more wills to be made?"

"That would make a pleasant change," said Hugh, and Georgina crossed the room to where he sat with Amy Russell.

"What have you two been talking about?" she asked.

"Fashions, actually," said Amy disarmingly. "Hugh said you had a very beautiful grandmother, and she must have worn dresses rather like this one I'm wearing. We go backwards and forwards, don't we?"

"Yes, we do," said Georgina. Backwards and forwards. Forwards and backwards. She was no longer seeing the girl with her shrewd provocative face and her virginal dress, but hearing the wind sweeping against the house, and thinking of Grandmother Amelia and the children listening nervously to stories about the marauding Boxers, and their inexorable advance on Peking. . . .

Dragon House, Peking

May, 1900

Chapter 6

It was getting unbearably hot in Peking. Usually May brought pleasantly warm weather, but this year the whole province was in the grip of a drought. The plains were scorched brown, the riverbeds dry, and the miracle of the spring, with almond and plum blossom, budding willows, singing birds, nothing but a memory.

One didn't know too much, in the heart of this dry dusty city, what went on in the country. Communications were unreliable, rumours prevalent. But it was certain that the rice crops had failed and there would be widespread famine. This grim prospect added to the unrest. It was said that the Boxers blamed the drought on the presence of the unwanted foreigners, and Sir Claude MacDonald wrote in an official letter to London,

I am now convinced that a few days' heavy rainfall to terminate the long-continued drought which has helped largely to excite unrest in the country districts would do more to restore tranquillity than any measures which either the Chinese government or foreign governments can take.

Lilian's last letter from Shansi had been disturbing, but it had taken six weeks to reach Amelia, so its news was already out of date. Nobody knew how much the situation she had written about had improved or worsened.

Lilian said they had had several scares at the mission, with small groups of Chinese soldiers bursting into the schoolroom and the church, waving rusty swords and spears. Thomas was awfully brave. So far he had been able to persuade the soldiers to leave peacefully. They were members of the terrifying Boxer army because they wore red sashes and red ribbons in their pigtails, or red turbans. Some of them were very young, merely high-spirited foolish youths. Lilian, however, thought them sinister, in spite of their youth.

They look as if they hate us unmercifully [she wrote]. They call us foreign devils, but their own expressions are far more devilish than ours. They grin evilly and make fearsome faces, and their eyes blaze with hatred. Thomas is such a saint. He says God will show them the error of their ways, but I am convinced they can't hear anything but their own war cries. Last week a church not twenty miles away was burned down, and we don't know what happened to Mr. Blundell and his wife, two Catholic missionaries. Although Thomas remains calm, I am terrified, not only for Thomas and Angel and myself but for all our converts working in the hospital and the mission school. I am urging Thomas to let us pack up and come to you in Peking, but he is so rigid, almost fanatical about his duty that I fear I shall never succeed. I am also fearful for Angel, but she is a remarkably independent child who does not seem to have any sense of fear. I envy you being in a fortified city. You can close the gates of the Tartar wall and be safe. The British government would never allow anything to happen to its legation, whereas a few missionaries are lost in this great wilderness. When you reply to this letter please don't mention my cowardice. Thomas would not like it.

Amelia discussed the letter and its disturbing news with Nathaniel. Formerly, he had paid little serious attention to the rumours of an uprising, saying, as Lilian had, that if a handful of mad Chinese peasants did attack Peking they were quite safe within the perimeter of the Tartar wall. Lilian and Thomas, of course, were a different matter, and Amelia might be wise to add her pleas to Lilian's and persuade Thomas to bring his family to Peking. It seemed that missionaries were a prime target for Boxers. Several of the unfortunate preachers had had their heads cut off.

Seeing his wife's face, he added hurriedly that he was sure Thomas could take care of himself. No one would dare to attack that crusty John Knox. If Thomas did die in that way it would be because he had secretly hoped for such a death, imitating his Maker. Amelia was wasting her sympathy on him. He was the stuff of martyrs.

"It's Lilian and Angel I'm worrying about," Amelia said.

"Then write and urge her to come. How old is the girl?"

"Angel? She's Lucy's age. Just eight. You know that."

"Yes, of course. I should have remembered. Then she can join the class in the schoolroom. Miss Deacon will look after her. I must say the children are getting on famously. Even our lazy son who's usually lost in daydreams."

"Has Miss Deacon told you so?"

"They have themselves. Haven't you seen me patiently listening to their display of knowledge?"

Nathaniel was a good but stern father. He liked to see his children clean, well-dressed, good-mannered and silent. He was proud of them, and went to a lot of trouble to think of an exhortation for them each morning. Lately he had followed a new practice, and instead of lecturing them at the breakfast table he did so in the schoolroom. He sat at the table beside Miss Deacon, discussed briefly their plans for the day, delivered his motto, "Be obedient. Georgie, Miss Deacon tells me you have a tendency to answer back. You must quell it. Remember, manners makyth man."

Amelia was acutely aware of this brief session, and felt excluded, as she had never done when Nathaniel's fatherly admonitions had been made at the breakfast table. She knew that Miss Deacon's large moody eyes would have their luminous look, for it had soon been apparent that the girl responded all too readily to masculine society.

However, apart from that characteristic, one had to admit that she had behaved impeccably during the three months she had lived in the house. She was an unorthodox teacher, the children appearing to learn their lessons by fun more than by industry. Peals of laughter frequently came from the schoolroom. One would think that nothing but games went on. Nevertheless, Henrietta could recite all the kings and queens of England, and do marvellous needlework, Lucy's reading had improved remarkably, and Georgie, for the first time in this life, was beginning to understand arithmetic. It was done by adding up dragons, he said engagingly.

Unorthodox certainly, but imaginative, and who could complain if Miss Deacon kept the children busy and happy. As Nathaniel pointed out, Amelia now had plenty of time to arrange the luncheon parties and soirées, which she enjoyed.

If it was tiresome having always to find a spare man to balance the table at a dinner party, there were many other compensations for having Miss Deacon living in the house. At first the nice young man, Rupert Fortescue, who had accompanied Nathaniel on his expedition to the

Ming tombs, had been available. But lately his apologies were more frequent than his appearances. Had he an objection to being partnered with Miss Deacon? Had they begun to dislike one another?

Amelia made an airy enquiry.

"Miss Deacon, have you any idea why Rupert suddenly has such a busy social life? He can't come to my dinner party next week."

Miss Deacon gave her small smile, her thin lips curved upwards. She looked very plain this morning.

"Don't blame me, Mrs. Carrington. I have nothing to do with it."

"I wasn't blaming you. But by the way you look you know something."

"Of course. Everyone does. Rupert has fallen in love with a Chinese girl. Her name is Almond Chen."

"Oh, dear me, that won't do at all," Amelia exclaimed, then saw Miss Deacon's look of cynicism and—was it derision?

"Why won't it do, Mrs. Carrington? Almond is very attractive and Rupert is a bachelor. Plenty of white men have married Chinese women happily."

"But they've not gone back to England happily."

"Oh, that's your cruel class system. Perhaps Rupert won't want to go home. Perhaps he'll choose to stay here, like Colonel Manners and Lady Comerford."

"Who are not the happiest people I know. Exiles never are. And it would be fatal to Rupert's career. You can't tell me that that nice but rather unimaginative young man would count the world well lost for love."

Miss Deacon's eyes were demure.

"Wouldn't everybody, if they could?"

"When they're extremely young, perhaps," Amelia said crossly. "Not when they've reached mature years like myself and my husband. We count other things, like companionship, similarity of interests, being parents."

Good heavens, she was defending herself and Nathaniel to this very young and silly girl who *was* looking at her pityingly. This wouldn't do at all. And what a nuisance about Rupert Fortescue and his unfortunate liaison. It was just one more pinprick of anxiety. Her initial enthralment with Peking was over and she knew that she would be glad when they could go back to England and safety. Here, there was the often slightly bizarre behaviour of exiled white people, the dreadful worry about Lilian and Thomas, the irritation—yes, it was certainly irritation, if nothing worse—of having Medora Deacon so firmly established in the house, and in everyone's affections. Except hers. She still had a deep uneasiness about the girl. Or, to be entirely truthful, was it uneasiness about the character of her husband?

What was fact was this very trying dry weather that went on and on, the heat intensifying each day, a black dust that smudged one's clothes and tasted bitter in one's mouth constantly hanging in the air, the great domes of the palaces of the Imperial City, burning golden and crimson, adding to the atmosphere of uncomfortable heat. The branches of Georgie's willow tree were hanging heavily, the leaves wilting already. The goldfish swam sluggishly in the dark green water of the pool. Even the gay little caged birds that the servants liked to keep on the balconies were almost silent. None of the white ladies ever ventured outside without a parasol, not even the boyish Medora who used to go about carelessly without hat or gloves. One wondered how much longer it would be before everyone got ill.

Amelia, having finished her letter to Lilian urgently begging her to set out at once for Peking ("Before anything worse happens, my darling. There are rumours that the railway trains may be attacked. Nathaniel and I can't contemplate you and Angel remaining among these dangers, even if Thomas is so brave"), turned listlessly to her dinner party list.

Sir Claude and Lady MacDonald
Lady Comerford
Colonel Manners
Mr. and Mrs. Conger
Rupert Fortescue (?)
Miss Deacon

Why had she ever embarked on this project? The evening after her party there was to be the party at the British legation celebrating the Queen's birthday. That would have been enough gaiety for one week. Not that her dinner party would be particularly gay, unless she succeeded in getting the house cooler, and persuaded Li to produce something spectacular in the way of ices and cold punch.

She would wear her lilac muslin. Nathaniel had always liked that gown. It belonged to a green English garden beside the cool Thames, he said. She was more than a little homesick just now. She wondered if he were, too, although this she doubted.

Georgie was elated at the thought of his cousin Angel coming to visit.

"She can tell us about the Boxers," he said. "She's actually seen them, lucky thing."

"It isn't lucky to see a Boxer," Henrietta said. "It's very dangerous. They have swords and guns."

"And they yell *'Sha Sha!'*" Georgie cried enthusiastically. "That means they want to kill you."

Lucy's fists shot into her eyes. The blank terror filled her, as it always did when the Boxers and their violent ways were talked about. When they killed her, she thought, she would die absolutely silently, her throat choked up, unable even to scream.

"Georgie, do shut up. You're frightening Lucy again. You know very well the Boxers won't come to Peking. That's why Angel and Uncle Thomas and Aunt Lilian are probably coming here to be safe."

"Miss Deacon says they'll come here." Georgie

marched up and down the courtyard, brandishing a bamboo spear. "She doesn't mind. She likes exciting things happening."

"That's just not true," Henrietta said indignantly. "The Boxers aren't coming. Sir Claude MacDonald says they aren't and he should know. And even if they do, Miss Deacon will be just as frightened as everyone else."

"I'm quite brave," said Georgie. "I think. I'm sure Papa is."

"Do stop talking about the Boxers, Georgie. You're making Lucy cry. Anyway, how could they be expected when there's the ball at the British legation for the Queen's birthday next week? Lady MacDonald says there will be paper lanterns in all the trees, and fireworks. Mamma says we can go for an hour and then Ah Wan will take us home because Miss Deacon will want to stay and dance. Lucy and I are to wear our muslins, and I suppose you'll be in your sailor suit."

"That's too hot. I don't want to wear that. You seem to know an awful lot, Henrietta."

"It's because I'm the eldest and Mamma confides in me," Henrietta said smugly. "What's more, if it goes on being so hot we're all to go and stay in a bungalow in the hills with Lady MacDonald's girls."

"Ugh!" said Georgie.

"What's wrong with that?"

"They're only babies. You can't play games with them. I'd rather it was Angel. She could show us how to fly."

Henrietta ignored this obvious lunacy and said, "We'll go in a Peking cart. You won't be frightened of that, will you, Lucy? We'll have the hood over our heads to keep off the sun."

"Isn't the hills where the Boxers hide?" Lucy asked fearfully.

"Not these hills. Anyway, Mamma says the heat's more dangerous than the Boxers. We might get sick if we stay in Peking."

"I wish we were in England," said Lucy flatly, but neither Henrietta nor Georgie took any notice of that lack of enterprise. In their minds they were already in the hooded cart trundling out of the big gates of the city, into the wild exciting country.

And in the rather dark and airless room in the basement of the trading emporium of James Carrington and Sons, situated in the street of silversmiths and jewellers, Nathaniel Carrington had taken out a small notebook with red leather covers and was adding to the list of his acquisitions since arriving in Peking.

1 Chinese jar, octagonal, blue and white, the decorations having a phoenix, a cockroach and a praying mantis among branches. (Almost certainly Mei P'ing, 14th century. Extremely rare.)

The jar had been brought to him that afternoon by a long-robed Manchu merchant, and after the prolonged polite haggling which the Chinese so enjoyed, he had paid more than he had intended, but much less than the jar was worth in the European market. He knew the collector in Geneva who would be tempted by it. That was if he decided to sell it. He would keep it himself, if he could afford to, and also the wine jar he had acquired on his trip to the Ming tombs with Rupert Fortescue. This had been standing on the floor in one of those notoriously dark and primitive inns on the way to the Mongolian frontier. He had noticed the unusual colours, copper red and cobalt blue in the moulded flowers and leaves, and had identified it as one of the rare successful experiments of fourteenth-century potters. Ching-tê-Chen, he thought triumphantly. What a find, even better than the one his grandfather had once made.

And whatever the Empress Dowager might say about treasures being taken out of China, wasn't he doing the Chinese a service by preserving their treasures? It was a miracle that this jar hadn't been shattered centuries ago. It was certainly never intended to be filled with raw rice wine, and handled carelessly by filthy Mongolian traders.

He had made a more than fair deal with the innkeeper, since the fellow had no knowledge of what he was selling, and was delighted with the small harvest of taels that had come his way. Then there had been the task of getting it back undamaged to Peking. He hadn't allowed Rupert to touch the well-padded package although Rupert was much more expert on mules than he was.

Now he had decided not to risk despatching either it or the Mei P'ing jar to England, but to take them and a few other select treasures with his personal luggage when he returned. In the meantime they would be carefully kept in the deep cellar underneath the shop. It should be safe from fire or other damage if trouble started. His grandfather had had the cellar constructed just before the Opium Wars, and had jubilantly reported that everything was safe, even after the looting and burning of the Imperial Palace.

Nathaniel didn't expect anything more than isolated acts of violence from the Boxers, and they could be quickly put down. He thought Amelia's fears unfounded, but women were prone to alarm. Amelia was a much more nervous creature than Medora Deacon, whose eyes flared with excitement when she heard rumours. Indeed, Nathaniel found it fascinating to have two such different women in close juxtaposition. Amelia was his, Medora, with her thin intense body, he thought fancifully, was the Forbidden City. Yet foreigners had before now fallen to the temptation of looting the Forbidden City.

These thoughts, combined with the brooding sense of danger and heat, stirred an excitement in him that he found difficult to quell. Or, indeed, that he wanted to quell, though he made a token attempt by going back to his little book of treasures.

1 white jade pair carp, fine quality (rare)

1 early Ming blue and white bottle painted with a single dragon

1 T'ang horse with rider and unidentifiable beast on back (very rare, have never seen another like it)

1 Hsuan Te blue and white ewer painted with peonies and three-clawed dragons

Nathaniel stroked the smooth round bodies of the little fish, feeling a sensual pleasure, perhaps identical to the emotions that had possessed the long-ago carver of this pretty toy. To have the ability to create and pass on these pleasurable sensations from century to century was a gift he would dearly like to have possessed. Since he did not possess it, helping to preserve such treasures was the next most satisfying thing. He would have no scruples whatever about robbing tombs if such a venture brought to the light of day delectable objects hidden for centuries. The dead had no sight, no sensitive feeling in the whitened bone of their fingers, no matter what the superstitious beliefs of the Chinese. It was one's duty to give these unique treasures to the world. Life was short enough. One must take and enjoy.

"Papa, Papa!" Unexpectedly that was Georgie's voice on the stairs. "May we come in?"

"Who is 'we'?"

"Miss Deacon and me. We wanted to go to the Mongol city. Miss Deacon thought you should come with us."

The two appeared, Georgie flushed and happy in anticipation of the expedition, Miss Deacon, that still puzzling young woman, looking very governessy indeed in a drab-coloured dress, with a little sailor hat tilted over her long sallow face.

Nathaniel wondered if she took a perverse pleasure in making herself look as plain as possible. It certainly had an effect, whether or not it was the effect she desired, for he had a sudden strong desire to throw away her prim hat and loosen the uncompromising bun of her hair.

"Mr. Carrington, would you come with us? Georgie has set his heart on seeing the camel trains coming in from the desert, or listening to storytellers or having his fortune told. Things like that. But with all these rumours of Boxers in the city I thought maybe we shouldn't go alone."

"You certainly shouldn't. I imagine Mrs. Carrington would be very angry indeed, and so should I. How was it she allowed you to come here?"

"Georgie had a little accident. Look." Medora lifted the hair from Georgie's forehead and displayed a reddened contusion. "It was to take his mind off that that we came."

"I fell out of the willow tree," Georgie explained. "That crooked branch I sit on broke. Mamma said it's like China, going rotten."

"Then you keep out of that tree in future," his father said. "But I don't see too much harm has been done. You'll heal."

"I thought it was the wizard," Georgie said compulsively, but under his breath. He knew his father didn't have too much belief in what he called babyish fancies. "I thought I had made him angry."

"No doubt if there was such a thing as a wizard you would certainly have tried his patience, as you do other people's quite frequently. Isn't that so, Miss Deacon?"

Medora's hand lay on Georgie's shoulder. All at once, and for the first time, Nathaniel observed its perfection. It was like the slim quiet hand of his little statue of Kuan Yin. Healthily browned but narrow and exquisite. Strange, on that boyish bony body. It was a hand for wielding a fan, for making fluent and fluid caresses. . . .

"Then if we're to do an expedition," he said abruptly, "we'd better begin. Just wait while I lock up things."

Since it was not a great distance to walk to the great

Ch'ien Men gate guarded by its stone lions, they set off on foot and had soon left the comparative quiet of the legation district to enter the broad highway, packed, noisy, picturesque, squalid and odiferous, of the Tartar city.

Georgie, although he had seen it on other occasions, was as entranced as always. He stared at the rope dancers, the puppeteers, the pedlars with their paniers of sweetmeats, rice cakes and toys, the water carriers, barbers and shoe cleaners. He wanted to look into every huddled dark shop with its watchful occupant. The dilapidation was appalling, but the vivid life of the ragged crowd was something unknown beyond the Tien An Men gate, the Gate of Heavenly Peace, leading to the Forbidden City, or even beyond the Ch'ien Men gate and the legation quarter with its spacious parks and flowering trees and orderly streets of silversmiths and jewellers. Peking carts drawn by coolies collided with one another, a string of camels laden and complaining padded through the dust, their Mongol drivers tattered, dirty and villainous.

Medora, although she had walked down these streets before, clung to Nathaniel's arm, perhaps pretending a nervousness she did not feel. He would not have put that pleasant little affectation past her. Georgie, however, resisted any control, and wanted to stop and watch everything, a small group of men in fearsome masks miming some story, a shaggy brown bear being led on a chain, a mandarin in brilliant robes carried in a chair by servants, clusters of half-naked children playing in the dust. Everywhere there was noise, the high shrill voices bargaining, the groaning of the camels, the distant blare of trumpets, the thin sound of wind-bells that was a haunting constant accompaniment to the life of the city.

"Isn't it fascinating?" Medora said breathlessly. "I just adore it all. Could we go shopping? I'd like to send Mamma some jade earrings. I just love bargaining. I might even find a peace offering for Aunt Agatha. But I don't know when I'll deliver anything because I don't ever want to go home."

"Not even if the Boxers attack? Can you imagine the chaos if they do?" Nathaniel waved his arm towards the huddled shops and shanties. "All this will go down like a house of cards. I must ask you never to come here alone, the way feeling is about Europeans at present."

Medora's eyes, Nathaniel saw, had got their strange brilliant shine. It was very infectious. He was almost imagining some Oriental romance among all the squalor though it would be hard to explain where he saw it. He had forbidden Amelia to go into this part of the city. Her fastidious senses would be outraged.

But Medora obviously revelled in the smell of spice and dung, colour and noise and heat. She was saying slyly, "Do you think I might be kidnapped and taken off to the Willow Lanes or the Flower Streets?"

"I hope you don't speak of those places in front of the children," he said sharply.

"I'm sorry, Mr. Carrington. I was only joking. Anyway, I'm not beautiful enough. Chinese girls are so small, like dolls."

Her eyelids were dropped with apparent modesty. Yet Nathaniel knew she had made that provocative remark so that he would look at her. As he inevitably did, seeing her trim waist, the flush in her sallow cheeks, those tapering fingers on his arm.

"It isn't a subject for joking," he said sternly. "I think it's time to go back. My wife will be worrying, especially since Georgie had that bump."

"I'm all right, Papa! It doesn't hurt a bit."

"You think so, old fellow. You can't be sure. I think rest is now indicated. Anyway, I find this overpowering stink a bit too much. We should have chosen cooler weather. Perhaps the rain will come soon. Then all this tension will end."

"But it mustn't rain tomorrow night," Medora said. "It will spoil Lady MacDonald's party. She's counting on fine weather."

"Oh, so you're invited? How did that come about?"

"Since my mother wrote to Mrs. Conger assuring her that I was a perfectly—well, reasonably respectable person, I guess I'm eligible for parties. Mr. Carrington, you're teasing me! You know very well that Mamma wrote to Mrs. Carrington too, and I expect you read her letter."

"The trouble is," said Nathaniel, "when to treat you like a governess and when to treat you like—"

"A social equal?"

"If that's how you like to put it."

"Shall we try it tomorrow night?" Medora murmured, her voice scarcely audible above the noise. She might almost have been suddenly shy.

But she wasn't, of course. She was plain devious. A devious woman was something he would have nothing to do with. It led to mischief, trouble, grief.

And diversion. If life were a little dull.

But life was far from dull in Peking in the month of May, 1900.

Chapter 7

At the appropriate moment toasts were drunk to her Britannic Majesty, Queen Victoria, and the Chinese band played the British national anthem.

Every representative of the eleven nations at Sir Claude and Lady MacDonald's reception stood politely to attention until the last brassy note died away.

The thoughts of the British present went loyally to the stout ailing old Queen, safe in the ramparts of Windsor Castle, but only for a moment. They were anxious to get on with the business of enjoying the party. Besides, did the Queen have any thought or even knowledge of this little enclave of her subjects marooned so far away? If hostilities broke out, would her government come to their rescue?

Colonel Manners was sceptical about that, and so was the Dowager Marchioness of Comerford. The British minister, Sir Claude MacDonald, was still convinced that there was no real cause for alarm, as were the ministers of the other powers. China was a country of firecrackers, little periodic explosions instigated by bandits or war lords that soon died down. This Boxer thing might make rather more noise, but it, too, would vanish into the endless annals of China's history. True, a report had come in today of a train leaving Tientsin being fired on by a band of rebels. That was getting uncomfortably near.

But the Empress Dowager was in her summer palace in the Forbidden City, and government seemed to go on as usual.

And this was being a remarkably successful party, heightened by the news of the relief of the British residents of Mafeking in South Africa that had just come in, proving that the protecting arm of Empire was still alert and powerful.

The paper lanterns glowed in the trees, the younger guests danced on the tennis court to the music of the Chinese band which had obligingly learned several Western numbers, there was no shortage of champagne and everyone was dressed in their very best party dress.

It was an uncomfortably warm, sultry evening, and several families were planning to leave the city the next day to go to the beaches or the hills. It would be a great relief to get out of this stupefying heat.

"For my part," Lady Comerford confided to Colonel Manners, "I'm putting my jewellery in the bank tomorrow."

"Going away, dear lady?"

"Most certainly not. I'm far too nervous."

"You! Never seen you turn a hair."

"Because you've never had occasion to. But this is different. If an attack comes I shall be like a jellyfish."

Colonel Manners stopped bantering. He stroked his moustaches thoughtfully.

"You think it's coming?"

"I'm convinced of it. My cook disappeared today. The

other servants said he was called home to his father, who was ill. If that's true, why didn't he tell me himself? I simply didn't believe a word they said. He's gone to join the Boxers."

"Would he scare you?"

"Indeed he would. He can look very ferocious when he's angry. And if he had a rifle or a sword—well, frankly, I shall never take him back again even if he comes in peace."

"I don't much care for the outlook myself," Colonel Manners admitted. "I think all these people have their heads in the sand. Deep. Look at that pretty Mrs. Carrington dancing with her husband. Hasn't a care in the world."

"That's not strictly true, Colonel. She's almost as nervous as I am. She's wondering whether to change her mind about taking her children away tomorrow. They were joining Lady MacDonald's party. Oh, she's looking happy now because she's dancing with her husband."

"In love, are they? Refreshing sight."

"Except that the husband is too attractive to women."

"Is he, by Jove?"

"Of course he is. He has that devil-may-care look women love. I suppose you, as a man, wouldn't notice it."

"I just think he's a strong fellow. Good to have on our side. I wasn't thinking of liaisons with the fair sex. I doubt if there's going to be any time for them, anyway. But I wouldn't like to see that nice lady hurt. Why is it good women marry philandering men?"

"Good women are often masochists. But I really wouldn't know how good or forbearing Amelia Carrington is. I fancy she could be quite a fighter. I wish, all the same, she hadn't taken that little troublemaker into her house."

"The Deacon girl? Surely you wouldn't call her a femme fatale. She's like a broomstick. And don't tell me that Nathaniel Carrington doesn't agree with me."

"He," said Lady Comerford drily, "will think that broomsticks have certain magical properties. Henry, I'm eighty. I know I've had to sit on the sidelines since losing my dear husband, but one sees a great deal from the sidelines. I've seen Medora Deacon's type before. Wilful, selfish, sexual." Her beautiful lavender-coloured eyes looked with sly innocence at Colonel Manners, who was beginning to huff. "Don't tell me you're too old to be aware of that."

"Dear lady—"

"You didn't think I would utter that word."

"There's nothing I'd put past you. You can't tell me you'd be afraid of a Boxer. Mere peasants in scarlet dresses, as the minister says."

"I shall be very afraid indeed," said Lady Comerford. "But I'll never admit that to anyone except you, old friend. And I only hope not to disgrace myself."

"You won't. You'll put on your war paint and out-face them."

Lady Comerford touched her papery delicately rouged cheeks.

"I'll try. Anyway, an old lady—now, what is this, Mrs. Carrington? Is something wrong?"

Amelia Carrington who had looked so lovely in her low-cut yellow silk ball gown was standing trembling in front of the two old people. Her face was ashen, her eyes full of fear.

"Lady Comerford, Colonel, I have to make my farewells. A message has just come. My sister has arrived with her little girl. Her husband—Thomas—"

"A missionary, isn't he?" said Colonel Manners bluffly, filling in the pause while Amelia found her voice again.

"My dear child, has something happened to him?" Lady Comerford asked.

"He's been murdered!" Amelia gasped. "In front of Lilian and that poor little Angel. They should have left the mission weeks ago. Lilian had begged him—"

Nathaniel Carrington was standing beside his wife. "Come, my dear." He held her trembling hands in his. His face was stern and angry, the hollow cheeks sucked in. "Let's just slip away quietly. I've explained to our host and hostess. We mustn't spoil the party. Colonel, may I ask a favour, that you see Miss Deacon is escorted home? No need to spoil her party, either."

The children had been taken home by Ah Wan some time ago. They had been reluctant to leave the fairy tale scene, but Papa's orders had been explicit. Children, when they became tired, were unwelcome at a party. And no, Miss Deacon was definitely not to go home with them. For once, pampered little beasts that they were, they could make do with the attentions of Ah Wan and Cassidy. Miss Deacon was enjoying herself, and looked different and exotic in her green silk dress.

That was Henrietta's opinion, and for once Georgie agreed with his eldest sister. Lucy, stumbling home half asleep, thought that the paper lanterns had been like butterflies in the trees, and that Mamma was far prettier than Miss Deacon. And that she would fall asleep with all those gay colours imprisoned beneath her eyelids.

But she was not to sleep for long. Nor was anybody.

For Aunt Lilian and Angel, dressed in shabby cotton dresses and straw bonnets, and with only one wicker travelling bag tied up with cord, had arrived and banged on the door so loudly and desperately that all the children thought the Boxers had arrived.

Georgie grabbed his toy sword and flew towards the front door. Henrietta followed more cautiously. Lucy stayed in bed, her face buried in the pillow, and therefore missed seeing the forlorn and travel-stained pair stumble into the house. Aunt Lilian immediately collapsed into the nearest chair and lay back looking as if she were dead. Angel stood in the centre of the room giving everyone, Cassidy, Ah Wan, Li, and Henrietta and

Georgie, a belligerent suspicious stare from fawn-coloured eyes.

She had a thin white face and a freckled nose. Georgie was immensely disappointed to see that she was ugly, and what was more, she had no wings, only two sharp shoulders hunched in a stiff awkward attitude.

She was no angel at all, just a skinny cat. What lies grown-ups told, Uncle Thomas boasting so often that he and Aunt Lilian had been blessed with an angel daughter. It seemed fairly certain that Uncle Thomas didn't know what angels looked like, although he was so good and taught the poor Chinese peasants, sunk in their dark and dangerous ignorance, about heaven. Those were his own words.

Georgie glanced briefly towards the door to see if Uncle Thomas was going to appear and explain this sudden arrival. Because it didn't seem as if Aunt Lilian was able to speak, and Angel looked dumb. Perhaps she was deaf, too, like that beggar who always sat outside the Ch'ien Men gate.

Cassidy was bending over Aunt Lilian, who appeared to be mumbling something. Suddenly she straightened and turned a shocked face to the children.

"Oh, my dear lord!" she muttered. Then she said sharply, as if they had been disobedient, "Miss Henrietta! Master Georgie! Look after your cousin. Ah Wan, will you go and make her a bed in the girls' room. She won't want to be alone. Miss Henrietta, you must lend her some of your night clothes. And show her where to wash. She might like a glass of milk, too. Go on, then. Don't stand staring. Li, please remain while I write a note. The master and mistress must be sent for."

"Poor Mamma," said Henrietta. "She won't like having her party spoilt. Do you realise that's what you've done, Angel? It's not very good manners arriving without warning like this."

She had one of Angel's stiff arms tucked firmly in hers, and was tugging the child from the room.

"Come on, you're not scared to leave your mother, are you? What's the matter with her? Is she sick?"

"Are you dumb?" Georgie asked in his gentle interested voice. "I know a dumb beggar. He looks like you do."

"Georgie, that's bad manners," Henrietta said.

"I like that dumb beggar. He has a kind face."

"Angel doesn't want to know about your silly dumb beggar. I say, you're awfully dusty, aren't you, Angel? Was it a long journey on the train?"

"Did the Boxers shoot at you?" Georgie asked eagerly.

A ripple of some emotion passed over the little girl's face. She opened her mouth, then shut it again. Her strange light-coloured eyes had a sudden hot misery. All at once she held out a portion of her grubby cotton skirt, thrusting it towards Georgie. He saw that there were two rusty smears on it.

"That's my Papa's blood!" she cried in a shrill voice. "They cut his head off. They cut it *off!*"

"Who?" Georgie asked, deeply impressed. Henrietta was silent with horror.

"The Boxers, of course, you silly little boy. They ran through our house and slashed it to pieces. Papa tried to stop them so they slashed off his head."

"She's telling lies," whispered Henrietta faintly.

The child's eyes blazed yellow.

"I am not! You don't know anything. That's my Papa's *blood!*"

Henrietta shrank away from the macabre skirt. "Hush, Lucy will hear."

"Who's Lucy?"

"She's our sister and you'd better be kind to her," said Georgie. "Because she's very sensitive. I think I liked you better when you were dumb," he added re-

flectively. "And I thought you'd be prettier and have
wings."

"She has to take that dress off," Henrietta said, trying
not to cry. "I wish Mamma were here."

"Or Miss Deacon," said Georgie. "Miss Deacon will
look after you, Angel. She's the only one who isn't
frightened of the Boxers."

No one had been able to persuade Angel to undress
before Miss Deacon came home. She arrived soon after
Mamma and Papa, saying how could she possibly go on
dancing when such a terrible thing had happened. She
·would take care of the children while Mamma and Papa
looked after that poor woman who had lost her husband.

Strangely enough Angel, who had resisted all attempts
to remove her travel-stained clothes, especially by Ah
Wan from whom she literally shrank as if the soft
wrinkled yellow-skinned hands would burn her, allowed
Miss Deacon to undress her. After her brief alarming
outburst she was silent again. Georgie sensed the respite
was only temporary. He longed to ask her if her father's
head had rolled like a football.

"I fell out of the willow tree," he said to the now
clean Angel, dressed in one of Henrietta's nightgowns.
"I expect I made it angry."

Angel was stung, by sheer curiosity, into speech.

"You can't make a tree angry."

"You can a willow tree," said Miss Deacon. "It's a
wizard. Isn't it, Georgie? Sometimes it's a good wizard
and sometimes I guess it's a bad one." She still had on
her green party dress, and she looked as if she were
almost enjoying what had happened, the sudden arrival
of the two refugees and their horrifying story. It was
exciting. Miss Deacon, Georgie knew, loved excitement.
"Now you're all to get into bed and I'll tell you a story.
Lucy, your eyes are as big as saucers."

"Not a frightening story," Lucy pleaded.

"I never tell you frightening stories."

Lucy nodded doubtfully. What she and Miss Deacon considered frightening were two different matters.

"Shall I sing to you?" Miss Deacon asked, and immediately began in her funny harsh voice that was yet curiously soothing.

> Rock a bye, baby, in the tree top,
> When the wind blows the cradle will rock. . . .

The children were silent, Henrietta and Lucy huddled in bed, Angel on a made-up pallet on the floor, Georgie lurking at the door of the girls' room which was usually forbidden territory. He wished Angel had been allowed to sleep in his room.

> When the bough breaks the cradle will fall,
> Down will come baby, cradle and all. . . .

That was what had happened to him when the rotten old branch of the willow tree had broken—when Uncle Thomas' head had gone rolling in the dust. . . . That was China, as Mamma said, this beautiful country that's rotten in the centre. . . .

Georgie crept up to Miss Deacon where she sat on the end of the girls' bed. He felt safe beside her because he didn't think there was anything in the world that could frighten her.

A few days later the people who had gone back to the hills to escape the city's heat came hastening back in Peking carts or riding on mules. It wasn't safe any longer. There were parties of Boxers roaming about threatening people with rusty swords. The governess to Lady MacDonald's children was scared out of her wits. The little party set out on the long journey back, bumping along in the heat, exhausted and fearful. Two days later they heard that their bungalow had been burnt. They had escaped just in time.

Aunt Lilian had spent a week in bed, at Mamma's

insistence, and then had got up and crept about, looking wan and haunted and crushed, as if she would never talk or smile again.

She had been so much under her husband's thumb, Nathaniel said a trifle impatiently. She seemed to have forgotten how to be a person without him. All those prayers and hymns. What good had they done? How did her faith help her now?

"Give her time," Amelia said. "She's suffering from a terrible shock."

"Well, if hostilities break out here, and I'm afraid they're going to, we can't all enjoy the indulgence of going into prolonged shock. I'm sorry to say this, my dear, but you ladies will have to overcome your delicate sensibilities. I'm transferring all my valuable stock into the cellars, and we must be prepared to move from here to the legation at any moment. All British residents are to go there. Luckily it's a great rabbit warren of rooms. There should be space for us all. And by the way, I want you to keep the children in sight all the time. Under no circumstances is Miss Deacon to take Georgie into the outer city."

"I should think not!"

"He can be very persuasive. And I fancy that child of Lilian's is going to lead him on."

"Angel? But surely——"

"Has she shed a tear for her father?"

"Cassidy said she was dumb with shock on that first night."

"Shock isn't grief."

"It's another way of showing grief. Anyway, although I shouldn't say it, Thomas was a very stern father. Perhaps the child didn't love him as much as she should have done. Lilian says she is like him in many ways. She has his inflexibility of purpose. All the same, we must be gentle with her. Can you imagine Henrietta's or Lucy's shock if they had witnessed—if it had been you—" Amelia's voice trembled at the nightmare possibility of such a thing, and Nathaniel's face softened as he put his arm about her.

"You're perfectly right, my love. Although I am afraid our own children may have to witness things not meant for young eyes."

Amelia clung to him. "Darling—couldn't we leave China while there's still time?"

"You still don't understand. There isn't any time. The Railway Station at Fengtai has been burnt. The Tientsin line will be the next. We're prisoners here now, like it or not. We'll have to see it through in the best way we can."

Chapter 8

Another boast made by the Boxers, "The mouths of the foreigners will be silenced," was circulating round the now thoroughly uneasy population of the legation compound. From information smuggled to him, Sir Claude MacDonald was convinced that the Empress Dowager was in league with the rebels. It was known that she had sent one of her eunuchs to spy. He doubted if the Tsungli Yamen, her government, had yet gone over completely to rebellion, although it was influenced by the Empress' powerful nephew Prince Tuan. Mysterious comings and goings were observed. At midnight the great Tien An Men gate would be opened by the Manchu guards and remain open until dawn when high officials in gorgeously decorated carts hurried into the Imperial City for a daybreak audience with the Empress Dowager. There was no doubt the time for listening to rumours and speculations was past and action must be taken.

In this Sir Claude was supported by the French Father, the Vicar Apostolic of Peking, who was convinced that the city was full of Boxer accomplices, only waiting the signal to attack first the churches and then the legations where the hated foreigners lived.

Sir Claude telegraphed to Lord Salisbury in Whitehall for troops, and then, to bolster up morale, suggested that the next Sunday service should be held in the open pavilion (so recently gaily decked with lanterns and flags for the Queen's birthday), so that there would be room for everybody who wanted to come.

The congregation exceeded even his expectations. It included many Chinese converts and a sprinkling of missionaries who had made long journeys, often in disguise, from the provinces in order to escape the fate of poor Thomas Beddow and others of his kind. They all had stories of burned churches and chapels, hospitals and dispensaries, of torturing and murdering. And of the terrible cries, "Exterminate the foreigners! Kill! Kill!"

The passions of ignorant people whose emotions were whipped up by the superstitions, rites and incantations of the Boxer cult were not to be dismissed lightly, even though these people were poorly armed and would be mowed down by modern guns. Witness the invincible strength of Christian martyrs, the French Father said. In their own primitive way, the Boxers had this strength. They sent leaflets into Peking which read:

The Catholic and Protestant religion being insolent to the gods and extinguishing sanctity, rendering no obedience to Buddha and enraging Heaven and Earth, the rainclouds no longer visit us. But 8,000,000 spirit soldiers will descend from heaven and sweep the Empire clean of all foreigners. Then will the gentle showers once more water our lands, and when the tread of soldiers and the clash of steel are heard heralding woes to all our people, then the Buddhist Patriotic League of Boxers will be able to protect the Empire and to bring peace to all its people.

Until all foreigners have been exterminated no rain can visit us.

Fortunately, a response to the British minister's appeal for troops came quickly. At the end of May the Ch'ien Men gate leading to the Tartar city was kept open and seventy-five marines on shore leave from warships anchored at Tientsin marched, with fixed bayonets, up Legation Street.

Nathaniel said the numbers were pitiful, but Georgie was immensely thrilled. An even greater and more fearful excitement was in store for him when he had his first sight of a real live Boxer.

The impudent fellow rode down Legation Street in a cart. His hair was tied back with a red cloth, he had red ribbons round his wrists and ankles, and a red girdle tightened his loose white tunic. He not only looked flamboyantly splendid, but he was sharpening a long knife on his boot in the most intimidating way.

The sight was too much for the fiery German minister, Baron von Ketteler, who tilted at him with his walking stick. The Boxer leapt from his cart and ran off swiftly towards the palace of Prince Su, disappearing in the grounds like a fox gone to earth.

But the bizarre sight had sent ripples of fear through the legations, and the next day several ladies decided to leave Peking, disguised as Manchu women.

Amelia would not have dreamed of leaving, even had Nathaniel encouraged her to do so. She preferred the compound surrounded by its forty-foot-thick wall, surely impregnable, to the wildness of the open country. Besides, nothing would induce Lilian to stir from the house. She could scarcely be persuaded to leave her bedroom. She was still in a state of shock, and sat a great deal of the time with her Bible in her hand, communing silently with God, or her dead husband.

Amelia had always considered herself a Christian, and brought up her children as Christians, but this extreme faith was unnerving and unhealthy. Thomas had turned Lilian, who had once been as pretty and frivolous as herself, into a gloomy sunken-eyed ghost of a woman whom the children shunned.

Nathaniel, who found it hard to feel sympathy for a woman who had lost her femininity and become so crushed and drab—he fancied he would expect his own wife to look clean and neat even at the height of the siege—nevertheless exerted his patience and tried to persuade Lilian to rouse herself. If things come to the worst, every pair of hands was going to be necessary and Lilian's were surely more experienced than most. She must forget her own grief and look after the refugees, and those who would fall sick or be wounded.

What was more, today, after the episode of that insolent Boxer, they must not put off any longer moving in to the British legation. They were completely defenceless in this house, situated so near to the Peking Hotel and the Ch'ien Men Gate. It might be attacked or burned. The Boxers had a way of throwing lighted torches which landed on the highly inflammable roofs and walls of buildings. Fire gave them some diabolical excitement.

"Burn! Burn! Kill! Kill!" Georgie shouted, pursuing Angel with lashing bamboo stems. This was a wonderful game. Angel enjoyed it, too. For a girl she was a good fighter. Her pale eyes glowed yellow, like a tiger's. He was glad now that she and her mother had come to live in Peking. He almost thought Uncle Thomas' death was a lucky thing to have happened. But it was a pity it was so hot. The air seemed to be full of black dust. Perhaps the gardens of the British legation would be cooler. He and Angel might even trespass into Prince Su's pleasure gardens, because it was said that he had abandoned his palace, leaving stealthily without any of his usual splendid trappings or fanfare of trumpets. There was supposed to be a heron that came to the lake in his garden. It would be fun to see that.

The Carringtons were allotted rooms at the back of the legation building, which was fortunate as it gave the children access to the grounds which should be relatively safe. Although Amelia gave strict instructions that they were not to wander beyond the bounds of the tennis court. She wanted them within sight. She really would have preferred them not to be outdoors at all, but one couldn't coop children up in this heat.

As it was, they were dreadfully overcrowded. There was one small room for herself and Nathaniel, an adjoining one for the children who thought it great fun to sleep on camp beds with Ah Wan on a pallet across the doorway, and the third had to be shared by that ill-assorted trio, Lilian, Miss Deacon, and Cassidy.

The other servants, Li, Ching and his menials, had suggested blandly that they would stay and look after Great Master's house. The issue now was far greater than cheating the mistress of a few eggs. One could not tell whose side they were on. They may well prove to be traitors. Nathaniel was not taking any risks. He paid the inscrutable little band their wages and sent them off. The house, he said, would be locked up and left empty.

His shop was a different matter. He hated to leave so many treasures unguarded. He could only batten down the trap door leading to the basement, spread the floor thickly with sand, as a protection against fire, and put up the shutters. After that he volunteered for military duties. Action, after all the rumours, would come as a relief. Besides, he had to get away from all those women crowded into three small rooms. He realized that Amelia was very afraid. There were tell-tale signs beneath her discipline, her paleness, her tense mouth, her inability to relax when the children were out of her sight. He knew that she was vowing not to go to pieces the way her sister had, and because he knew this he treated her with consideration and tenderness.

Lilian still sat inertly, uninterested in anything, showing the symptoms of profound shock. If all the women behaved like that when hostilities began, and their eyes had to dwell on brutal sights, they were going to be a tremendous problem.

But Nathaniel was sure this would not happen to his wife, who had always had admirable self-discipline and pride. Neither, he surmised, would it happen to prim old Cassidy, British to the backbone. As for Medora, she apparently thrived on danger. By common consent the children's lessons were abandoned, and she spent most of the day occupying them in more lighthearted ways, playing energetic games with them, shouting and screaming as loudly as they did. She had become a grown-up child, a delayed adolescent, but her gleaming eyes, when they met Nathaniel's, had a sly wild expression that was far from adolescent. He wondered, not for the first time, if the girl were entirely sane. She had two distinct personalities. Interesting. He found he responded to her wildness with a secret affinity. It was part of this bizarre adventure.

The legation, as refugees poured in, was going to become uncomfortably overcrowed. Especially after a Manchu servant reported that he had seen three long carts full of swords and spears passing through the Ha Ta gate into the outer city. That was the day that it was announced there would be no more trains from Tientsin, and great clouds of smoke in the distance came from the burning grandstand at the racecourse.

Spies reported that the Empress Dowager had returned from the Summer Palace to the Winter Palace, and was deep in plots with the evil Prince Tuan. Even more alarming, the Kansu army was encamped in front of the Temples of Heaven, and it was optimistic, in the extreme, to think that they would attempt to repel an invasion of

Boxers. They were hand in glove with the rebels, Colonel Manners was convinced. He privately urged the British minister to telegraph urgently to the admiral of the British fleet for more reinforcements. Never mind the dilatoriness of the other foreign ministers. Let them have some reliable British troops.

For everyone, eventually, would converge on the British legation. It was situated in the safest position and moreover was the most commodious building in the whole of the compound. Already it was filling up with refugees, weary and hollow-eyed missionaries and their helpers, and an immense band of Chinese converts who, with nothing but knapsacks holding their meagre possessions, pots and pans and precious bags of rice, were camping in the grounds.

All those people would have to be fed. They would be down to horse flesh, Colonel Manners surmised, although there were plenty of supplies at present, and the Peking Hotel had apparently unlimited cases of champagne, as well as a small stock of exotic tinned foods to be doled out to the privileged. But if the siege lasted several weeks, and the water supply ran out, and they were all drunk on champagne, including the children, it was going to be a fine picnic.

After the burning of the racecourse grandstand, guards from all the legations were placed on the Tartar wall, keeping a round-the-clock vigil. In the British sector five hundred marines and soldiers cleaned rifles and checked supplies of ammunition. There was one ancient machine gun which jammed far too frequently. Colonel Manners strode about, his elderly bones locked in a proud military posture, longing to rap out commands to what he considered a pitiful rabble of an army. His time would come, he was convinced. His eighty-odd years would count for nothing when the real war began. He wouldn't be condemned forever to marshalling the children together and instructing them in the essential rules of siege behaviour. Conserve food and water, don't wander far from the legation, take cover and keep your heads down if the enemy breaks in, don't panic, don't scream.

The parents thought he was doing a great service. Lady Comerford, who had established herself in a tiny room, a pantry, she fancied, with her bits of finery about her, was full of admiration, and felt almost safe when that spare upright figure was near. Alone, she twittered to herself like a frantic bird, newly caged. Her servants had deserted her. Anyway, she didn't trust them. Her maid, Lily, was married to a palace eunuch of alarming size who wanted her only for her children (of whom she had three by a previous husband now deceased) so that he would have descendants to worship at his grave. Lady Comerford did not trust him an inch, and made no bones about indicating her feelings to Lily, who bowed and expressed polite regrets that Mistress was "aflaid." Nothing to be "aflaid" of. Lady Comerford thought otherwise, and made herself devote all her thoughts to dying with dignity.

It was very wrong, said Henrietta indignantly, for a little boy to share a room with three girls. Georgie's camp bed must be put in a corner beside the wardrobe and a screen put up.

There was no screen, however. Mamma said distractedly that it would be enough if Georgie turned his back while undressing. There were times when allowances must be made. Anyway, he was their brother.

He wasn't Angel's brother, Henrietta thought. It was really rather shocking that Angel should see Georgie undressing, even with his back turned. It wasn't as if she had brothers of her own.

But Angel gave Henrietta her insufferably adult contemptuous look, and remarked that you couldn't live in a mission without seeing thousands of bare little boys. Henrietta really was rather old-fashioned, wasn't she?

The only important thing was not to get your head cut off. And the way not to think about that was to keep inventing new things to do. Exciting dangerous things in which Georgie was a willing partner.

More than lacking privacy in undressing, Henrietta was horrified at not being able to have a bath or even to have fresh underclothing every day. Water from the wells in the compound grounds was scarce and had to be rationed. An enamel basin was filled each evening and all the children were expected to wash in it, no matter how dirty the water became. Henrietta longed to go first. She couldn't bear to follow Angel or even Lucy, and Georgie was always as dust-grimed as a chimney sweep. Besides, she was the eldest and the most fastidious. But being the eldest carried responsibilities, as Mamma frequently told her. So it was essential that she be fair and that meant making the suggestion that lots should be drawn for the privilege of first use of the water.

Mamma praised her for her cleverness.

"That's my good girl," she said, and added that Henrietta was a great comfort to her.

But Angel muttered what a bore, and who cared whether you washed or not. God loved you just as much with all your sins. That was what her papa had always said. And look at the way he had had to go to heaven, without a head. So a little dirt was of no consequence. She disliked Henrietta for her smug superiority, and Lucy was a scared little ninny. She and Georgie intended to be really brave tomorrow and join the soldiers on top of the Tartar wall.

Henrietta gasped.

"You can't do that! I'll tell Mamma and Papa."

Georgie gave his wide gap-toothed grin.

"Don't be silly, Hen. She's only joking. The soldiers wouldn't let us past. We know, because we tried today."

"Georgie! You bad boy!"

"We only tried. We wanted to see if there were any

more fires. Ah Wan said the fire-cart stopping-place was going to be burnt."

"Whatever is that?"

"The railway station. You really don't know anything. I say, it's going to get awfully dull if we've got to hang around here all the time. We've been all over the gardens and we've never seen the heron. We thought we'd go to Prince Su's palace tomorrow. You and Lucy can come if you want to."

"I'm sure we wouldn't be allowed."

"Miss Deacon would let us. She's not afraid. I say, don't get angry with Angel, Hen." Georgie gave his endearing smile. "She says her mother won't talk to her, and she'd rather be naughty than scared."

Henrietta tried to understand this, but failed. Being naughty got you nowhere, and that Angel really was a bad influence on Georgie. The two disappeared for hours at a time, and she was left with Lucy, who followed her like a shadow, and really did whimper too much.

Mamma and Cassidy spent a lot of the day cutting up sheets and rolling them into bandages, and it was useless to try to talk to Aunt Lilian. When you looked into her eyes there was no one there. But Lady Comerford was always glad to see them in her tiny room. She gave them sips of champagne, and told them long incoherent stories. She was drinking a good deal of champagne, and it made her very gay until she fell asleep.

Miss Deacon was here, there and everywhere. She was really supposed to stay with the children, but Papa had decided that in such a time of emergency the children, especially Henrietta, were old enough to behave with sense if they were left alone for part of the day. The chancery was being made into a hospital, and Miss Deacon had volunteered to scrub floors and dispatch tables which were to be used for operations. Fortunately, there were doctors, and one of the Germans was said to be an excellent surgeon. It was very hot and airless in this makeshift hospital, and the flies were a great nuisance. But luckily there had been only one patient so far, a marine, who had fallen over some obstacle in the dark and broken his leg.

Papa said he was very careful in the dark. If he ended up in hospital it would be because of an honourable bullet wound. Carelessly he added, would Miss Deacon wipe his brow?

"Miss Deacon is here to look after our children," said Mamma rather sharply.

"We are all here to look after each other," Papa answered. "I trust the children will have enough sense to stay indoors when bullets start to fly."

"I wish I could do more than scrub floors," Miss Deacon cried, her eyes full of a brilliant intensity. "Couldn't I learn to fire a gun?"

"No," said Papa curtly. "Damn this heat! I'm sorry. I've been on that wall staring into a heat-haze for six hours. It's made me short-tempered. Isn't there anything to drink?"

"Only warm champagne," said Mamma. "Or Cassidy may be able to make you some tea."

"Jasmine?"

"I'm afraid so."

"What sort of drink is that for a man? I'll go down to the Peking hotel and see if they have any beer. By the way, there's been a meeting of all the ministers, and Sir Claude MacDonald has been given the supreme command. Thank heaven for that. Colonel Manners will be pleased. I believe he was trying to steel himself to serve under a German or a Russian or even a Japanese. But less good news—I must tell you—"

"What?" Mamma asked breathlessly.

"In the last hour the Boxers have been pouring into the city, setting fire to churches and houses and silk stores and what they call foreign medicine shops. They're apparently very superstitious of foreign medicine. The London Mission and the school for the blind have been destroyed, and the Roman Catholic cathedral is threatened. They're trying to destroy everything foreign. They're a long way off still, and we have all the gates shut, but if you hear roaring and shouting in the night, don't panic. Just stay under cover. You're all safe here."

Mamma sprang up, her eyes enormous with apprehension. How, Henrietta wondered admiringly, could she look so clean, her white blouse immaculate, her beautiful bronze hair smoothed back like a well-groomed chrysanthemum.

"You, Nathaniel—you'll be with us?"

Papa stood there, tall, handsome, the light of excitement in his black eyes.

"I told you, I'm just going to see if I can find some beer."

"But then?"

"Back to my post, my love."

Miss Deacon moved compulsively.

"Oh, couldn't I—isn't there anything—"

"Your job is to put the children to bed and to keep them quiet. Isn't that important enough for you?" Papa spoke with a sharpness that made Miss Deacon flush unhappily. He seemed to think she was being rather silly. Then he added, in his normal voice, "Henrietta, have you remembered the motto for today?"

"Yes, Papa. Be brave and obedient."

"And have you been?"

"Yes, Papa. I think so." Her gaze flicked to Georgie and Angel, who may have been brave, but had certainly been far from obedient. She said virtuously, "We all have been. And we drew lots for who washes first. It's Angel's turn tonight."

"Then she must be thankful for small mercies. In a few days no one may wash at all."

In the stifling black darkness Amelia could not sleep. She kept trying to re-create her first rapturous feelings about China. There was that morning when one first realised it was spring, with the almond blossom and the plum blossom breaking into a pale rosy light over the dun landscape. The flowers came first in this country, the greenery much later. But the birds arrived with the plum blossom, and the spring sunshine turned the marvellous rooftops of the Imperial city to gold and vermilion, a richness of colour that was sensually satisfying.

This spring, alas, had been drought-stricken, and the lovely profusion of bloom had turned brown far too quickly. Even so, one had seen the miracle and read poems about it.

Lying in the dark Amelia tried to calm her mind by saying the poems over to herself aloud.

> In the month of peach-bloom and plum-bloom, in the
>   silken-screened recess
> Love is the burden of sweet voices, and the brief night
>   melting, and the long caress. . . .

But the cool delicate words had lost their magic, she was simply repeating them senselessly while her ears strained for the sounds Nathaniel had anticipated. She fancied she could hear roaring, rising and fading like the sea crashing on rocks. Occasionally there was a far-off crack, like rifle fire, although never in her life had she heard rifle fire and therefore could only guess the origin of the sound. She thought of Nathaniel on top of that great towering wall in the menacing night, and found all her bones set in rigid angles of anxiety.

In the small hours of the morning she got up to look at the children. They slept soundly, Henrietta with her arm protectively round Lucy, Angel face downwards on the pillow, sleeping with the same ferocious intensity that she lived. Georgie, on the other hand, carried his sublime innocence into sleep. His lips curved upwards, his lashes lay on his tender cheeks.

How she wished she could spare them the almost inevitable horrors ahead. What effect was it going to have on their lives? She feared that Angel, poor child, was seriously disturbed, expending her fears in manic activity. Timid Lucy was the most vulnerable. Henrietta would determine to behave well at all costs, and Georgie just possibly might find the whole thing an enthralling adventure, although that seemed too much to hope for.

It was a terrible responsibility protecting the children and calmly doing the useful things women did in a siege, while all the time her anxiety about Nathaniel ate into her. Lilian, withdrawn into shock and seemingly oblivious of what was happening, was almost lucky. So was Miss Deacon, with her lack of fear. Nathaniel admired that, Amelia knew. It was one of the reasons she tried so desperately hard to remain calm and serene herself. One could not have one's husband making unflattering comparisons.

Her thoughts dwelt compulsively on what Nathaniel was experiencing, the moonless night on top of that great wall, the smell of smoke from the city, and the distant fanatical cries, the stealthy movement in the gloom that straining sleepless eyes must watch for, the sudden flare of a torch, and the imminent danger of fire, the crawling hours of the long night. . . .

When Nathaniel came in just before dawn, he threw himself on the pallet on the floor, smoke-blackened and unclothed as he was, and fell immediately into an exhausted sleep. Even long after daylight Amelia wouldn't move for fear of disturbing him. She lay gazing at his grimy face, his curved black brows, his bony cheeks, in love and a strange sad longing that she didn't understand. When Cassidy tiptoed in with a miraculous cup of freshly brewed tea she signed to her to be quiet. A tired man was much more vulnerable to danger. She was not going to allow Nathaniel to take up his post again until he was fully rested. She would fight off the enemy herself, if necessary.

It appeared that there had been alarming developments in the night. A great crowd of hostile Chinese had surged up the street outside the Ch'ien Men gate, carrying lighted torches and shouting. The besieged nations decided to take action, and the gate was opened and a machine gun run into the street. After a flurry of shots, the German and Japanese contingents charged with fixed bayonets and bugles blowing. Either intimidated, or as part of their tactics, the enemy melted away, leaving only the burning torches stuck in a line along the edge of the road like a fearful garden border. There wasn't a sign of a Boxer. If they had been there, among the swarming crowds, they had disappeared, like phantoms.

However, no phantoms could have caused so much destruction. The Roman Catholic cathedral was in flames, there were burned and mutilated bodies in the streets, and in the delicate pink dawn a flood of refugees began pouring in through the open and heavily guarded gates. They were filthy and shocked, some of them barely alive. Nightmare stories began to circulate. The Boxers were devilish, ferocious, merciless, shouting their ceaseless *"Sha! Sha!"* and wielding their deadly curved swords. They also had the ability to vanish into thin air. Perhaps they really were supernatural.

The hospital in the chancery buildings began its first serious day's work. And Medora, with a private sense of pride, found that she could stand the sight of blood much better than most of her compatriots. There was a young Austrian soldier who was likely to lose a leg, and an enormous bearded Cossack who had made too conspicuous a target. He had sustained a nasty sword wound across the back of his neck while he had been helping to load the ancient machine gun. Tendons and muscles had been cut. It was likely he would be permanently paralysed, although he had not been told this. Medora wanted to help him to die, there and then. She couldn't imagine that magnificent body propped up uselessly for the rest of its life.

Instead, she smiled, letting her eyes get their luminous look, and helped the half-conscious man to swallow a little cold tea.

"Sorry it's not vodka," she said. She was wondering how she would behave if this were Nathaniel Carrington lying helpless on one of those narrow makeshift beds. Now that he had become one of the fighting force and exposed to danger, she was filled with an enormous sense of urgency. For a long time she had known she wanted physical contact with him. Just his casual touch on her arm had been wildly exciting. Then, from the night of the Queen's birthday party, she had become recklessly determined to flirt with him more seriously. He must be persuaded to kiss her. Secretly, and whenever the opportunity offered. The secrecy would make the act so much more exciting.

Now, however, considering the danger in which they all lived, she wanted much more. There might be so little time. Who knew? Tomorrow Nathaniel might be lying helpless like the giant Cossack. Or dead.

One must live to the uttermost while one could.

As she had always done, Medora indulged in dreams and fantasies. But now they were also plans for the future. The nights were dark and some of them, surely, would pass without hostilities. She could easily find out the time Nathaniel was due to leave his post on the wall. Last night she had known when he returned, and had lain listening until she had heard the thud of his tired body on the bed. Only a thin wall separated them. She was nearer to him than his own wife, in terms of space. This knowledge was pleasing as well as maddening. One night she would go out and wait for him. What might never have been possible in peace time, in the well-run house in Legation Street, was now on the verge of happening.

She had not failed to recognise the look in Nathaniel's eye. She had seen it often enough in other men's eyes. In spite of her lack of looks she had a powerful attraction for men. It had been no use her mother, and then an embarrassed and shocked Aunt Agatha, telling her this was not so, she was a silly girl making up fancies to compensate for her plainness. She had too much evidence to prove otherwise. It wasn't beauty a man wanted, not even the lovely clear-skinned auburn-haired beauty of Amelia Carrington. It was this other thing, this deep violent response that they unerringly recognised.

No one had aroused it in her as much as Nathaniel Carrington did. She dreamed of that bony intense face when it would become full of lust, a look that had never been turned on his gentle wife, she was certain.

It was the look she wanted. She knew she was bad. Not all the time, not when she entered into the children's games with spirit and imagination, or now, when she was full of pity for the bearded Russian. But when the impulse for what she knew to be wickedness came over her she was swept along on a wild beautiful stormcloud, and life was irresistible and magnificent and must be lived to the limit of one's breath. Imagine living and then dying, as those wretched eunuchs did, never having known the final expression of love.

The month of May, the month of Queen Victoria's birthday, was still not over, but so much had happened. Things had changed so much. Morals could surely be forgotten.

Dragon House, England

May, 1975

Chapter 9

The early May sunshine was as yellow as butter in the cheerful little dining room where Georgina and Hugh were having breakfast. The newly leaved plane trees gave an exuberant fresh green colour to the quiet Kensington street.

As always on a beautiful spring morning Georgina's spirits were high. She wore a pink gingham housecoat with a frilled neckline. Her hair hung loose, her face without makeup had a very young look. She was very dear to him, Hugh thought, but entirely familiar, and if the spring sunshine made her happy and contented it made him restless. He wanted a small adventure. Just a small one. He knew he was going to keep that appointment this afternoon.

Well, because he was intrigued, and life had been too routine lately. Difficult and squalid cases in court, and predictable evenings at home, with television, and Ben doing his lessons, and Georgina quiet and dreamy. She was in one of her more than usually dreamy phases and he longed for some aggression, a good fight, a bit of excitement. Marriage, no matter how solidly based it was, shouldn't be dull. Though one couldn't ride on a crest all the time. After nine years of cohabitation with one woman, did the crests have to come from elsewhere?

Hugh rustled his half of the *Times*, with a sudden tetchy uneasiness, and hardly heard Georgina's exclamation.

"Good heavens! What a price! Grandfather must be turning in his grave."

"What price and what for?"

"A Chinese wine jar sold at Sotheby's. A hundred thousand pounds!"

"I don't believe it. No piece of pottery can be worth that."

"This is, according to the dealer who bought it. A Ching-tê-Chen fourteenth-century wine jar with under-glaze copper-red flowers and cobalt-blue decoration. Only the third known sample of such a work. My grandfather was ahead of his times when he guessed how valuable Chinese art would become. Even seventy years ago he must have realised that because he started keeping the best pieces he discovered."

"Which means your Aunt Suzie is sitting on a fortune."

"That's just what I was thinking," Georgina said slowly. "Only she doesn't think of her things in terms of value. She just loves possessing them."

"Are you sure? I suspect there was more to it than her acquisitive instinct when she cannily chose them instead of cash from your grandfather's estate."

"No, I don't agree. She didn't need money. Like all dedicated collectors, she just couldn't bear anyone else having what she wanted."

"Then it's a pity your father hadn't had a little foresight about values."

"It wasn't foresight he lacked, Hugh. It was an actual dislike for those possessions. He thought . they were stained with blood—if that doesn't sound too melodramatic."

"It does."

"You have to understand that as a little boy, no older than Ben, he saw so much blood. That's why he expressed his memories of Peking by planting almond trees and willows, and chrysanthemums and peonies and little dwarf firs. I suppose that represented a sort of cartharsis for him. Anyway, it made him a lovely gentle endearing man."

"I know," said Hugh. "He was a scholar and a dreamer. His daughter"—he patted her head as he got up—"is just a dreamer."

"Did you want a scholar as a wife?"

"Heaven forbid."

"Well, then. By the way, Hugh, don't forget it's Aunt Suzie's birthday next weekend."

"No! Not again!"

"Once a year only, like other people."

"That means we've got to go down to Dragon House? Count me out."

"Darling, we haven't been since January. Really, it's not an awful lot for Aunt Suzie to expect of us. Aunt Lucy will be there, too. We haven't seen her for a long time."

"A May weekend spent in that dreary house."

"If it's fine you can go on the river. Ben is longing to see how his yew dragon is getting on. And after reading this"—Georgina tapped the newspaper—"you could have a talk to Aunt Suzie about getting her things revalued, and increasing the insurance. I'm sure that big old house is never locked up properly."

"We don't want to scare the old girl, do we?"

"Nothing would scare her. Indeed, it would be disastrous if she came face to face with a burglar because I know who would come off worst. He'd have his head lopped off in no time at all."

"More blood on those ill-gotten treasures," Hugh said.

"Not on Ben's little jade pony," Georgina murmured in distress. "We have to protect Ben, too. He'll inherit some of the things. Aunt Suzie has promised. She won't change her mind about that, no matter how often she changes her pretty young men."

Hugh sighed heavily.

"Is she still cherishing that actor?"

"Hal Jessel? I believe so. He's lasting longer than most. As far as I know she hasn't made her will lately, so I guess he's hanging around hopefully."

"And his girl friend?"

"The one who wore the prim Victorian dress? That was clever. Surprised you, didn't she?" Georgina nuzzled her head against Hugh's stomach. "I saw the look on your face."

"What look?"

"Just a man's look. I like my husband to be a man."

Georgina's voice had its usual dreamy innocence. Now, Hugh thought, if she started to protest jealously as most women would he might cancel that appointment this afternoon.

Might. Not likely, though. He had kept a small clear picture of Amy Russell in her white dress in his mind. Not because he had wanted to but simply because he couldn't dislodge it. He knew she had gone to Switzerland on a job because he had telephoned once and been told by the person who answered his call. A long job of three months or more.

Fine, Hugh had thought. By that time he would have got over his niggling desire to see her at work or take her out to lunch, perhaps. But this hadn't happened, because when out of the blue she had called him yesterday, he had got terribly tense and excited and knew that he had an overwhelming curiosity to see her again.

So it was just as well that Georgina remained placid and unsuspicious.

"By the way, I'll be a bit late tonight. I've got to go out to Wandsworth gaol to see a client."

"I wish your clients weren't all gaol birds, Hugh. So depressing."

"They're not all. Some are innocent."

"Can you tell the innocent?"

"I pride myself on being fairly perceptive."

"Yes, you are, but it gives you a suspicious mind."

"About chaps like Hal Jessel? And the prevalence of burglars and the dangers of being your Aunt Suzie?"

At that Georgina laughed.

"Don't be afraid for Aunt Suzie. She's the Empress Dowager. Indestructible like the Boxers. Protected by spirits."

"Who apparently haven't yet had their miraculous powers tested. Well, all right, if we must go, pack whatever the fashionable punting man wears nowadays."

"Bless you, darling." Georgina nuzzled against him again. Her forehead was cool and silky against his hand. The little white picture in his mind blurred, but only for a moment. It was sharp and clear as he left the house.

Amy had decided that it was time she had some fun. She deserved it. Free of obligations, delighted to reopen her shop after her absence, and hoping for some customers not sent by Hal or his friends, she dusted and polished, and filled old Worcester tureens with flowers. There wasn't a Chinese object in the place. Her nicely judged blend of old and modern English presented a bland pleasant façade. She was longing to become established in her own right, free of Hal and others. A girl had to grasp chances at the beginning to get a little necessary capital, but now she had received generous rewards for her recently finished job she intended to try for independence.

Not that she would ever lose her interest in Chinese antiquities. However, at present it seemed wise to submerge her considerable knowledge on that subject and concentrate on being English.

She had thought that Georgina and Hugh Morley might be of use. They were an attractive couple with surely the sort of friends, thriving young professionals, who would occasionally want the services of an interior decorator.

At least this was what she told herself when impulse had made her telephone Hugh at his office. Her basic reason, however, had been rather different. That weekend at Dragon House Hugh had attracted her quite a lot. She had fully intended seeing him again, and was only sorry circumstances had prevented this. Now she was back in London, lonely and bored. Boredom was a condition she could not endure. As soon as she felt its onset she quickly invented measures to get rid of it. She took after her grandmother, who had been a decidedly original and strong-minded character. One couldn't fight heredity, could one?

She suspected she had chosen an inspired moment to telephone Hugh Morley because he had responded so readily. Perhaps he was bored, too. She would have to move warily, of course, showing Hugh her shop, talking furnishings and fashions, discussing Geneva, the January weekend at Dragon House, Georgina and the little boy. What was his name? Must remember. What sort of criminals he had been defending lately. Wasn't the crime wave terrible, etc., etc.

Then they would have drinks, one thing would lead to another. Another meeting? Lunch? Dinner? Bed? Not falling in love. She didn't fall in love. She just amused herself in the slightly dangerous way she enjoyed. That would be all Hugh would want, too, if she guessed right. He was basically conventional, and had his career to think of. But a love affair on the lightest of levels would pass the summer.

The telephone rang just as she was putting out the drinks in the sunny living room behind the shop. She picked up the receiver lazily, thinking that that new picture, an innocuous Victorian river scene with punts and parasols, over the mantelpiece, was just right for the atmosphere she wanted to create.

"Amy Russell speaking."

"I'm glad to hear it."

The deep gravelly voice with its underlying cynicism sent a shudder of premonition through her. Oh, no, she was through with him.

"Are you checking up on me?" she asked tensely.

"Just welcoming you back to London, my angel."

"Isn't everything okay?" She was angry with herself for having allowed the tension to creep into her voice.

"Everything is absolutely splendid."

"Then what is it, Bunny?"

"Just a little matter. We can't waste brains like yours."

"They're not being wasted."

"But not extended, either."

"I think so, Bunny. Really."

"What, are you tired already of our little ploy?"

"Our little ploy is over."

"Oh, goodness me, no." The gentle rumble of the laugh she already knew too well made her move the receiver away from her ear. "It's only beginning. Did Hal mislead you?"

"Anything Hal wants is his own affair. The old woman's mad about him. Or was."

"Still is, fortunately. But Hal hasn't your superb judgement. He has to be watched in case he does something precipitate."

"Like stealing?" said Amy sharply.

"I'm delighted you understand."

"So what do you expect me to do?"

"The old lady has a birthday party next weekend. Just like Queen Victoria. Troops on standby orders. Hal is going. So are you."

"I'm not invited."

"You will be."

"But honestly, Bunny—"

"Are you really so surprised, angel? Did you think we'd stop where we did? Don't tell me you don't enjoy this as much as I do. You're a charming and gifted young woman, but luckily one for whom love affairs simply aren't enough. Now are they?"

"You might give me the chance to find out."

"Don't be silly, you found that out years ago. You don't care for wasting your talents."

Amy drew a deep breath. She was tingling with fright, but only because he knew her so well. No one had ever read her as he did. He knew that if he went on dangling temptation, risk, excitement, pitting one's wits against that formidable old woman's, she would succumb. And not for the money, but for the sheer love of intrigue.

Also, she was nervous of Bunny Beaumont. She had only met him twice. Both times he had hidden behind dark glasses so that she had never really seen his face or been able to guess what he was thinking. It had been enough, however, to make her realise that she could never risk his being an enemy.

"What is it you want me to do, for God's sake?"

"Just a small matter of an inventory. And to keep an eye on our mutual friend, Hal. As I said, he isn't renowned for patience, and the old lady may take longer to die than he would prefer."

"Don't build hopes on her dying at all."

"She's like that, is she? But in the end everybody does die."

"For heaven's sake, are we to hang around Dragon House for years?"

"I'd say for the summer. Maybe a short summer."

Amy's eyes went to the picture over the mantelpiece, the serene sunlit scene, the languid ladies beneath their pastel-coloured parasols, the drooping willows, the glass green river. Could it be like that at Dragon House the first weekend in May?

She doubted if, in this stage of evolution, anything so innocent and idyllic as that scene existed.

But who wanted innocence or idylls? One was a creature of one's time, unless one was a dreamy romantic like Georgina Morley. Bunny was absolutely right. The adrenalin was flowing through her blood, giving her a most pleasurable high.

An inventory. What harm was there in that? She could include the jade pony and get rid of her sense of grievance.

"If I do this, Bunny—"

"Ah, you're still there, I'm glad to hear."

"I was thinking."

"Fair enough."

"If I do this—"

"Is there any question? You will come and have tea with me when you return to London, and receive your reward. Perfectly simple and harmless, isn't it?"

"What does Hal say?"

"Hal does as I tell him. What a foolish question."

She remembered her first meeting with Bunny Beaumont in the Hôtel Richmonde in Geneva. That was when she had been working for the Far Eastern Art Galleries, a shop that had once belonged to the famous family firm of James Carrington and Sons, but had passed into other hands on the death of the last active member of the family, Nathaniel Carrington.

There had been the large cigar and the outsize dark glasses, an unhealthily yellowish skin and a squat figure, expensively dressed. And the gravelly voice and the proposition.

It seemed that Bunny Beaumont knew all about her past life and her qualifications. He knew, worst of all, that she was both tough and vulnerable. Not emotionally weak, but with the vulnerability of ambition. Greed, too, perhaps. Revenge, perhaps. The victim of heredity, if it were possible to be such a thing.

She was also young and acceptably attractive. He had been watching her. He saw that she would fit at any level into that most class-ridden of all societies, the English. And she was not hampered by a husband or an inquisitive or possessive family. She was alone, and very capable of being alone. But she was twenty-eight, although she still had a waif-like appearance, with sharp shoulder blades and elbows, and therefore must be wanting more than the comparatively modest rewards of an expert on Chinese ceramics. Besides, there was the connection, the heredity, the envy, the grievance. Bunny Beaumont had done his homework. He even knew about the jade pony. Or had she told him that on their first meeting when she had been both bewildered and intrigued and had swallowed the drink he had recommended, a deceptively innocuous frothily pink mixture, too quickly?

Anyway, the chance of acquiring her own business in London had proved irresistible. He had guessed that would happen. He probably, she reflected wryly, had guessed also that she would endeavour to keep her connection with Dragon House, that very English house on the Thames, by starting a liaison with one of her fellow guests.

Was that the subconscious reason for her sudden impulse to telephone Hugh Morley?

God, if it were, that mysterious powerful Bunny who existed only as a squat figure sitting in the smart bar of the Hôtel Richmonde, and as a voice on the telephone, had a rather terrifying knowledge of her motivations, more than she had herself.

It was a sunny late spring day and she had merely been thinking of love. Yet Bunny had uncannily telephoned. And now Hugh was here.

He sat on the chintz-covered couch and stared at the Victorian painting, and said that it wasn't what he had expected her taste in art to be.

"Surprise you, do I?" said Amy lightly.

"If it is your taste. But I expect you hope to sell it to a customer."

"What artist would you expect me to admire?"

"Chagall?" Hugh hazarded.

"Nice, yes. If I could afford one. I'm not likely to while I earn my living this way."

"Wasn't the Geneva job lucrative?"

"Oh, that, yes. Aging film star. No names. But I didn't earn enough to buy a Chagall."

"I imagine one thing leads to another in your job."

"Leads back to Chelsea and South Ken, and designing trendy drawing roms for not particularly well-heeled TV producers. And banal punting scenes on my wall. No, not banal. I like it. I don't intend to sell it. Anyway"— Amy watched Hugh's face—"I imagine we might be re-creating that pretty scene this weekend."

"At Dragon House? Are you coming?"

The leaping interest in his face—he *was* attractive in his English way—was almost immediately followed by a flat look of disappointment.

"Is Hal Jessel taking you? I wouldn't have thought—"

"That he was my cup of tea? Actually, you might be wrong. He's so beautiful. I just gaze at him."

"So does Aunt Suzie," said Hugh drily.

"Poor old duck. Gorgeous old duck. I love looking at her, too. That place sort of turns me on. Doesn't it you?"

"I think it's a ghastly mausoleum. That ridiculous old woman, and her poor wreck of a son. And this weekend, for a bonus, Aunt Lucy as well."

"Who is Aunt Lucy? Not another Suzie? Or should I say Tz'u-Hsi?"

Hugh looked at her sharply. She realised she had had her tongue round the Chinese name too expertly.

"Aunt Lucy is my wife's eldest aunt. Sweet, but gaga. A little elderly woolly lamb." He paused and looked at Amy again. "The river's nice, though, at this time of year. And the garden, if the dry weather lasts. We won't be prisoners indoors. I'm so glad you're coming."

He *was* attractive, even more so than she had remembered. That direct look, with its total absorption in her. Her feeling of tense and irresistible excitement mounted. She could use him as an unsuspecting ally in discovering the geography of the house and the distribution of its treasures. As well as laying the foundations for her self-promised summer's love affair.

"Why did you come today, Hugh?"

"I wanted to see your setup."

"And are you going to give me some work? Recommend me to friends?"

"Perhaps."

"Do you like it, then?" She waved her arm round the room.

"It's an improvement on the interior of Wandsworth gaol—where I'm supposed to be. I do like it. But it's still not you, is it?"

"Who is it?" Amy took a long drink, and said deliberately, "Your wife?"

"Georgina? Oh, no, she's far too disorganised. Braque and Lowry and Marie Laurencin. Lithographs, of course. It actually works, but that might just be Georgina."

Amy's mouth tightened. Was that a stab of ill-tempered jealousy? She surprised herself.

"Another drink?"

"No, I really must go. I only dropped in."

"I'm sure you give your criminals far more time."

"Have to, unfortunately."

"Then I must commit a crime."

"You do that, and I promise to get you off."

"M'lord, it has come to our knowledge that counsel for the defence is a personal friend of the accused."

"Yes. Too bad. So you had better be good."

He held her hand for a moment, looking at her with that attractively direct gaze. It now, however, held a hint of uncertainty, of shyness. He still wasn't quite ready to be unfaithful to his wife. The insane decency of the English. She had lived abroad too long. She would have to give lessons. This weekend was promising to be really something, the first manoeuvrings before the outbreak of hostilities.

Yet Hugh, leaving earlier than he had intended, couldn't explain why he had wanted to go. Amy Russell had been even more intriguing than he had remembered. Not pretty, but chic in that odd gamine way, original, quick-witted, a girl any man would enjoy being seen with. Unpredictable and funny. But with a look of sharpness, a well-honed little silver knife. Too dangerous if he wanted an extramarital affair? He only knew that suddenly he wanted to be back with Georgina. The weekend might bring other ideas. At least it was now something to be looked forward to.

But tonight he wanted Georgina, with her tumbling hair and her plain lawn nightgown and her mouth loose with sleep, in his arms.

Coward, he thought to himself. Square. Faithful old married man, settling for the status quo.

But not altogether. He had a vision of himself pushing

Amy Russell overboard from the punt, then dragging her out of the water, kissing her cold lips back to life.

Was he catching Georgina's habit of dreaming?

Lying on the yellow velvet couch in the drawing room, two pugs sprawled in her lap, Suzie let the telephone ring several times before she answered it. Lazy servants, where were they?

Then she languidly stretched out a beringed hand, the long nail shield on her little finger clicking against the plastic receiver. Holding it to her ear and answering in her husky voice, she instantly dissolved into delight.

"Hal! My dear boy!"

"Highness! Dear lady!"

She grew petulant. She detected the wheedling tone in his voice. He was about to ask a favour. She detested being asked favours, preferring to bestow them unasked and when she was in the mood.

"Yes, what is it?"

"I was only about to suggest the teeniest thing about the weekend."

"Nothing that will spoil it, I hope."

"Oh, no, no. Just permission to bring Amy Russell. She enjoyed it so much in January and absolutely longs to come again."

"You're not involved with this girl?"

"Goodness me, no. She's only a rather lonely little thing, and there's poor old Charles sitting on the sidelines. Didn't you notice the way he looked at her? I thought a birthday party, everyone being jolly, let Charles and Amy be jolly, too."

Suzie's eyes narrowed to slits. What was Hal up to? Devious young man. They all were.

"My son," she said cruelly, "is a eunuch."

"But not blind."

"And poor, too. Entirely dependent on me. Does this girl know that?"

"Oh, dear, oh, me, we are getting our lines crossed, Highness. Amy isn't at all mercenary. She's just a nice lively girl who will add life to your party."

"Georgina and Hugh and my grandnephew Ben will be here to do that."

"And poor Charles glooming. And your sister Lucy, who you know drives you up the wall. Are you going to hang out Chinese lanterns for a senile old woman? You know it only brings on an attack of her Peking memories."

Suzie grunted, then, beguiled as always by Hal's impudence, gave her brief croak of laughter. Hal was so right, she didn't want a bland polite weekend. She hungered for conflict.

"Very well, bring the girl. But if this turns out to be for your selfish pleasure, then you're out, both of you."

"You old tyrant, you know me better than that."

"I thought I did. Old women and young men. Am I wrong?"

"You can leave the young men out. Absolutely none. And if you despise my devotion—" The hurt in his voice was so real that one had to remind oneself he was an actor. And hope, eternally suspicious as she was, that this was not acting. He really was quite the most charming of all her young men.

"I don't despise it, dear boy. I simply want it proved."

Constantly. She could be lonely, too. Didn't these self-centred young men realise that?

Chapter 10

Luncheon. A difficult meal. Everyone newly arrived and not settled in. By evening, when twilight hung over the garden and lights had been lit on the terrace and in the big drawing room, and everyone was mellowed by drinks, the uneasy assortment of people would have begun to mix.

But now Aunt Lucy was nodding with the fatigue of her unaccustomed journey. Georgina had her mind on unpacking. Charles, white and pinched, was never at his best until later in the day, and even Aunt Suzie was not in the sunniest of tempers. One of the spoilt pugs had misbehaved on her favourite Chinese carpet. He was growing old and incontinent. It was depressing.

Ben was not depressed. He was fidgety with excitement. He had made his birthday gift for Aunt Suzie himself. It was a scarlet banner trimmed with gold braid and, after laborious instructions from Ho Ming at the

159

Chinese restaurant in Cromwell Road where his parents occasionally took him for a treat, he had printed "Exterminate the foreigners" in Chinese characters in white paint on the banner. Aunt Suzie could either tie it round her waist or wave it from behind a tree when they played Boxers. They were sure to play sometime this weekend because it was not only Aunt Suzie's birthday but the anniversary of the beginning of the Boxer Rebellion. Actually, Mother said, both anniversaries were a little suspect. The Boxers had begun their intermittent war in the provinces long before hostilities in Peking in May, and there had been a slight vagueness about Aunt Suzie's birth. She had arrived after the other children had been sent back to England in the care of another English family. So it was several months before they saw either their parents or their new sister. And then that odd forgetfulness had occurred about the date of Aunt Suzie's birth, a fact that had rankled with Aunt Suzie all her life. It just proved that she had been an unwanted baby, she said.

Actually her birth hadn't even been entered in the family Bible until her mother was dead. On writing the melancholy words, "On the 1st day of August, 1909, my beloved wife Amelia departed this life," Suzie's father had discovered that in the flurry of getting ready to leave China no one had remembered to record the new baby's birth. He made up for the lapse by writing "Suzie, daughter of Amelia and Nathaniel Carrington, born on 24th May, 1901, in Canton, China."

They had only given her one Christian name (not that that wasn't enough for her since she was obviously named after the great Empress Dowager), but no one had explained why she had been born in Canton instead of Peking. Her father must have had business there, before leaving for England, and he had taken his wife, heavily pregnant, with him.

Anyway, the doubt existed that after all that time he

had remembered Suzie's birth date correctly. For it did seem a coincidence that it had been not only on the anniversary of the harrowing Boxer war, but on the anniversary of Queen Victoria's birthday. This last fact when she discovered it, pleased Suzie immensely. It gave her the importance which she needed. It was then that she began to develop her aggressiveness.

While Ben was devoted to Aunt Suzie in a curious half-fearful way he did have a kindly regard for Aunt Lucy, whom he saw much less frequently. He thought she was probably over a hundred years old, and that one day she would simply float away like a puff of thistledown. But, when she was thinking clearly, she was a wonderful source of stories about Peking and the Boxers, and the family. She talked a great deal about her brother, Georgie, and almost always called Ben Georgie, in spite of his patient correction of her error.

Then she would laugh and say what a forgetful old woman she was. Georgie had been the same. He had frequently called Suzie Plum Blossom.

Why Plum Blossom? Ben had wanted to know.

Well, one supposed it was because Suzie was the only one of the four of them with dark hair and dark eyes, and she apparently reminded Georgie of a Chinese child he had known.

This subject came up again at luncheon, when Aunt Lucy made her inevitable error and addressed Ben as Georgie.

"That was my grandfather," Ben explained, his eyes earnest behind his owlish glasses. "I'm Ben. Can't you remember, Aunt Lucy?"

"Ben?" Aunt Lucy's large eyes, as pale a blue as the heat-hazed noonday sky, were bewildered.

"Georgina's boy," Aunt Suzie said impatiently.

"Georgina? Oh, of course, dear Georgina. My memory is a little unreliable. And yet I can remember all that dreadful time in Peking so clearly. And after we came home, and Mamma was always poorly. China ruined her health, you know. She had a very bad bout of typhoid during the siege and she never completely got her strength back. After she came home she kept to her room a great deal. We three children used to spend hours with her."

"You see," said Aunt Suzie, "you speak of yourself and Henrietta and Georgie. The sacred trinity. I wasn't in it."

"Because you were only a baby, Suzie. Poor Mamma wasn't well enough to look after you."

"I was a deprived child."

"Nonsense," said Aunt Lucy with sudden brisk lucidity. "You had all the things Henrietta and I had. Clothes, school, parties. Papa took very good care of you."

All the same, Ben understood Aunt Suzie's point of view. He could see the scene in the big bedroom, Great-grandmother propped up on pillows, tenderly loving to Henrietta, Lucy and Georgie who clustered at her bedside, while downstairs poor Suzie, with none of her mother's golden beauty, was a demanding screaming baby who was more of a nuisance than anything to the closely knit trio upstairs.

Ben, personally, knew that he would hate it if his mother had another baby, so one couldn't blame the three older children. Although Georgie must have been fond of Suzie since he called her by the pet name of Plum Blossom.

The other guests at the luncheon table were bored with the reminiscences, for Ben's father was saying in a pleasant but slightly edged voice that when he came to Dragon House he was never sure whether he was in England or China. It was a very hot day and—

"Just like the drought in Peking before the rebellion," Aunt Lucy interrupted obstinately. "The Boxers blamed the foreign devils for the failure of the crops and the famine."

"And I personally intend going on the river," Hugh continued, looking at Amy Russell before he turned to the others.

"I'm doing nothing more energetic than lying in a hammock," said Hal Jessel, also looking at Amy.

"Tomorrow," said Aunt Suzie, "I have planned a picnic. We'll go down the river to a very pleasant little island. You men can fish. I'll take my sketching materials and the dogs. We'll have a packed lunch, cold salmon and chicken and champagne. Does everyone agree?"

"Certainly, Highness," said Hal Jessel. "This island sounds just like your Highness' pleasure gardens in the City of Heavenly Peace."

"That's what it is, dear boy."

Amy pressed her temples as if she felt a headache about to begin. Aunt Lucy smiled vaguely and said that she would probably like to rest. The heat was so enervating. Mamma had never let them go outdoors at the hottest time of the day. Oh, that was in Peking, of course.

Neither of Ben's parents said anything. They had always emphasised to Ben that these weekends were to please Aunt Suzie, and therefore they must go along with her whims.

Charles said nothing either, but then nobody expected him to go on a river picnic. He was relegated to Aunt Lucy's regimen of old age and sleep.

"And then tonight," said Aunt Suzie, with the eagerness of a child, "it's my birthday dinner party. I expect everyone downstairs by seven sharp. I'll leave you to your own devices this afternoon. I am going in to Maidenhead to my bank."

"On Saturday?" Hal queried. "Isn't it closed?"

"I have an appointment with the manager. He sees me at my convenience."

Aunt Suzie's eyes were narrowed. She was enjoying the speculation she had evoked. What was she up to, with an appointment with her bank manager? Who was most concerned? Charles, her loving son, who couldn't wait to get his hands on enough money to be free of her and Dragon House? Her beautiful greedy Hal, the foxy-faced Miss Russell who could well have the kind of morals that would allow her to seduce and marry a hopeless cripple for his money? Georgina and Hugh, thoroughly nice but not unaware of family interests? Ben, who only wanted the jade pony?

The perennial game was in full swing. She was enjoying it more than ever. She had to, for its climax was inexorably approaching. She was seventy-four years old. Death, once no more than a faint shadow on the horizon, was now visibly nearer. She had to crowd all the amusement she could into her remaining years.

Aunt Lucy had the room next to Georgina and Hugh. This pleased her. She was very fond of Georgina. Sometimes, when half fallen into one of her frequent dozes, she thought she was a little girl again and Georgina was her mother. Gentle and quiet-voiced and loving. Now that Henrietta had gone she needed someone to take care of her. There were menaces.

No, there were not, she reminded herself sharply. Henrietta had been very firm with her about that. Her fears existed only in dreams. She would wake in a fright, but only because she had been carried back in her sleep to those traumatic eight weeks of childhood. The vague menace that seemed to hang over her came only from memory, not from the modern dangers of burglars, muggers, hooligans. None of those evils had yet struck her, thank heaven, so why should she be so nervous? Especially in Suzie's house.

All the same there was no doubt about it, someone was tiptoeing over her head. There was the faint creak of floorboards, silence, then another creak. Something moved. It sounded like furniture. Then there came a rasping sound. Ah, she knew what that was. The wardrobe door. It had stuck all the years she had known it. It was a massive oak piece put up in the schoolroom out of the way. Since it was not used for anything special, nobody had ever bothered to fix its warped door.

So the sounds definitely came from the old schoolroom, a large room under the eaves that Aunt Suzie now used for junk.

Everyone had gone on the river, she seemed to remember. Who could be up there?

No one would ever know what enormous courage it needed to go along the corridor and mount the stairs to the second floor. A flight she had known so well in the past when, as often as not, they had slid down the bannisters, Georgie first, Henrietta next, and Lucy clinging to Henrietta's waist. Now she was creeping up, a very old lady with creaking knees and thumping heart. She was suddenly in such a state of terror that she fully expected to encounter a Boxer, pigtailed, red-sashed, waving a sword and grinning ferociously.

Only there were no Boxers in England. Hadn't Henrietta kept telling her so?

Something fell on the bare floor and skidded across it. In the doorway, clutching the door frame, Aunt Lucy saw first a Canton enamel box, one of Papa's treasures, then the form stooping over it, and slowly straightening to look full into Aunt Lucy's face.

"Angel!" Aunt Lucy gasped incredulously, the shock taking the breath out of her lungs. She fought for breath, then collapsed into welcome darkness.

After all, Georgina had gone on the river with Hugh because he had been disappointed that no one had accepted his invitation. Ben too, when he found Aunt Suzie was not going to be available for games, was ready for any alternative suggestion. Hal had reiterated that he was exhausted after a week's filming, and Amy had murmured that the garden was such bliss.

So Georgina, leaning luxuriously on cushions, had glided down the river while Hugh had given Ben a somewhat precarious lesson in how to manage a punt. It was an idyllic hour, drifting beneath hanging willows over the gloomy green water, startling the shyer water birds into flight, fending off a hissing swan, letting the dappled sunlight fall on her face. She was getting like Ben, she was dreaming of that other family. Delicate Amelia holding a parasol to keep the sun off her face, the two little girls, Henrietta and Lucy in white muslin with floppy hats, Georgie begging his father to let him handle the pole. That was if Nathaniel ever unbent enough to do such a lazy summertime thing as punting on the river. Suzie, the baby, would have been left behind, probably screaming in her perambulator. Poor Suzie, the last dilatory and not particularly welcome arrival.

Amelia, Nathaniel, Henrietta, Lucy, Georgie. . . .

She was thinking of them as a family of strangers, not as poor Grandmother who had died before she was forty, Grandfather who became so stern and short of temper, dear Father, a gentle absent-minded elderly man who revered all forms of life (because once in the siege of Peking he had been so aware of death?), and the two quaint old-fashioned aunts, Henrietta and Lucy, recluses in their Sussex cottage, avoiding life because it could be too shocking.

"Glad you came?" Georgina asked Hugh.

"I admit I can take plenty of this."

Georgina craned her head backwards to look up at him. She wanted to say "I love you," and did say it, adding, "I love you both," because Ben was there, hanging over the side of the punt, trying to grab some unidentified shape that had slid through the water.

"Euphoria," said Hugh tolerantly. "It'll disappear when we get back to that crazy house."

"I don't know. I think it's going to be nice this time.

Aunt Suzie seems happy and even Aunt Lucy is talking more sense."

"Aunt Suzie is going to light lanterns in the trees," Ben said excitedly. "How late may I stay up, Mummy?"

"Quite late, little owl."

"Oh, good. Aunt Suzie might play Boxers with me."

"Not in the dark, surely."

"She might when she sees the banner I've made for her."

"Well, perhaps. But you must be careful. You know Aunt Lucy gets upset if there's screaming and yelling."

When they returned they found Charles, Amy and Hal in the walled garden. Hal, as he had promised, was stretched out in the hammock. A little distance away Amy sat on the grass at Charles' feet, or, more correctly, at the foot of his wheelchair. Obviously she had coaxed him to talk, for she was looking at him with close attention. He did seem more than usually animated, and was pointing out some shrubs and flowers to her. When Georgina came up he said, "I took your advice about gardening. I've done quite a lot of this myself. Smythe did the things I couldn't manage. Do you like my peonies? Have you heard the Chinese legend that they have mandarins' eyes?"

"Well, that's fine if you want your garden full of crafty mandarins," Georgina said lightly. "The Chinese have a legend for everything, like that haunting one that chrysanthemums are the ghosts of children."

"And the willow is a wicked old wizard," shouted Ben.

"Really," said Amy, laughing, "is this place English or an offshore island of China?"

She looked attractive when she laughed, vivid, and with that strange air of repressed excitement. Was she always like that, Georgina wondered, or was there something about Dragon House that excited her? Poor Charles, who would one day be rich Charles, if his mother didn't reward too many hangers-on, was going to be her victim, Georgina was afraid.

No, that thought was unworthy. But looking sideways at Hugh who was watching Amy, Georgina wished he would have the same thought. It might make the interest in his eyes more clinical, less admiring.

One thing seemed certain. Amy was not at Dragon House for the weekend because of the somnolent Hal.

"Charles, I'm so glad you've found the garden interesting," she said. "It's making you get outdoors, and you look much better."

"Nurse Jenkins sees I get outdoors. She's a great one for a daily tour of the estate, as she calls it."

"Nurse Jenkins? Isn't she new?"

"Not according to my turnover of the nursing profession. She's stayed three months. A record."

"Then I take it you aren't brandishing swords at her?"

"Wouldn't dare. Isn't Mother back yet?" Charles' face, which had been momentarily animated, relapsed into peevishness. "I want my tea."

"There's someone coming now," said Georgina. "I think it's your Nurse Jenkins."

"My dragon," said Charles.

"Is she really a dragon?" Ben started up eagerly to look at the figure approaching through the shrubbery. "Oh, no, she isn't," he said disappointedly, as a plump young woman with a jolly smiling face appeared.

One of those, thought Georgina. Her perpetual cheerfulness would soon irritate Charles as much as bossiness or ill-temper did. However, she thought there was less hostility than usual in his face. Perhaps he hadn't been able to intimidate this nurse and the fact still intrigued him. It wouldn't go on doing so. He enjoyed using the tyranny of an invalid as much as his mother enjoyed the power of her possessions.

"Mr. Charles, I think you ought to come indoors for

a rest if you're going to stay up all hours tonight," Nurse Jenkins said. "I'm sure everyone will excuse you."

"Isn't he to wait and have tea with us?" Amy said disappointedly.

"I think not." Nurse Jenkins turned her smiling gaze briefly on Amy. Did anyone else, Georgina wondered, notice a cool glint in her bland blue eyes? It suggested an instant disapproval of Amy's waif-like figure, perhaps because of her own generous curves. Or because Amy seemed to have entertained her patient too successfully?

Rubbish, Georgina told herself. All nurses got possessive of their patients, and how nice it was that Charles at last had one who didn't seem too abhorrent to him.

"He was gardening all morning. Now he really must rest," Nurse Jenkins said firmly.

"The boss dictates," said Charles.

"Charles, I haven't had time to see your garden properly," Georgina said. "But it does look charming. Will you show it to me tomorrow?"

"If we're all still here after Mother's high jinks tonight."

"We'll all be resting, I fancy," said Nurse Jenkins. She seized Charles' chair and began briskly pushing it towards the house, a pale white hand raised over its arm in a departing salute.

"Heavens," said Hugh, "she's making him almost human."

"Yes, we've been talking for hours," said Amy. "He's really quite a fascinating person."

"So it's you who's been making him human," came Hal's voice lazily from the hammock. "That sounds more likely to me. I wouldn't trust that female gorgon an inch."

"Why not?" Hugh asked. "She seems pleasant enough."

"She's a brainwasher. Poor old Charles is getting the treatment."

"He's happier and that's what matters," Georgina said

rather sharply. She didn't quite understand the undercurrents, but they were definitely there.

"I must go in and bring Aunt Lucy down to tea. I don't think we should wait for Aunt Suzie. Will you all come in in a few minutes?"

So that was how she happened to find Aunt Lucy creeping shakily down the stairs from the old schoolroom. Her hair was dishevelled, her face ashen.

"Oh, Georgina, darling! I'm so glad you're here. I've seen a ghost."

"A ghost? Whose?"

"Angel's, my dear. You remember our cousin Angel? Such a naughty little girl. An awfully bad influence on Georgie."

"Aunt Lucy, what *are* you talking about?"

"She was in the schoolroom interfering with Papa's treasures. She always was a thief. I remember that day she and Georgie went to Prince Su's palace. But Mamma said one must make allowances for Angel since she had seen the Boxers slash off her father's head. Too dreadful!"

"Aunt Lucy, you've been dreaming."

"Have I?" The forlorn frightened eyes looked hopefully at Georgina. "Then I must have been walking in my sleep. I had a fall, I think. I became dizzy."

"I'll help you back to your room."

"No, no, I'm perfectly all right. But do just run upstairs, dear, and see if Angel's still there."

Georgina stood in the long low-ceilinged room, full of furniture, pictures, certain large and small objets d'art discarded because of their ugliness or lack of value, children's toys—the rocking horse with the wispy moth-eaten mane and tail, the tin soldiers, the miniature rickshaw, the shabby French doll with the kid arms and legs. A room full of memories, and therefore surely full of ghosts. Aunt Lucy had drifted back into the past. Angel had died long since in the province of Shansi. She had never visited this house, except as a projection of a senile old lady's imagination.

All the same, there was a feeling in this room. That was why Georgina didn't like Ben coming up here. He was too susceptible already to atmosphere. He would have said someone had been disturbing his family's things. Weren't those recent fingermarks in the dust on that old bureau?

No, she mustn't begin seeing with Ben's eyes, or she would have wraiths in pinafores and sailor suits coming out of the corners. This had been the children's room. It had been virtually shut up when they had grown and scattered. Nobody came here except Aunt Lucy, wandering in her sleep. Those would be her fingermarks in the dust. She must have had a particularly vivid dream. She had better rest before dinner, and get rid of that disturbingly shocked look she had. Ben looked the same when emerging from a nightmare.

Hugh was calling from downstairs.

"Georgina! Teatime. Is Aunt Lucy all right?"

"She's just seen a ghost, but she's all right. Ask Kate to bring her a tray of tea in her room."

"Darling, what *are* you talking about?"

"Aunt Lucy's tea."

"You said ghosts."

"The constant companions of the old, dear boy," came Aunt Lucy's voice, surprisingly strong. "This house is full of them. Is Suzie back?"

"Not yet."

"Ah! I fancy she's up to something. She likes surprises."

In his room, sitting beneath the curved Chinese sword on the wall, Charles began to laugh silently, his thin shoulders shaking. Nurse Jenkins looked at him enquiringly.

"What's amusing you?"

"That little tramp. Where does Mother find them? Well, I know where she found this one, of course. She's an accomplice of that rat Jessel."

"An accomplice, maybe. But a girl friend, no." Nurse Jenkins was stooping over the bed, smoothing its covers. Her generous haunches were just out of reach of Charles' hungry fingers. He began to move his chair.

"So what do you think they want?"

"Jessel wants a large legacy. Believe it or not, I think Amy wants me."

"You!"

Nurse Jenkins spun round, her pale blue eyes sparking.

"As a second iron in the fire, supposing Mother changes her mind about the legacy to Hal, and leaves everything to me."

"Long-term planning like that, the villains!"

"And pickings on the way. Or am I being too suspicious?"

"No one can afford not to be suspicious in your position."

"No," said Charles flatly. "I even suspect you."

"Oh, sir—"

"Charles, Eileen."

"Charles. I have to watch my tongue when I'm with other people."

"You do that very well."

"But you don't really suspect me? Aren't I good to you? Won't I go on being good to you?"

A kind of wary hopefulness touched Charles' face.

"I almost believe you, Eileen."

"Then why don't we tell your mother? Get little tramps like that out of your hair."

"Not yet. We haven't made half our plans yet."

Nurse Jenkins took his hand in her warm capacious one.

"Are you coming to bed, then?"

"Are you?"

"Oh, I don't think so. Not with a tiring evening ahead for you."

"God, do stop being a nurse!"

"I want to, but—"

"But lock the door. You know my mother's prowling habits. Mustn't give her the shock of finding her son isn't a eunuch, after all."

Nurse Jenkins gave a surprising giggle.

"She is rather horrible, isn't she?"

"She's an evil old woman who has to be outwitted. But no more gardening this weekend, eh?"

Nurse Jenkins was plumping up pillows.

"That's right."

"It's too hot, anyway. Hot and dry and dusty as they said it was in Peking seventy-four years ago today."

"You never forget that old siege in this house, do you?"

"Never. My family brought it home with them. It really should have been called the siege of the Carringtons. . . ."

Dragon House, Peking

June, 1900

Chapter 11

The enemy was at the gates. There was no longer any doubt about the gravity of the rebellion. The mobs had moved up from the burning and ruined city and were hammering on the great Ch'ien Men Gate, shouting *"Sha! Sha!"* The gate trembled but did not fall. The Tartar wall was so immense it seemed impossible to be breached, and gave an illusion of safety. But missiles could be fired over it, either bullets or flaming torches, and determined and fanatical men could scale it. Everyone not on military duty was ordered to keep well out of the vicinity of the wall. Many of the legations were in vulnerable positions. It seemed as if eventually all the besieged might be forced to take refuge in the British legation which, fortunately, was large and occupied the most protected position. Nearly a thousand people had gathered there, congregating in the vast number of rooms or camping on the grounds. There were meetings of the ministers hourly, and urgent diplomatic protests were sent into the Imperial City where the Peking government, the Tsungli Yamen, was keeping suspiciously silent.

In the meantime, the hammering and yelling went on, undeterred by the midday heat. If only it would rain, the hot, dirty and terrified besieged said. That would surely calm the mad frenzy of the Boxers. Their rebellion had been precipitated by the drought. If the heavens would open and pour down a cool drenching rain it would quiet their hysteria, and calm everyone's bad temper, including Colonel Manners', who had been told, none too tactfully, by an arrogant German *Kapitän* that a gentleman of his venerable years would be a liability rather than an asset on guard duty on the wall.

Dammit, he could still fire a rifle. There was nothing wrong with his eyesight, and he didn't know the meaning of the word "fear." Yet he was discarded. He was useless. He was condemned to fetching and carrying for the women and teaching the children a bit of essential drill. He wanted, he said wryly, recruits up to the age of twelve years. Over that age, they were required by the army to do some real work.

"Don't worry, my old friend," said Lady Comerford. "Let us organise a concert. We must keep people occupied. Isn't that important? Otherwise they'll go to pieces like poor Lilian Beddow."

"One thing is certain, you'll never go to pieces," said the Colonel gallantly.

"Won't I?" Lady Comerford twisted her rings on her bony fingers. She had taken to putting on more makeup, hoping it would hide her pallor and the way her skin had shrunk and wrinkled in the last few days. She didn't realise that she was beginning to look like a painted doll. The light was bad in the slit of a room which she insisted on occupying because at least she could be alone there. A larger room shared with others would have meant disclosing all her pathetic secrets. So if her rouge and her rice powder and her eye shadow got a bit mixed up it was because she couldn't see. Anyway, she would have preferred looking like a circus clown to showing her arrant cowardice.

"There's Madame Leonora longing to give us some arias," she went on. "I'm sure we can find plenty of other talent. I'll ask Amelia Carrington to help. And Lady MacDonald and Alice Conger."

"Show we're not a sinking ship, eh?"

"That's exactly what I mean. Do you know, Colonel, I never thought one could get so tired of champagne. We're also going to be eating mules, Sir Claude tells me."

"There are worse things, dear lady."

"Oh, I know. Cats and rats as in the siege of Paris. I doubt if that knowledge will make mule steaks taste any more palatable."

Amelia begged the children never to go out of the legation gardens. She also ordered Miss Deacon never to let them out of her sight, unless Cassidy or Ah Wan was with them. She could trust Henrietta and Lucy who were content to play with their dolls. Indeed, Lucy could hardly be persuaded to set foot outdoors, even in the nearest and most secluded courtyard. The noise hurt, she said. Henrietta was braver, and consented to go at least as far as the willow tree that dipped its graceful fronds in the goldfish pool. Georgie spent most of the day in this tree, saying that since he wasn't allowed on the wall he must have some kind of lookout. He longed to see a Boxer running across the lawn or invading the tennis court.

Angel, a skinny rebel figure herself, with her hair always tumbling over her strange yellow eyes, paced backwards and forwards beneath Georgie in his leafy perch, shouting *"Sha! Sha!"* until her voice grew hoarse. Henrietta said it made her dizzy. Why couldn't Angel play dolls, as girls did? She was glad when Angel, after beckoning to Georgie and whispering something in his ear, set off in the direction of the tennis court, with Georgie, a plump hot little figure, plodding obediently in her wake.

It was very hot indeed, and no day to be running about. Henrietta stitched at a new petticoat for her best French doll, and told Lucy not to just sit rocking her shabby Topsy. Couldn't she be doing some useful work? Aunt Lilian peered out from the doorway saying anxiously, "Where's Angel?" but was gently pulled back by Mamma, who said in her bright calm voice, "Don't worry so, Lilian. Cassidy's there, and Miss Deacon. Come with me and help to roll bandages. We're going to need a great many, I'm afraid."

"Have there been many wounded?" Aunt Lilian asked.

"Not yet." Mamma sounded cheerful, because that was the longest and most sensible sentence Aunt Lilian had spoken since that dreadful night when she had arrived. Perhaps, now that she could speak again, she would be able to make that naughty Angel behave.

In the meantime, Angel had led Georgie on a daring expedition right across the grounds of the legation, across the canal and into the Su Wang Fu, which was a large park of gardens, lakes, palaces and pagodas. They were not allowed to go there, Georgie knew, but he suddenly spotted a heron standing like a statue in a small lake, and he rushed forward joyfully.

"It's the first I've seen. I wonder if it will fly."

Disturbed by the children, it did indeed fly, spreading its wings and tucking back its long neck, floating overhead like a small galleon. Georgie watched entranced until it was out of sight. Committed now to the adventure he shouted, "Come on, Angel. Let's see what else we can find."

The white pine, the snowy trunk shining among its dark green needles, the tamarisks swishing in the breeze, the crows giving their harsh cries, a hoopoe running with short fussy steps, the mounds and pathways and small marble pavilions with vermilion roofs and then, joy of joys, a dove with the clever Chinese device of small pipes tied to its tail so that it emitted an ethereal music.

All these enchantments were like a dream after the dreary, hot, overcrowded legation. When Angel shouted that she had found a door open in one of the deserted palaces, Georgie followed eagerly, as intent as she was on what could be discovered.

In the end, among all the empty rooms with their collection of lacquered tables and screens, porcelain vases and bowls and ticking clocks, the only thing they both coveted was the green jade pony asleep with its head tucked against its side, its rounded haunches as darkly gleaming and smooth as the water of the small lakes.

Angel held it in her cupped hands.

"I'm going to take it," she said.

"That's stealing."

"I don't care. Anyway, no one else wants it or it wouldn't have been left behind."

"Papa will be angry."

"You're not to tell him."

Georgie hesitated, remembering uncomfortably one of Papa's maxims, *Tell the truth at all times.* But if Papa didn't ask, if he didn't see the delectable little pony, no one would be obliged to confess to a misdeed. And Angel deserved something from the wicked Chinese, for cutting off her father's head.

Anyway, he could see it was not much use arguing with her, for she had gathered up her pinafore to hold the pony.

"You find something, too," she urged.

"I don't want anything else." This was true. It was only the pony he wanted. He thought Angel might get tired of it later, and give it to him. She was a girl and ought to like dolls best. Besides, they couldn't stay here too long in case someone came. In fact, a sharp cracking noise had begun outside. It sounded frighteningly like guns, which meant the Boxers must be trying to break in. Papa said the Fu would be the most dangerous place if the Boxers managed to get over the wall. "Come on, Angel. We ought to go."

Angel had heard the noises, too.

"I think it's the Boxers. We'd better run. Come on."

Halfway across the pleasure grounds, in the burning sun, they stumbled beneath a crooked pine tree to get their breath. Something smacked in the dust a little way off. A bullet! Georgie gave a suppressed whimper of fear, but Angel said stoically. "It's swords you have to be afraid of, not bullets. The Boxers are bad marksmen, my papa said. They couldn't even hit a church spire. Come on, we'll be all right."

There were no more of those menacing cracks. Almost back in the legation grounds, Georgie had to stop again to get his breath.

"You're not a very good runner, are you?" Angel said. "You're too fat, that's the trouble. And your face is as red as the roof of the Imperial Palace." Now that the danger was over she was giggling rudely. "It was a good adventure, though. We'll go again and find another treasure."

"Share the pony with me," Georgie said.

"I didn't think you liked stolen things."

"I don't, but—"

"But everyone does if they get the chance," said Angel shrewdly. "Now don't you dare tell where we've been."

Lucy was crying, and Henrietta cringed with discomfort as Papa paced up and down scolding everybody, Mamma, Aunt Lilian, Cassidy, Ah Wan and particularly poor Miss Deacon, who stood looking at the ground and muttering that she hadn't seen the children leave because she had been helping in the hospital.

"That isn't your business," Papa raged. "Your business is to look after my children. There are dozens of women able to do hospital work." He turned on Mamma. "And where were you?"

"Don't get into such a state, Nathaniel," Mamma said. "I was in the kitchen helping with the food. We're establishing a rota. There are hundreds to be fed, and a lot of the cooking will have to be done outdoors. Lady MacDonald can only have forty at the very most sitting at her table."

"So you'd feed the hundreds while your own son gets lost."

"They're not lost, Nathaniel." But Mamma was looking rather white, all the same. "They'll turn up any minute. Georgie's almost certain to be up a willow tree."

"We've looked at all the trees over a radius of two acres," Papa barked. "If the children have strayed farther they can be in great danger. Fighting has broken out in the Fu, as you must have heard."

Mamma bit her lips, trying to stay calm.

"I know. We must look again. Henrietta, didn't they say anything to you or Lucy?"

"They were playing on the tennis court, Mamma. I told you. Then I didn't see where they went."

"You women stay here," Papa said abruptly. "I'll get Rupert Fortescue to come with me. We'll have to go as far as the Fu. Miss Deacon, where are you going?"

"To look for Georgie and Angel, since it's my fault—"

"Will having you hit by a sniper's bullet improve matters? Stay with my wife. Do as you're told for once."

Miss Deacon stood still, her eyes tragic. It was all being singularly horrid, Henrietta thought. She loved Georgie, of course. He was her brother. But she didn't care if that Angel never came back. She longed to go back to England now, this minute, and so did Lucy. They were hot and frightened and dirty, and Ah Wan had just told them, with some secret relish, that little missies needn't think they were going to have any more baths, because there was not enough water. So they would begin to smell, too. How appalling.

Fortunately, however, just as Papa picked up his rifle, preparing to face the dangers of that wilderness of lakes and hillocks and ornamental trees called the Fu, a flicker of white beyond the willow trees in the distance was seen by Mamma.

"I believe it's them," she cried. "That's Angel's white pinafore. Yes, look, there's Georgie. Oh, thank God!"

Papa put down his rifle. "Now don't rush to welcome them, Amelia. They've been extremely disobedient and must be punished."

"But they're safe!"

"By great good luck. I hope they've had a good fright."

"Why is Angel holding up her dress?" Henrietta asked. "Look, Mamma, she's showing her bloomers. How rude."

"Don't be such a little prig," Mamma said so sharply that tears rushed into Henrietta's eyes. Then, ignoring Papa's wishes, Mamma hurried out into the hot sun to welcome the children. Georgie, quite unaware of his disgrace, was grinning cheerfully, patently relieved to be home. Angel's face remained pale, the heat made her go paler, but there was the familiar gleam of aggression in her eyes.

"Why are you all staring at us? We haven't been doing anything wrong."

"Haven't you?" came Papa's voice ominously. "You've been out of bounds, if I may make a guess, and what is Angel hiding in her apron?"

Angel clutched the small object closer to her, but Papa seized her hands and made her relinquish the treasure.

He held up the little green pony, turning it this way and that. A covetous look crossed his face. It was gone at once, and he was frowning angrily.

"Where did you get this, Angel? Did you steal it?"

"No, I did, Papa," Georgie said quickly.

"Angel, is that true? Did Georgie take it, or did you?"

Angel's eyes flickered. "It was only there in that empty palace. There were lots and lots of things that nobody wanted. We didn't think everything should be left for the Boxers," she added on an inspiration.

"In Prince Su's palace?"

"It was just a house," said Georgie. "There was no one there, not even a eunuch. We saw a heron, too. But then the Boxers started shooting so we ran home."

"And did you remember you were expressly forbidden to wander so far?"

Georgie's head hung. "I'm sorry, Papa. We just sort of got bored around here. May Angel keep the pony? Because she doesn't like dolls, and she needs something."

The gleaming jade carving lay in Papa's large hands. His fingers kept smoothing it. He was assessing its quality.

"This isn't a child's toy," he said briefly. "It's a work of art, and probably several hundred years old. Besides, we do not loot. The Boxers may. They're ignorant peasants. But we know better. Or I hope we do. I shall have to confiscate this and in due course return it either to its owner or to the Chinese government."

Angel stared longingly at her lost treasure. Suddenly she burst into sobs and ran to her mother who was sitting silently in a corner.

"Mamma, Mamma, let me keep the pony? Please! It's all I have. I so badly want it. Mamma!" she screamed, looking into the empty face. "Mamma, *where are you?*"

Her mother did nothing more than stroke the tangled hair and murmur, "Poor fatherless child," which did nothing at all to calm Angel's frightened sobbing.

It was Amelia who drew the hot tear-stained child away, saying the trouble was she was hungry, it was long past time for tiffin. If they didn't hurry there would be no food left.

As it was, it was not especially palatable, fried rice and pony meat and warm champagne, and a little tinned fruit from a supply that was being kept for the children. Angel refused to touch any of the rice or meat. Perhaps because it was pony, Henrietta thought. She didn't care much for it herself, but virtuously swallowed as much as she could. Angel would be sorry, when she began to starve long before supper time.

And where was Papa going to keep the jade pony until he was able to return it to the mysterious and disappearing Prince Su?

It was altogether a horrible day, for Miss Deacon sulked all afternoon, sitting over Georgie and Angel who were made to do lessons. Lucy, exhausted by the heat, slept, and Mamma and Cassidy joined the other ladies sewing sandbags for the trenches that were being dug in the grounds. Lady Comerford, Lady MacDonald and Alice Conger, and the wives of other ministers were all there, as well as a few young girls. Henrietta was the youngest, but Mamma said she was a good little seamstress, and she was given a beautiful piece of red silk to work on. She would dearly have liked to make a dress for her best doll, instead of a sandbag to get filthy and wet, but they had to use the materials to hand, Mamma said. She herself was pushing her needle in and out of a stiff piece of brocade that had been a mandarin's robe. The beautiful hand-painted silk curtains had been stripped from the windows and cut up. War, Henrietta thought, in a moment of forlorn maturity, desecrated everything.

There was, however, an excitement late in the afternoon. The shouting in the outer city died down, and five ministers from the Yamen came with eleven red envelopes, each containing an ultimatum, for the eleven legations.

China, the ultimatum announced, could no longer protect the legations. Therefore, they could only protect themselves by leaving Peking within the next twenty-four hours. Would they be given a safe conduct over the ninety-mile road to Tientsin through a countryside swarming with bandits? the ministers wondered. Just imagine a convoy of one thousand white people in the slow hooded Peking carts crawling down the long road, followed by a trail of Chinese Christians. They would be at the mercy of roving hordes of Boxers.

It was a trick of that evil prince Tuan to get them all slaughtered, Colonel Manners said. He, for one, did not intend to move an inch. The legation was British territory and there he stayed. He hoped his friends, Lady Comerford and the Carringtons, would have the sense to follow his example. Some people were packing boxes and sending their servants out to buy carts at exorbitant prices. Well, good luck to the poor devils. But what chance would they have of not being molested when it was known that the Empress Dowager herself was feeding the Boxers with rice from the imperial granaries?

All the same, the eleven ministers met to discuss the possibility of a safe conduct being granted, and when the meeting broke up in disagreement, the German minister, Baron von Ketteler, said he had an appointment with the Yamen for the following morning, and he intended to keep it. Let the decision wait until he returned.

He never did return. Smoking a cigar, sitting relaxed in his red and green official chair, with two Chinese outriders, he gave a debonair wave of his hand as he set off. Fifteen minutes later his outriders came galloping back on their ponies, saying the Baron had been shot dead. A German detachment, with fixed bayonets, went to verify this terrible story, and to retrieve the body, but they found nothing. Sedan chair, bearers, Chinese soldiers, all had disappeared. There was only a dark stain of blood seeping into the dust.

It wasn't until much later in the day that another official message arrived from the palace. It was regretted that Baron von Ketteler had met his death at the hands of the brigands. Perhaps the Baroness would be pleased to know that an elaborate coffin was being made for his burial.

After that subtle piece of torture, there was no more talk of anyone leaving for Tientsin. All the food and materials that could be found were brought in, rice, maize, wheat, a little flour, coffee, not much else. The Chinese shopkeepers, while maintaining their polite smiles, were quietly putting up their shutters and vanishing. The streets were rapidly emptying, the dust settling. At dusk, the defenders in the legation compound put up barricades at strategic points, and reinforced lookouts on the wall. Everything was suddenly too quiet.

Chapter 12

Sewing sandbags and rolling bandages (which were now in demand in the hospital), looking after fretful children, using all the ingenuity one possessed to make the meals palatable, trying not to worry constantly about husbands, brothers, friends, who were guarding the wall and making forays into the outer city to disperse blood-thirsty bands of Boxers—these occupations for the women paled into insignificance the day the Hanlin Museum was set on fire.

It had been reported by lookouts that incendiaries were getting into the legation compound and creeping about in the dark like cats. The legations on the far side of the compound, the Belgian, Austrian, Dutch and Italian, had all been badly damaged by fire, and the occupants had sought refuge in the already overcrowded British headquarters. But the Hanlin Museum was a much more serious matter for the British, for it was

situated beneath the Tartar wall and in the immediate
vicinity of their own territory.

Apart from the danger of the fire spreading, the destruction of manuscripts dating back to the earliest dynasties was a tragedy of proportions only to be
appreciated by future generations of scholars. Something
had to be done to salvage at least a proportion of these
priceless treasures. Though serving the enemy in this
respect, Lady Comerford said sourly, was a characteristically quixotic British attitude.

Nevertheless she joined the chain of ladies passing
water scooped out of lily ponds into any sort of recep-
tacle available, to be flung more or less ineffectually on
the blaze. Soldiers and clerks and old men tried to save
some of the books, rare silk-covered illuminated volumes,
by throwing them into the pools. What the fire did not
destroy, water surely would. But the effort was commend-
able. At least Amelia Carrington, smudged with dirt and
fatigue, said so. Chinese scholars would thank them in
time to come.

"If we live to see such a time," Lady Comerford muttered. The world was swirling about her in hot eddies of
smoke and flame. She tottered and eventually sank to the
ground, an elderly rag doll, whom Amelia called to Henrietta to rescue.

"Help Lady Comerford, darling. She should never
have come out here."

"Mamma, will we all be burnt up?" Henrietta gasped.

"Of course we won't. The fire is dying down already.
Take Lady Comerford indoors. And look after the
younger ones."

Look after the younger ones! That was the constant
cry. Really, they were quite able to look after themselves, for Georgie, watching the salvage operation with
passionate interest, meant to fish in the pool for some
of those precious books when the excitement had died
down. He also had a story he was relating with frankly

unholy relish. There was supposed to be a human head
stuck on one of the city gates. It belonged to an Englishman and was meant to frighten people in the way
the grinning lion dogs did. The Englishman had been
killed in the Fu. So it might just as easily have been
Georgie's or Angel's head that hung up there, grinning
horribly.

Amelia hoped that ghastly story would be an effective
deterrent to Georgie and that tiresome child Angel. Now
they must realise the importance of staying within bounds.
Indeed, it seemed they might have to be confined indoors,
for now that the incendiaries had wreaked such havoc,
the wall had been breached in several places, and outbreaks of fighting were occurring beyond the Imperial
Carriage Park, and across the wilderness of the Fu. The
hastily dug trenches and the barricades made of upturned
Peking carts manned by Austrians, Italians, French and
British, were sorely needed. The brilliantly coloured silk
and brocade sandbags, festooning the trenches as if for
some mad orgy, were already stained with blood. The
wounded had been coming in for several days.

Colonel Manners had lashed a carving knife to his
only weapon, a walking stick, and others of the volunteer garrison were imitating him. Unfortunately, both
guns and ammunition were in short supply, and too
many of the Boxers were armed with extremely efficent
Mausers. If the relief forces, urgently telegraphed for,
didn't come soon, the besieged might indeed be defending themselves with carving knives.

After the burning of the Hanlin Museum the attack
intensified. The uneasy quiet was like a forgotten dream.
Now the yelling and battering at the gates and fusillade
of gunfire was almost continuous. This was punctuated
at intervals by the rattle of a machine gun, the American
Colt and the elderly Nordenfelt owned by the British
which kept jamming. Lookouts on the wall said the
streets in the Chinese city were littered with bodies.

In the European cemetery the first mass grave was dug. Among those buried, shrouded austerely in white cloth and strapped to planks, was Rupert Fortescue, the fresh-faced eager young Chancellery clerk. He had been shot through the head while on guard duty on the wall. There had been that rumour of a Chinese girl called Almond, Amelia remembered. Where was Almond now? No one knew, but it was discovered later that willow fronds, the symbol of immortality, had been laid beneath the rough wooden cross bearing Rupert's name.

Lady Comerford wept, the tears making white tracks down her rouged cheeks. For a few moments she had lived in her own past. But her tears soon dried up. There was not sufficient moisture in her body to sustain them. She was sad and frightened and dehydrated, and far too old, but no one should guess her devastation. She persevered with her work on rehearsals for the concert to be given the next evening. Lady MacDonald and Amelia Carrington had persuaded her to do this, and she had whipped up all her energy in an effort to wring decent performances from her volunteer artists.

After it was all over she knew she would have the greatest desire to retire to her room, as to a quiet dim grave.

Amelia wept at Rupert's death. She clung to Nathaniel that night and begged him to stay with her. She was so afraid. It was bright moonlight and he would be too visible at his post on the wall. It wasn't fair that he should be doing so much night duty.

"It's quieter at night, my love. Fewer bullets flying about."

"But so lonely. And the nights are so long. I feel as if you're never coming back."

"It's something to see the dawn rising behind the Imperial Palace. The pink sky and all those coloured roofs. It has a barbaric splendour."

"Too barbaric for me. When can we go home, Nathaniel?"

He smoothed her hair. His touch was gentle.

"When this is over."

"Really?" Her voice trembled with hope. "You don't mean to stay in Peking?"

"I will. For a time. But perhaps I'll send you and the children home. You could stay with your parents, couldn't you?"

"Without you? Oh, no!"

"We'll be lucky to get through this siege without an epidemic. Lucy's looking far too delicate already."

"It's her colouring. She has my pale skin."

"And you're not exactly blooming either."

"If you can see beneath the dirt." Amelia edged slightly away. "Do I smell?"

"We all pong a bit."

"Nathaniel, I can't bear it, being filthy like this!"

"When you're back in England you can have three baths a day. At the moment what I'd put first would be a large steak, rare, with baked potatoes and a bottle of Château Lafite. All this boiled water and tepid champagne. I fancy the curried pony we had tonight was from that nice little beast that won the last race a month ago. Damned shame."

He lay back, relaxing. Amelia could feel the tiredness in his body. He had only talked because she had wanted to. He really wanted to sleep.

"Georgie been behaving?" he said, with a last effort.

"Moderately."

"Miss Deacon?"

"Behaving? Oh, yes. But I let her go to the hospital for two hours a day since she so much wants to. They say the flies are such a pest. Someone is needed to keep them off the more serious cases. It's terribly hot in there."

"Good heavens, can't some coolies do those things?"

"Some of the European patients get upset by Chinese faces. One can understand. But I keep the children with me when Miss Deacon is away. She seems to burn up with energy. I think she imagines she's a sort of Joan of Arc."

"Who?" mumbled Nathaniel, drunk with sleep. He didn't seem to know what he was saying. "That French virgin? Far from it. Not our Miss Deacon."

Medora never took off the ring the Empress Dowager had given her. It fascinated her. When she wasn't dreaming of Nathaniel she was imagining what it would be like to be that stout dumpy lady who wore her power so visibly and effectively. She had only to beckon with one of her grotesquely long fingernails, or give her hooded glance, like some deadly bird of prey and people fell on their faces before her. It was said that for political reasons she disapproved of the Boxers, but that secretly she loved them. Their barbarism and colour would appeal to something in her own nature. Medora understood that. She had to confess to unholy thrills herself when she heard the chanting and the harsh blare of trumpets. She was still not in the least afraid, and had been quite a heroine during the salvaging of books from the Hanlin Museum. That had been enormously exciting, the leaping flames and the smoke and the poor bewildered old Mandarin scholars, torn so abruptly from their quiet philosophies and plunged into that inferno.

But apart from dramatic episodes like that, Medora was appallingly bored and depressed. Nathaniel hadn't looked at her since the day he had been so angry with her for letting the children out of her sight. She suffered secret agonies that he would be killed, shot through the head like Rupert Fortescue, or dying a slower and more cruel death from stomach wounds.

In the brief times that he came in to eat and rest he was with his wife. Medora was beginning to hate Amelia Carrington and inventing ways of revenge. She sat rubbing the large baroque pearl in her ring, and wondered what methods the Empress Dowager would use towards a woman of whom she was jealous. Especially if that woman were all the things one both envied and despised. Good looks, good manners, charm, courage, Amelia Carrington had them all. But was she an exciting lover, or was she too ladylike for the sexual lust Medora recognised in her husband? Medora brooded, was short-tempered with the children, and took little interest in her appearance—who did?—as everyone became dirtier, and children, suffering from the heat and a depleted diet, began to fall ill.

However, the night of the concert, the beleaguered residents of the legation did make an effort to look their best. It had begun to rain at last. The people who had believed that the long-awaited rain would cool the passions of the Boxers were proved wrong, for the attacks from the outer city were increasing in violence, and instead of dust there was now sticky mud, and a stifling humidity. But at least the clean rain could be gathered in receptacles and drunk, and it was possible to wash again.

There was an air of festivity in the big reception room where the concert was held. The older children had been allowed to stay up. Georgie and Angel got an unfortunate attack of the giggles when the majestic Madame Leonora took the stage. Her powerful voice must have carried beyond the legation walls, for it precipitated a fusillade of shots, and the women with husbands in the fighting lines became tense with anxiety.

Amelia hissed angrily at Georgie and Angel for their bad manners. Cassidy promised to remove them from the room, but they hastily agreed to behave and fidgeted sleepily through a long piano solo, and then through the slightly off-key singing of lieder by one of the German attachés. It was boring, but better than trying to sleep in the suffocating heat of their horrid dark bedroom.

And Mamma had put on her scarlet slippers, and little scarlet jacket so that she would look like a party. Miss

Deacon hadn't bothered to change into her long green dress. She said she hadn't brought it with her. She would remain in her daytime blouse and skirt. Who was going to notice anyway?

She no longer looked like a mermaid but like a Peking crow, Georgie thought disappointedly. But, as she said, who would notice? Papa was on guard duty out in the dark noisy night. Indeed, all the able-bodied men who were not on duty were getting some necessary sleep, so none of them attended the concert. Georgie wondered if ladies only wore nice dresses to please men. Didn't they want to please children? Or very old gentlemen like Colonel Manners who was sporting an ancient dinner jacket and wearing all his medals?

Lady Comerford, despite her eighty years, was here, there and everywhere. From a distance she looked exquisite, blue tulle swathing her shoulders, diamonds at her throat. But close up one saw her ravaged face, her glassy eyes, the artificial colour thick on her cheeks and lips. Henrietta, although too good-mannered to say so, was remembering a Punch-and-Judy show she had seen at a fair in England. Lady Comerford looked exactly like Judy, all shrill cries and gestures, her over-painted face looking quite common.

At the end of the concert the British minister thanked everyone. He said it had been a splendid effort, and to crown the evening's enjoyment he had had telegraphs from Whitehall and confidently expected reinforcements in the very near future. It was only a matter of holding out for a few more days.

The Russians and Japanese also expected reinforcements. And this evening, everyone would be glad to hear, some Mausers and a Krupp gun had been captured from the Chinese. Not without casualties, unfortunately, but victory always had a price. It was essential now for women and children to stay indoors, for there were Chinese snipers in the trees. They were excellent marksmen.

"Do you hear that?" Amelia whispered to Georgie.

Georgie nodded. He dearly wanted to see a sniper in a tree.

"Georgie! You promise to obey Sir Claude and stay indoors?"

Georgie wriggled, restlessly. If a Boxer got into his willow tree at the edge of the goldfish pool he would have to shake him out, like a ripe plum. He and Angel together.

"Georgie!"

"Yes, Mamma," he said reluctantly. "But it's not because I'm frightened of snipers."

As a retaliation for the minor victory the foreign devils had had in capturing guns, the Chinese set fire to the remaining houses in Legation Street. There was a thick pall of smoke and flames, and when it died down Nathaniel Carrington saw what he had feared. His shop was a mere skeleton, a few upright timbers, and a sagging roof. But with luck his treasures in the cellars would be safe. He congratulated himself on his foresight in laying that thick carpet of sand over the ground floor. Now he must just wait with what patience he could until this stupid and costly siege was over and he could go and investigate.

Indeed, that very evening the first hopeful event for several days occurred. There was a resounding blare from the long brassy-toned Chinese trumpets, announcing a truce. A Chinese soldier, carrying a white flag, deposited a placard on the bridge over the canal. Translated, the script read, "In accordance with the Imperial commands to protect the Ministers, firing will cease immediately and a despatch will be delivered at the Imperial canal bridge."

The cessation of noise was a benison. Palefaced people emerged from indoors and strolled nervously in the devastated grounds. The guard on the wall maintained a sharp watch, wary of a trap. But the silence continued as the light faded, although a great gathering of soldiers was reported in front of the Imperial Palace. Manchus and Bannermen, in brilliant colours, dragons embroidered on their tunics, and armed with great two-handed swords or bows and arrows, stood in orderly lines. There were also Kansu horsemen on tough little ponies, carrying banners and flags. With the rose-red walls of the Imperial Palace behind them, the scene was like a larger than life stage setting. But the weapons were real, and so was the ferocious attitude of the soldiers. An even more ominous factor was that there didn't appear to be a single Boxer in that war-like gathering. They obviously were having no part of the truce. It seemed to be a quixotic decision of the Empress Dowager's. And one of which she quickly repented, for no despatch arrived, and by midnight the blessed silence was over. The cracking of rifles began again, the hopeful lights in the windows of the legation and the nearby Peking hotel were quickly extinguished, and a great fire started by a flaming arrow blazed beyond the canal in the grounds of the Su Wang Fu.

The siege was not over, and Amelia could not help weeping from despair. More children were beginning to fall ill. The heat, the poor diet, and the pervading nauseating smell of death raised fears of cholera. The children of the Chinese refugees camping in the grounds had sad wizened faces, the Europeans grew pale and large-eyed and too quiet. Lucy scarcely spoke, and had a waxen look that was alarming. Even Henrietta, who had always been a little too good and something of a prig, had occasional outbreaks of temper. Georgie, probably because of his intense interest in every new event, was the most cheerful. He found the flaming arrows shot over the wall, like shooting stars, fearfully exciting. And one couldn't blame Angel for her defiant disobedience, because one recognised she was a deeply disturbed child. She had so suddenly lost both her mother and her father, her father horribly beheaded, her mother retreated beyond reach, shut within her nightmare.

How awful it all was. One simply had to keep busy, like that indomitable old Lady Comerford, taking one's turn in the kitchen, or the hospital, or the sewing room, and trying not to think of the children falling sick or the danger Nathaniel was in.

It would all end before very long. Relief forces would arrive. That megalomaniac old woman, the Empress Dowager, and her gang of brigands, couldn't go on defying all the great Western powers.

Chapter 13

Georgie had meant to keep his promise not to go outdoors, especially after there had been a battle on the
tennis court. People had danced there by the light of the
paper lanterns on the night of the Queen's birthday
party, and now dead bodies lay there. Papa came
in, his rifle in his hand, his face blackened, his eyes red-
rimmed, and said, before he realised the children were
listening, "I picked off a couple of the devils. It's all over
now. We're letting Jung Lu's men carry off the wounded
and dead."

There were too many large and fearful eyes watching
him.

"Now why are you all staring at me?" he asked, with
false joviality. "I know I'm as black as a chimney sweep,
but that's due to unavoidable circumstances."

Mamma said tensely, "You're all right, Nathaniel?"

"Absolutely. Not a scratch. Why aren't the children at their lessons? Miss Deacon—"

"We were listening—" Miss Deacon began.

"War isn't a game to provide distraction," Papa said curtly. He added in a low voice, to Mamma and Miss Deacon, "Keep the children occupied, for heaven's sake."

"Yes, of course," said Mamma brightly. "What a pity we didn't bring more games with us. But never mind, let's make some up. What about pinning the tail on the donkey? Dearest, aren't you going to rest? Or get some food?"

"Later," said Papa, striding out.

Georgie and Angel found it difficult to settle to the game. Henrietta played industriously, until Lucy, without any warning, was suddenly sick on the floor. That caused a commotion. While Mamma comforted her and Ah Wan mopped up, and Cassidy found clean clothes, Georgie felt Angel's hand in his. He knew by the yellow flare of excitement in her eyes what she wanted to do. To creep out and see the signs of battle on the tennis court.

"We mustn't. We promised Papa."

"I don't like your papa. He's mean and unkind."

"Why?" asked Georgie in surprise.

"He took our toy pony. That's stealing." Angel's chin was stuck out, hard and unforgiving. "Come on," she said.

Georgie followed her, not because he meant to break his promise of good behaviour, or because he couldn't stand up to Angel, but because he couldn't bear to look at Mamma's face as she gazed at Lucy. Georgie knew she thought Lucy was going to die, like those soldiers of Jung Lu's on the tennis court. He had to run away from that knowledge.

All the same he was not prepared to go far. Just to the willow tree. It had a curved bough, rough and scaly like a dragon. Perched up there, with the green fronds dripping around him, he always felt safe.

There were no bodies on the tennis court, Angel reported disappointedly, after a cautious foray. But there had certainly been some, for there were dark mucky patches that must be blood. It was the first time Georgie had seen human blood. He sniffed the hot odorous air, with its lingering smell of rifle smoke, and things going bad. (Horses, Mamma said. The strong little ponies that the Kansu soldiers rode. Some lay dead in the streets of the native city.) He wondered, for an uneasy moment, if he were going to be sick, like Lucy. But Angel distracted him from his queasiness by calling in a low excited voice, "Georgie, come here! Quickly! Look what I've found."

She was peering into a clump of bamboo at the edge of the goldfish pool. Georgie found his footsteps dragging. He was afraid she had found what neither of them really wanted to see, a dead Chinese.

"Come *on!*" Angel hissed.

She was on her knees when he reached her, bending over what looked like a large red poppy. Not a poppy, for it stirred and emitted a faint wail. Now Georgie could see that it had a tiny dark head, and a minute lemon-coloured face and dark slitted eyes that gave an unfocussed black stare. Of all miracles it was a baby. A live baby wrapped in a piece of red silk and tucked into the undergrowth as if it had been carefully hidden.

"It's Moses!" Georgie cried.

"No, it is not. Moses was a boy."

"How do you know this isn't a boy?"

"Because only girl babies are put out to die. Mamma and Papa were always saving them and telling their mothers not to be so wicked. We can look if you don't believe me," Angel added practically.

Georgie imagined that might be rather rude, although he didn't know whether rudeness counted with such a small creature as this, no bigger than a puppy.

"Can we save it?" he asked eagerly. "It'll need milk, and there isn't any."

"We're not taking it indoors," said Angel. She was crouching over the infant in a fiercely possessive way. "It will only be taken from us like the pony was."

"The pony didn't have to be fed, though."

"I'll feed this baby. When I start nursing it milk will come out of my chest."

"Truly?" said Georgie in amazement.

"Of course. When you start nursing a new baby God puts milk in your chest."

"Then try," Georgie urged with deep interest.

Angel whipped up her pinafore and her dress, undid her bodice, and exposed two pale brown points on her chest. They were no bigger than the ones Georgie had himself. He didn't see how they could suddenly spurt milk. However, he awkwardly picked up the bundle of red silk and pushed it into Angel's arms. The baby stirred and whimpered as Angel guided its mouth to her flat breast. It nuzzled feebly, a small fist groping. When no miraculous stream of milk appeared its cries grew louder.

"It's cross because you haven't got any milk," said Georgie.

For the first time since her arrival in Peking, Georgie saw Angel's face crinkled up with anxiety and tenderness. She laid the whimpering infant back in its nest of rushes, and drew fronds of reeds across to hide it from sight.

"We'll have to find something else for it. Perhaps my milk will come by tomorrow."

"We can't leave it out all night."

"Yes, we can. It's only in the winter the babies put outdoors die. Let's save some rice from our supper."

"It's too small to eat rice."

Angel stamped her foot.

"Oh, you don't know anything. You're only a boy. We can squash up rice and push it down its mouth."

"I think we ought to take it to some grown-up ladies with milk in their chests."

Angel's face contorted angrily.

"No, we will not. It's our baby. It's the only thing we've got. You're its father and I'm its mother. It'll sleep here tonight and tomorrow morning first thing we'll feed it. We can come out before Ah Wan wakes up. So just shut up, will you."

When Angel looked like that there were no alternatives but to shut up. Besides, they were probably in deep trouble already for being outdoors. Unless, by some fortunate chance, everyone was too busy to notice their return.

This actually happened, although the circumstances were far from fortunate. Lucy had had to be taken to the hospital. She might be sickening for typhoid fever, the doctor said, and that would be serious. So serious that Henrietta had insisted on lending Lucy her best French doll, hitherto not allowed to be touched by any hands but her own.

No, no, of course Lucy wouldn't die, Mamma said. They would all be praying for her. Just now she must return to Lucy's bedside and stay with her all night. Everyone must promise to be obedient and quiet, and to say their prayers.

"What shall we call her?" Angel whispered to Georgie as they lay in their beds in the dark.

"Our baby? I expect she's got a name."

"No, she hasn't, because we haven't given her one. What about 'Plum Blossom'?"

"Yes, that's a nice name."

"We'll christen her tomorrow," Angel said.

"When she's been fed." Georgie was still haunted by the baby's cries. He had a funny idea that the scrap of red silk and pale lemon flesh in the bamboos had come to take the place of Lucy. He didn't think he cared for that. He had also decided that the baby's real mother must have been killed by the wicked Boxers when there was that fighting going on around the tennis court. There had been a lot of Chinese refugees camped about there. The mother must have hidden the baby to try to save it when she had to lie down and die herself.

All the same, he wasn't at all sure that he and Angel could keep it alive and safely hidden. Babies needed so many things, clean clothes mostly. He was afraid that eventually they would have to ask Miss Deacon to help. He was sure they could trust her.

The next morning, when it was scarcely light, Angel was awake and tugging at his arm.

"Come on, we have to hurry. I've got the rice and a sponge."

"A sponge?" Georgie said sleepily.

"We'll have to wash Plum Blossom."

In the scummy water of the goldfish pool? Georgie didn't think the baby would like that, but he could see that Angel was in one of her bossiest moods, when it was useless to argue with her. Actually he was eager to see the baby again, and got up with alacrity. Henrietta slept without stirring. So did Ah Wan, a neat bundle across the doorway. They had to step carefully over her, holding their breath.

It was quiet outdoors. All the soldiers must be asleep because no one was shooting or yelling, and no alarm bells were ringing. The air might have had a dawn freshness had it not been for the smell of bad rotting things. At least it wasn't raining, so the baby would be dry in her nest of leaves, like a young bird.

She was dry, certainly, and still sound asleep. Angel nudged her to wake her. When she didn't stir Angel whispered with that surprising tenderness one wouldn't have thought she had, "Wake up, baby dear. We've got something for you to eat, and we've called you Plum Blossom. Look, here's nice rice."

Georgie tentatively drew the wrapping back from the minute black head, and saw the wizened lily-pale face, the shut eyes. And knew. With a great dropping of his heart he knew.

"She's dead," he said flatly.

"Oh, no, she isn't!" Angel cried. "No! She's only asleep." She unfolded the red silk and lifted one of the naked arms. As skinny as a heron's leg. Stiff. Like Henrietta's china doll.

"You said you'd seen dead people," Georgie said.

"She's not dead! She mustn't be dead!" Angel snatched the baby into her arms and shook it, at first gently, then angrily.

"We'll have to bury her," said Georgie. He suddenly felt strong and practical, as the man of the family. "We can scrape a hole here and cover her with leaves."

The furious tears streamed down Angel's face. But when Georgie had scooped out a shallow hollow in the dust, and lined it with reeds, she resignedly laid the baby, in the gay silk, in the sad little nest. They both carefully covered it with bamboo shoots and willow fronds, which Georgie had torn savagely from the willow tree. Silly old wizard, he had become an enemy, why hadn't he protected their baby? Then, over the tiny grave, he bowed his head and mumbled, "Gentle Jesus, meek and mild, look upon a little child. This is Plum Blossom, God," he added, in mild reproach. "She was ours, but You took her. It isn't fair, really. Both the jade pony and our baby."

"God's supposed to know best," Angel said bleakly. "But He doesn't."

Was He going to take Lucy, too? No, she was a lot better. Her temperature had fallen, and she hadn't got typhoid fever after all. Just some form of gastrointestinal disturbance, the doctor said, which would be all too prevalent in the compound as time went by.

Mamma was so thankful Lucy was better that she didn't scold Angel and Georgie when she saw their grubby hands and the dust on their shoes, the last signs of their ill-fated adventure. She just said, "Children, do be good. It will help Papa and me so much."

Papa, when he came in, sunken-eyed and with rough whiskery jowls, and heard that Lucy was recovering, cried a little. Georgie could see the tears shining on his cheeks. It was very embarrassing because grown men didn't cry. However, he was still able to speak brusquely.

"Now, you children, your sister being ill doesn't mean you can have a holiday. Lessons as usual. And no going outdoors."

Georgie nodded meekly. Even Angel had lost her mutinous look. Neither of them had any desire to go outdoors at present.

Lucy was brought back two days later to convalesce. Her big blue eyes had eaten up her face. She clung to her mother and scarcely spoke. She had hated the hospital although she had not been in the room with the wounded soldiers. She had heard them groaning, however, and the sound had terrified her. The interesting thing was that Angel, who had hitherto ignored and obviously despised shy Lucy, suddenly became excessively protective of her. She read stories to her and dressed and undressed dolls for her, and even carried her about, her skinny figure staggering under the weight of someone almost her own size.

Georgie was put out and jealous. But he knew exactly what Angel was doing. She was pretending Lucy was Plum Blossom and being her mother. What a silly game. All the grown-ups, who knew nothing of the real reason, were delighted that at last Angel seemed to be repenting of her wild ways and showing consideration for others. And Lucy, her thin arms clasped around Angel's neck, adored the attention. She was very content to go back to babyhood.

It was extremely bad luck that at that time, with all

the children as well as could be expected, Amelia should fall ill. She succumbed to the same malady that Lucy had had. Within twenty-four hours her temperature was soaring dangerously and she had to be carried, not on a stretcher, but in Nathaniel's strong arms, to the hospital.

It was even worse that fighting had reached a crescendo, and the noise from the native city, and in the vast reaches of the legation compound, was unceasing and appalling. No active man could be spared from his post. No anxious husband could sit at his wife's bedside, even though she was critically ill. The British legation might follow the fate of the others, and be burnt to the ground. They might all be dead before the end of another day.

"Don't worry, I'll look after Mrs. Carrington," said Miss Deacon to Nathaniel. "Cassidy and Ah Wan can take care of the children."

"Will you?" said Nathaniel gratefully. "Will you promise not to leave her?"

"Certainly I promise. None of those bossy nurses will drive me out. So far they think I'm only capable of brushing the flies off their patients. I'll look after your wife, Mr. Carrington."

"I'll bless you forever. Don't let her worry. If she heard that explosion this morning, tell her the Chinese blew up a mine under the wall of the French legation, but they killed more of themselves than us. We're well able to defend ourselves."

However, Amelia, by this time, was too sick to worry. The distant shouting and rifle fire, the occasional boom of the temperamental cannon, the harsh blare of trumpets, and the ringing of alarm bells from the gate tower was a confusion in her mind, part of an incomprehensible nightmare. In more peaceful moments she thought she was back in England, sitting under the willow that drooped over the slow green water of the Thames. She could hear the children playing on the lawn, and her mother's gentle warning voice, "Amelia! Lilian! Don't go so near the river. You may fall in."

They had both fallen into something, not the cool river, but a black hot pit of sadness and pain and screaming noise and nightmare.

She knew someone sponged her face. And sometimes she was aroused to sip warm unpalatable water. Flies buzzed revoltingly over her face and were brushed away. Once she thought that strange American girl she had taken in bent over her. She would know that face anywhere, long and plain, with its curious shut-in fervour. A danger, that girl. Why? The children liked her. She had gentle hands.

What was she doing here, at Amelia's bedside, in this sticky heat in this awful place, full of flies buzzing and other more sinister noises? In her emerging consciousness, Amelia heard her saying, "Just another mouthful, Mrs. Carrington. You mustn't get dehydrated. That's the real danger, the doctor says."

Amelia turned her head weakly.

"My husband? The children?"

"They're all well. Go to sleep now."

The reassuring hand she clutched at for strength, the husky American voice. Medora Deacon! That was tremendous, she had remembered who someone was.

"What are you doing here?"

"I'm taking care of you. You've been pretty sick."

"I'm—better now?"

"Oh, yes. You're talking sensibly for the first time in a week."

A week! And the fighting was still going on. How many had been wounded or died? How many more burials in that sad little cemetery where Rupert Fortescue had been laid so long ago? And who? Amelia had an overpowering desire to retreat into the haven of unconsciousness. She forced her eyes open.

"My husband?" She forgot she had already asked that question.

"He's well. Not a scratch. Tired, of course. They all are, those brave men."

"Have you—saved my life?"

"Not just me, Mrs. Carrington. Everyone has helped."

It had, however, been mainly Miss Deacon, Nathaniel told her, when at last her dizzying foggy weakness began to leave her and her brain cleared. The girl had spent days and a good part of the nights as well at her bedside. She had wanted to do it. She had been perfectly splendid. They would always be in her debt.

Medora could never have explained why she had looked after Amelia so devotedly. It must have been the better side of her nature operating. She had been filled with self-sacrifice and a genuine desire not just for Nathaniel's approval but for Amelia's recovery. But seeing Amelia return to life and to a shadowy resemblance of her former beauty had not in the least lessened her consuming desire for Nathaniel. She knew that if Amelia had died and Nathaniel had become a widower it would not have been the same. This hidden passionate illicit love was another thing altogether. She wanted not only the challenge but the knowledge that she could lure Nathaniel from his wife. She was just wicked. Her spirit fed on the delicious guilt of it all.

She suspected that Nathaniel's did, too, for although he was less abrupt with her since her care of his wife, he still avoided looking at her directly, and never so much as laid a finger on her arm. As if he dared not succumb to either temptation. At least, this was what she told herself, when all the time it was probably that he was just too tired.

Everybody was tired. The siege was in its seventh week, and the poor diet, the heat, the increasing casualties and deaths, and the enforced confinement were making people ragged with nerves. There was a horrible little room at the back of the hospital where the dead, wrapped in white cloth, often still booted, and strapped to planks, lay awaiting burial. Funerals now took place every day, and whether the victims were British or American or Russian or any other nationality, they were followed to their mass grave by members of all the legations.

Lately it had rained without ceasing. The men came out of the waterlogged trenches black with mud. They didn't talk of the bloated corpses, or the ponies and mules trying to subsist on the scanty grass in the gloomy gardens of the Fu, before they were slaughtered for food. Prince Su's palace had been struck by a flaming arrow and destroyed, all its treasures vanishing with it. Except one small jade pony carefully hidden by Nathaniel Carrington.

Gruesomely, starving dogs gnawed at the bodies of the Chinese dead in the streets. Two thousand Chinese refugees, damp, starved, miserable, crouched in their makeshift shelters in the legation grounds. They had little rice left. The children stripped leaves off the trees and chewed them, or lined up at the doors of the British legation, waiting for bowls of gruel or precious horse meat stew.

But there were also a thousand Europeans to be fed, and food supplies had to be carefully rationed. One knew there were still tins of such delicacies as oysters and pâté de foie gras with truffles in the Peking hotel, which Monsieur Chamot doled out like gold bars. And the supply of champagne appeared to be inexhaustible. It was desirable, M'sieu Chamot said, to have something left with which to celebrate the arrival of the relief troops. If, of course, they arrived in time and the battered half-destroyed hotel still stood. In the depths of the night he had heard Chinese officers shouting to their men to climb over the wall and kill all the foreigners. There was now scarcely a respite from attack. Bullets were flying all night and Sir Claude MacDonald wryly reminded the besieged of General Gordon's advice to the Chinese years earlier in the war against Russia. The best tactics were to wear out the enemy by constant firing all night long so that they would get no rest.

Would relief never come? Rumours were followed by contradictions. A courier, exhausted and half-starved, a message rolled up and plaited in his hair, arrived from Tientsin, having been three weeks on his journey through Boxer-infested countryside. His message was encouraging. It said that 24,000 troops, Japanese, Russian, British, French and American, had landed and were on their way. All would be well if the besieged could keep themselves in food for a little longer.

Food. To everyone's immense surprise a gift arrived from the Empress Dowager. Baskets of watermelons and vegetables for the children. Then some enterprising Chinese from the outside city began selling eggs to the soldiers on guard duty for rolls of dollars. It was a trickle of nourishing food to be kept strictly for invalids and children.

Amelia was persuaded to eat an egg. With greedy relish, Henrietta, Lucy, Georgie and Angel demolished a watermelon. It was the best day they had had for a long time.

Other rumours spread, not that the eagerly awaited troops had been sighted, but that a great many carts were coming up the ruined streets towards the Imperial City. It was said that the court was preparing to flee. The wicked and conniving Prince Tuan, perhaps, but surely not that indomitable woman, the Empress Dowager Tz'u-Hsi. She would never consent to such a humiliation.

It became a new game for the children to play. George and Henrietta turned a chair upside down and Angel, wrapped in a piece of yellow brocade that had somehow escaped transformation into sandbags, sat in the chair and was carried from room to room. Lucy was the outrider, a role of which she soon tired. So she was allowed to be the Empress wrapped in the imperial yellow robes, with Angel galloping enthusiastically on a broomstick at her side. She made a poor little defeated Empress, however, and the game usually ended with her in her now favourite position, being hauled about in Angel's arms, sucking her thumb like a baby.

This was a vaguely disturbing development on Lucy's part, but Amelia was still too weak and tired to worry about it. These problems could be resolved when the siege was over. Children were resilient, and recovered from bad experiences.

Lady Comerford and Colonel Manners were sharing a meal. Colonel Manners had a tin of pâté de foie gras and a tin of asparagus which he had been carefully hoarding for a special occasion such as the arrival of the relief forces. But his old and good friend, Blanche Comerford, was virtually shrinking away in front of one's eyes, damn those dastardly Chinese. Naturally she couldn't eat that disgusting pony meat, and was existing on a little rice and gruel. Heaven knew what the gruel was made of. Boiled pony's hooves, no doubt. It was better not to surmise.

"Will you go home when this is over, dear lady?"

"To my own home, yes, if it's still standing. And if my servants will come back."

"I was referring to England."

"Then don't confuse me by calling it home," she said tartly. "It hasn't been for sixty years, and what would they make of me there now? An absurd ancient Chinese doll. No, I'll stay here. Terrified out of my wits as I am. In spite of everything, you know, I'm attached to the Chinese."

"So am I, butter-faced devils. But no one can cook better than my Li Chen. I'll have to take him back even if he's been killing the foreigners. If he's still alive, of course."

"Who's going to be left alive?" Lady Comerford asked. She could only toy with the delicacies on her plate.

"Most of us, have no fear. The whole nonsense is petering out, you know."

Lady Comerford tilted her head, listening to the crackle of rifle fire.

"I can't say I've noticed."

"Oh, yes, it is. We'll wake up one morning very soon and find the Imperial Palace deserted, that devious old queen fled."

"I wonder," said Lady Comerford, "how Queen Victoria would behave in similar circumstances."

Colonel Manners snorted. "She'd have more sense than to get into such a situation. But I'm damn sure she'd never run away."

"I rather fancy those nice Carringtons will go back to England as soon as possible. A pity. I like her so much."

"He's made a damn fine soldier, I must say. Otherwise I can't say I've taken to him. He's an arrogant beggar."

"But very attractive to women."

"Women are masochists."

"Really, Colonel! Such wisdom from an old bachelor. And I don't entirely agree with you about Nathaniel Carrington. He has very strict moral values. At least, he preaches them to his children."

"Seeing himself in the image of the correct father. Well, perhaps you're right, dear lady. Perhaps I misjudge the man. Have a little more pâté. It's doing you good. Your eyes are brighter."

"That comes from the illicit pleasure of gossiping."

"Well, at least it's taken your mind off Jung Lu and his villains."

"Colonel," said Lady Comerford impulsively, "have you noticed how cowardly I have been? Has it showed?"

"Cowardly! You! Utter nonsense. You're the bravest

woman in this compound and I can't speak higher than that, for there are some brave ones. Including the beautiful Amelia, and the odd American girl who I must say has kept her head remarkably well."

"Medora Deacon? Yes, she's been a brick, especially when Amelia was ill. She saved her life, Nathaniel says. But me—" Lady Comerford laid her hand on the Colonel's with affection and gratitude. "Thank you, you dear man. You've reassured me. It would have been so awfully bad to have let the side down. That's why I deck myself out like a tart. Concealing my craven heart."

"You decorate the scene. And I must say I'm glad you don't plan to run off to England. Peking wouldn't be the same without you. You're like a paper lantern. Always liked them. Gay and warming."

Lady Comerford began to laugh gently, the heavy layer of paint and powder on her cheeks cracking.

"I think I rather like that. A paper lantern. Terribly inflammable, though. When I go up in smoke or flame, will you put a willow branch on my grave, Colonel?"

"I certainly will, dear lady. I certainly will."

The day after that tête-à-tête luncheon, in the eighth week of the siege, it was all suddenly over. The first troops came in through the water gate, Indian Cavalry led by a British officer, tough brown men who seemed to have made little of the long march from Tientsin. They were followed by turbanned Sikhs, Bengal lancers, and later in the day by American marines, Cossacks, and Japanese.

The Chinese city, the besieged realised with incredulity and dazed astonishment, was suddenly utterly silent and deserted. So was the Forbidden City. The rumours of the Empress Dowager's flight had been true. Stripped of her jewels and dressed in blue cotton like a peasant, she had slipped away through the northern gates some time during the night, and was well on the way to a planned exile far beyond the Great Wall, in the province of Shensi. It was an ignominious disappearance. She must have hated it. Her jewels and rich garments left behind, her long nails clipped short, sitting in a Peking cart like a peasant, facing the long jolting journey, wondering if she would ever see her palaces, her pleasure gardens, her vast horde of treasures (which she had ordered to be buried), her retinues of eunuchs and waiting women again.

Yet her spell was still present and palpable.

Dragon House, England

May, 1975

Chapter 14

When she arrived home from the bank, Suzie rang for some jasmine tea, then settled back on a couch to rest for an hour before dressing for dinner. Not that she was tired. She was too excited for that. But the evening would be a long one, and she must remain in full possession of her wits.

For the first time in her life she intended to wear in public the famous black pearls that had been looted from the apartments of the Dowager Empress Tz'u-Hsi of China.

"Keep them in the bank," Papa had said that long-ago day, her twenty-first birthday, when he had dropped them into her eager hands, a pool of smokily gleaming richness. "They're your insurance for a rainy day. Don't wear them. For one thing, awkward questions might be asked, and for another no one knows I have them, so they're my special gift to you."

That she, the ugly duckling in the family, should be chosen for such a magnificent present had overawed her. Why not Henrietta, the eldest, or Lucy, the prettiest?

Because, said Papa, they were both young ladies of tiresome consciences. They would immediately want to return the pearls to the Chinese government, or something quixotic like that. He thought he could trust Suzie to treasure them and gloat over them in secret. After all, she bore the Empress' name, didn't she? Besides, he had always felt guilty about Suzie. She had been the odd one out, the plain one, the motherless one.

This stern unknown man, her father, had never before expressed such sentiments, and Suzie had been moved by them, although she had thought them entirely deserved. She *had* been the odd one out, so much plainer and more graceless than her sisters, and motherless to the extent that Mamma had always been too frail and ailing to handle such a strong and stubborn child.

So she regarded this unexpected treasure trove in the same way Papa did, as amends for her childhood and as a perfectly marvellous piece of loot. The secrecy appealed to her, too, as he had known it would. "People have been murdered for less," he had said. "So hide them safely. Keep them for a rainy day."

And as a weapon, Suzie had thought to herself, precociously. She had locked her bedroom door, and sat before the mirror, twisting the gleaming rope round her neck, and having the perception to know that then, with her gauche young face, they looked nothing. But when she was older, when she had a strong ugly impressive face, and the clothes to complement them, the pearls would look sheerly magnificent.

She had seldom been tempted over the years to bring them out of hiding. Her carefully kept secret had been too precious to share with the rest of the family. Besides, both of her husbands had been rich enough and she had feared their generosity might dry up if they had known too much about her superb treasure. She had always been a schemer.

On her seventy-fourth birthday she determined to wait no longer. The time had come to exhibit them as they should be exhibited, to make her spectacular entrance.

And let anyone who knew the value of a rope of perfectly matched black pearls, not to mention their unique provenance, admire, envy and desire.

She had a feeling that everyone at dinner tonight, except innocent Ben, and poor senile old Lucy, would have a fairly good idea of their value.

The bank manager had enquired anxiously about locks on her house, and had even suggested adding a security man, as a waiter, to her staff for the night. But she had pooh-poohed that. She would be wearing the pearls. She would even sleep with them round her neck if she thought it expedient.

No one would dare to touch her person, she thought, as she lay brooding in the quietness of her room. Her eyes narrowed to slits, her long face took on the bland inscrutability of the Oriental. She put on her nail shields (removed for her visit to the bank), and lay with her hands folded on her stomach in an attitude of relaxation. She was deep in her royal dream. She was the great Empress Tz'u-Hsi, and tonight, arrayed in her splendid dragon robe, she would hold court.

It was Ben who made the discovery. He came bursting into his parents' bedroom, his eyes sparkling with indignation.

"Mother, I can't find the horned dragon. Uncle Charles says Aunt Suzie must have hidden it. May I ask her for it?"

"Not tonight, Ben," Georgina said. "It wouldn't be very polite on Aunt Suzie's birthday. Wait until tomorrow."

"But why should she hide it, Mother?"

"I don't know. Perhaps she's afraid of thieves."

"There have been thieves already," Ben said. "The umbrella stand in the hall has gone."

"Come off it, old man," Hugh said. "I saw it when I came in. Stuffed with umbrellas, as usual."

"Not the same one," Ben insisted. "It hasn't got red flowers on it. It's just an old blue basin with cracks."

Georgina's eyes met Hugh's in a swift question. The Ching-tê-Chen bowl at Sotheby's, she was thinking. No, that thought was too wild for words.

"Ben, are you sure of this? The dragon *and* the umbrella stand? Or are you making up a story about thieves?"

"Thieves hardly bring replacements," said Hugh thoughtfully. "Now, look here, Ben, not a word about these funny discoveries of yours tonight. We mustn't spoil the party. You know how Aunt Suzie gets if she thinks any of her treasures have been mislaid."

"They haven't been mislaid, they've been looted," said Ben with conviction. "I expect there are some of those old Boxers prowling about. *Sha, Sha, Sha!*" he shouted suddenly, making Georgina jump.

"Oh, darling, be quiet. If you don't behave you won't be allowed to stay up. Now run along and wash yourself properly and brush your hair, and put on your new shirt."

"Probably it wasn't the Boxers. Probably it was that Angel who did it," said Ben, lingering at the door.

"What angel?"

"The one Aunt Lucy saw. Don't you remember, Mother? You told me about her taking the jade pony from the Prince's palace. I expect she's still stealing."

"And she would be exactly eighty-two years old," said Georgina. "Rather elderly to be creeping about stealing things, don't you think? Silly little sausage you are."

When Ben had gone, however, Georgina turned to Hugh, frowning.

"Don't laugh at me, but from the moment we arrived I've had this funny feeling."

"I always have a funny feeling when I arrive at this ridiculous Dragon House. It's like being in limbo, poised between two worlds."

"I wonder if Aunt Suzie was putting that dragon in the bank."

"After all these years of leaving it and other valuables lying about? Not unless she really distrusts her current favourite. After all, her treasures are her weapons. You don't want to lock away the ammunition when there's a war on."

"Is there a war on?"

"Permanently, in this house."

"But it was nice on the river today," Georgina murmured. She laid her cheek briefly against his shoulder, and he patted her head.

"What are you wearing tonight?"

"Something you haven't seen."

"Nice?"

"Rather wicked."

"Do I suspect you of trying to outshine Miss Russell?"

"You do, and I will."

"As long as it's not Aunt Suzie you're competing with." Georgina began to giggle.

"Heavens, I have no aspirations to the celestial throne. But, Hugh, I do have suspicions about Amy Russell. I think I know what she's up to. She's making a dead set at poor Charles, either to amuse herself or because she thinks he's going to be very rich. It's cruel and heartless. Supposing he falls in love with her. He's still got all his emotions. Too many of them, I suspect. I think he's enormously vulnerable. And he will be rich if anything in this house is as valuable as that Ching-tê-Chen wine jar that I told you about at Sotheby's. There very well could be something like that, you know."

"I think I'll just go downstairs and check on our imaginative son's story," Hugh said.

He was gone only a few minutes. When he came back he said that there had been no one about and he had been able to take a good look at the bowl in which the umbrella had been left partially open and had almost concealed what it stood in, which was the cracked and chipped blue and white bowl Ben had described. He didn't recall having seen it before, but it could have been there for a long time, couldn't it? Who but Ben, with his obsessively observant ways, would ever have noticed?

"Hugh, when we get back to London—" Georgina began.

"You're going to do a little detective work?"

"I think so." Georgina's eyes were troubled. "I think everyone in this house tonight has some secret scheme. Even us, to preserve things for Ben. I believe I feel just as they must have done in Peking that night of Queen Victoria's birthday party. On the brink of something ominous."

"Look, Georgie," said Aunt Lucy, only to be patiently corrected by Ben.

"I'm not Georgie, Aunt Lucy. That's Georgie in the photograph."

Although the French windows were open and the night air flowed in, it was still enervatingly warm. There were too many lights, Georgina thought. All those Chinese lanterns strung along the trellis, so that it glittered like the Albert Bridge over the Thames in the tourist season. The garden lay bleached and dry beneath the artificial light, and gloomy dark towards the river. The drawing room smelled of nightstocks and roses and incense. The lights burning everywhere made it seem as if they were all on a stage and presently the curtain would go up. Aunt Lucy showing Ben her old photographs. Charles, in his black velvet jacket and frilled white shirt, looking like an ivory figure of a mandarin. Amy Russell in the simple white Victorian dress she had worn previously, making Georgina feel too formal in her elegant black. Hal Jessel in a theatrical ruby red jacket and trousers prowling about the room, his handsome head thrown back, his nostrils twitching occasionally. He had a fine expressive nose that might have been smelling the odour, not of garden scents but of money. Nurse Jenkins, buxom in floral silk, lurking possessively behind Charles. Hugh, dear Hugh, sprawled in an armchair pretending to be relaxed but hating being dressed up in his dinner jacket. Such formality, for a simple dinner party on a hot night.

Everyone was awaiting the entrance of Aunt Suzie.

"Yes, dear boy, that's Georgie and Henrietta and myself, and Miss Deacon, our governess," Aunt Lucy said.

"Miss Deacon's ugly," said Ben.

"Yes, she was quite plain except when she wore her green mermaid dress. That was what Georgie called it. She wore it to the party at the British legation for our Queen's birthday. I remember that night so well because it turned out to be the night Uncle Thomas had his head cut off. He was a missionary, you know, and the Boxers didn't like missionaries. Look, here we are riding our ponies."

"Where's Angel?" Ben asked. "Why isn't she riding a pony?"

"Angel?"

"The one you saw today."

"Oh, her. She'd gone back to Shansi with Aunt Lilian by then. We never saw her again. Henrietta and I were glad. She was a very mischievous child, a bad influence on Georgie, Mamma said."

"Where was Miss Deacon when you were riding ponies?"

Aunt Lucy frowned, peering at the faded brown photographs.

"I think she'd gone by that time, too. We didn't need

a governess any more because Mamma had decided to send us to the English school. Mamma said Miss Deacon had been a mistake, anyway."

"So did she find another family?"

"Yes, I believe she did, in Canton. Papa would have seen to that. He was very strict about the welfare of servants. Oh, and look—"

"Mother!" exclaimed Ben suddenly. "Your back's *bare!*"

Georgina revolved slowly, beginning to laugh. The low-cut black dress was the most sophisticated she had ever had. Already, however, tendrils of hair were escaping from her pinned-up topknot, and she had the faintly dishevelled look that Hugh found both exasperating and charming.

"My best party dress, Ben. Don't you like it?"

Hugh looked at her lazily.

"Darling, you're quite hopeless as a femme fatale. Even your son agrees."

"Mother, your skin's showing!" said Ben in embarrassment. "Down to—down to—"

"Aptly put," murmured Hal in amusement. "It's not exactly a mermaid dress, is it? Like that governess' you are talking about. No scales, no tail. But it's devastating, nevertheless."

"Oh, don't be silly," said Georgina. "I only dressed up for Aunt Suzie's party, to please her. But I'm not really the type, as my husband says."

"What type? The mysterious Miss Deacon's?" Hal was still intrigued. "I must say a governess suddenly becoming a mermaid fascinates me. And I thought the Carrington household was so respectable."

"It was," said Georgina shortly.

"Especially after Miss Deacon left us to go to Canton," said Aunt Lucy mysteriously. "She was only with us for six months. After that we all went to school—"

"Oh, those ghostly children are a bore," exclaimed Amy Russell suddenly. "You're all living in a dream. People grow up and get old and die and become forgotten, with luck. Can't you let that lot go? I must say I came here to be with people who are still alive."

"But this is their house and their things," Ben cried.

"Hush, Ben," said Georgina. "I think Amy may be right, you know. We do get a little obsessed with the past in this house. It's Aunt Suzie's fault. It's this eternal game she plays."

"And my God, she's playing it now," Hal murmured, as the door swung open with deliberate slowness, and the squat glittering fantastic figure of Aunt Suzie, no, surely the Empress Dowager of China, appeared.

She wore her stiff imperial yellow robe, the mandarin collar encrusted with embroidery making her hold her head high. Her skin was slightly yellowed (artificially, surely), her eyebrows darkened, and eye pencil had skilfully slanted her eyes. Her ebony hair was scraped back into a knot on the top of her head and secured with a jewelled pin. The nail shields protected her grotesquely long little fingernails. The rest of her fingers were loaded with rings, including the familiar baroque pearl one. But the most unexpected feature of her apparel were the pearls twisted twice round her neck and hanging to her waist. Georgina never remembered seeing them before.

Aunt Suzie must have been satisfied with the impact her entrance had made, for everybody stared and for a long moment nobody spoke. Even Charles, used to his mother's theatricality, seemed astonished and without words.

Then Ben said happily, "You have your best dragons on, Aunt Suzie," and the uncomfortable silence was broken.

"And the Empress' pearls, or surely I'm mistaken," Hal drawled.

"I've never seen those before, Mother," Charles said sharply. "Where have you had them hidden?"

"In the bank, of course." Aunt Suzie was highly pleased with the effect of her entrance. It was all she had hoped. Her guests were goggle-eyed, as they well should be.

"Not always!" Charles said, with complete disbelief.

"Always. You don't keep a king's ransom lying about in a drawer. Actually"—she fingered the pearls caressingly—"I've scarcely ever worn them in public. Once or twice in Biarritz when it was fashionable, once to a ball in Venice. But never in England, since the day Papa gave them to me."

"Papa!" Aunt Lucy had a sudden startled intelligence in her usually vague eyes. "Why should he give you such a valuable present? Why not Henrietta or me?"

"Because, frankly, you were not the type, dear sister. Nor was Henrietta. Where would you, two spinsters, have worn the Empress of China's black pearls? To church?"

"From what you say you don't seem to have flaunted them much yourself, Mother," Charles pointed out.

"I always wait for the right occasions," Aunt Suzie said in her harsh confident voice. "I decided my seventy-fourth birthday was one of them."

"Looted treasure?" Amy Russell murmured, almost inaudibly.

Aunt Suzie heard, however, and shot her a searing glance. (*Last time she'll be invited here,* Georgina thought.)

"How they came into my father's possession has nothing whatever to do with my not wearing them. Since my sister has questioned my ownership, I will tell you Papa gave them to me to compensate for my being rather plain. The ugly duckling, as you might say. Does that satisfy you, Lucy?"

"Were you ugly like Miss Deacon who had a mermaid dress?" asked Ben with deep interest. "Is that why you wear your dragon dress and black beads?"

It was one of the rare times when Georgina saw that Aunt Suzie was angry with Ben.

"I have no idea how ugly Miss Deacon was," she said icily. "I never saw the woman. And I am wearing my dragon dress"—she drew herself up haughtily—"because this is a party. And nobody is looking after me. Why haven't I been offered champagne?"

Hal turned to the sideboard.

"No one has had any yet, Highness. We were waiting for you, to drink your health."

"My health?" Aunt Suzie queried ironically. She fingered her pearls. "How intriguing."

"Your absolutely splendid health," Hal said, unperturbed. "Shall I officiate?"

"Isn't she a marvellous old antiquity?" he murmured later to Amy, refilling her glass. "You'd better put her on your list."

"She's a marvellous old ham," Amy retorted. "Even you can act better than that."

Hal's sunny blue eyes gleamed with some private pleasure.

"Aren't you enjoying yourself, sweetheart? Has our little Georgina upstaged you, wearing her Givenchy."

"A copy. And she hasn't the poise to wear that sort of thing. She giggles and her hair falls down."

"And her nice unsophisticated husband has discovered that he adores her like that. You hadn't got him on your mind, had you? You stick to your job. A little flirting with poor Charles, okay, but no other complications, or there'll be hell to pay."

"With Bunny? That rabbit?"

"Rabbit, did you say?" said Hal in a queer voice. "Oh, my!"

Amy took a long swallow of her champagne.

"Are you scared of him?" she asked contemptuously.

"Yes, I bloody well am, and you'd better be, too. Just stop thinking you fancy little Georgina's husband and make do with Charles. Or me."

"But Aunt Suzie wouldn't care for it. You're her favourite, and God help you if you stray. You'll be cut out of her will as fast as her beloved Boxers slashed off heads."

"But it won't matter, will it, if you do your stuff? By the way, watch that kid. Don't be fooled by his glasses. He's got eyes like laser beams."

Amy drooped her eyelids innocently.

"And how do you propose to get the pearls? They're a surprise, aren't they?"

"I'll say. Such a plum on old Plum Blossom."

"Are you going to tell Bunny? Or count on inheriting?"

"Give me time. Keep your mouth shut in the meantime. We just might get a brilliant idea, the two of us. Eh?"

"What are you two over there talking about?" came Aunt Suzie's voice, as strident as a brass gong. "Soft nothings, I'll be bound. That's why I don't trust champagne. It makes everyone too sentimental. Anyway, it's time to go into dinner."

"When are you going to open your presents, Aunt Suzie?" Ben asked eagerly.

"After dinner. You see how thoughtful I am. I don't care to have my guests starve. Lucy, why are you staring like that? Have you seen a ghost?"

"Oh, not another, Aunt Lucy," Georgina exclaimed.

"No, this isn't Angel again." Aunt Lucy seemed breathless and flustered. "It's the rings, Suzie's and mine. Look!" She held out her tiny crumpled hand, exhibiting the large pearl ring worn on her middle finger.

"It's exactly the same as the one Suzie's wearing. And there was only one, you know."

Everyone was now looking with interest at the two identical rings, one on each elderly hand.

"This is what the Empress Dowager gave to all the ladies of the legations when she held her tea party," Aunt Lucy explained. "When Mamma was dying she gave hers to Henrietta. Henrietta never wore it, and told me not to. It reminded her too much of that awful time, you see. But I thought just for tonight I would bring it out. I never knew it was exactly the same as Suzie's."

Aunt Suzie was genuinely bewildered. She frowned.

"I've always worn this one. Perhaps it was looted." She put her hand on the magnificent pearls again. "Papa seems to have been quite naughty."

"But it isn't mentioned in the little red book."

"What little red book? Mao's?" Hal's flippancy received a fiercer scowl from Aunt Suzie and he had to mutter an apology.

"I've never heard of any little red book, Aunt Lucy," Georgina said.

"You wouldn't have because Henrietta hid it very carefully and told me to do the same. You see"—the old head shook distressfully—"it recorded all Papa's most valuable thefts, well, possessions. The jade pony, the horned dragon, and so on."

"The pearls?" Hugh asked.

"No, not the pearls. I don't understand them. Although there is an item scratched out. Henrietta and I tried often to read it. But then we gave up and pretended none of the things existed. Loot was really rather abhorrent, no matter what the Boxers did."

"Some day you must show us the book," Hugh said.

"I'd like to see it, too," Aunt Suzie said thoughtfully. "Lucy, you secretive old squirrel."

Aunt Lucy looked even more distressed.

"I hadn't meant to tell—"

"Tell? You've told nothing."

"About Papa being so dishonest. It grieved Henrietta and me, and Georgie, too. I don't think Mamma ever knew, thank goodness. But this, Suzie"—she twisted the ring on her finger, her eyes again had a surprising lucidity—"is the genuine ring the Empress gave Mamma. Yours must be a fake."

"A fake! I'd never own a fake."

"Well, I admit you don't need to. You have so much else."

It was plain that Aunt Suzie was disturbed. She sat at the head of the table, toying with her food, darting sharp suspicious glances at each of her guests in turn.

The warm night air flowed in through the open doors, the coloured lanterns swayed, the wind-bells gave their ghostly chimes, and in the candlelit room all the light seemed to be drawn to the brilliant yellow-clad figure as regally erect on her chair as if it were a throne.

It was a pity, Georgina thought, that the ownership of treasures made one perpetually suspicious. Why should it upset Aunt Suzie so much that she might not be wearing the genuine ring bestowed on Amelia Carrington by the Empress Dowager? Or was she worrying as to the mysterious circumstances that had produced two of those unique rings in the same house? Or was she becoming doubtful that the marvellous black pearls were genuine?

It was only when she began to open her birthday presents that she regained her ebullience. She kept Ben's until last, and gave a cry of pleasure as she unfurled the scarlet banner.

"Oh, Ben, how clever! Chinese writing, too! I'm so ignorant I can't read it. What does it say?"

Ben had gone pink with gratification.

"It says 'Exterminate the foreigner,' Aunt Suzie."

"Ho, ho, ho! What fun! What a lark! When are we going to play Boxers? Tonight, in the dark? Are you brave enough?"

Ben's eyes were enormous with fearful anticipation.

Georgina said hastily, "Not tonight, Aunt Suzie. It's too late, and if Ben gets over-excited he has nightmares. Besides, I don't think it would be very safe in the dark."

"Safe! In my garden! What are you afraid of, Georgina? Bats? I would only be up the willow tree, wearing my new sash and sniping at the foreigners." She looked round the room aggressively. "I suppose you all think I'm mad."

"You would look magnificent perched in the willow tree dressed like that, Highness," said Hal. "Like a great golden Chinese pheasant. It would be a pity to waste such a sight in the dark."

Aunt Suzie began to give her slow croaking chuckle.

"You mean I'm to dress like this again tomorrow just for your benefit? Pearls and all?"

"Oh, do, Aunt Suzie, please!" Ben begged. "And I'll get out Georgie's sword."

"Would you like a real Chinese sword?" Charles asked laconically. "I have one in my room."

"Don't be ridiculous," Hugh said. "Giving a child a dangerous weapon like that."

"Oh, I have no doubt Charles would enjoy seeing me decapitated," Aunt Suzie said. The game was in full swing and she was enjoying her birthday at last. "But you need to be a little more subtle about it, dear boy. Don't boast about your proposed weapon."

Aunt Lucy was suddenly cringing, her hands knotted together.

"I remember how they stood lined up outside the Tartar wall in their tiger skirts and their red sashes, and blowing those awful loud trumpets, and waving their curved swords."

"Who, darling?" Georgina asked gently.

"The Boxers and the Manchus and the Bannermen. The colours hurt my eyes and I got earache from the noise. Don't let us talk of it, please. It makes me very confused. I don't seem to know where I am."

"You're on your way to bed, Aunt Lucy," said Georgina. "And so is my warrior son Ben. Really, Aunt Suzie, you're very naughty. Can't we ever talk of anything but Boxers in this house?"

Aunt Suzie lifted her head in a contemptuous gesture.

"Lucy always was a coward. Let her go to bed, then. Tomorrow it will be hot again. Just the right sort of weather for us, Ben. Goodnight, soldier."

Because he was already over-excited, and had been up far too late, Georgina sat beside Ben's bed and read to him.

> I was a child in Yung-Yang,
> A little child I waved farewell.
> After long years again I dwell
> In world-forgotten Yung-Yang.

Ben always asked for that poem. He knew it by heart, but wanted to hear it again and again.

> Yet I recall my play-time,
> And in my dreams I see
> The little ghosts of May-time
> Waving farewell to me. . . .

It had the usual soporific effect, and presently Ben's eyelids were drooping.

"I wish I had known them all," Georgina heard him mutter.

"Known who, darling?"

"Henrietta and Lucy and Georgie, of course."

It was a constant wish that was never far off fulfilment in this house. The past became only yesterday. Or it was even the present.

Chapter 15

When Georgina came downstairs she found the company in pairs, Aunt Suzie on the high-backed Victorian sofa, with Hal gracefully and theatrically arranged on a cushion at her feet, Charles in his wheelchair by the open French windows, Nurse Jenkins sitting watchfully near, and on the terrace, strolling up and down beneath the rainbow light of the Chinese lanterns, Hugh and Amy.

She was the odd one out, thought Georgina. Even in her sexy black dress. She debated whom she would interrupt, then decided she would quietly sit alone and absorb whatever snatches of conversation were audible.

Hugh and Amy on the terrace were quite inaudible, although Amy was doing a lot of gesticulating with her hands, the snowy ruffles of her sleeves falling back to her elbows. She was being animated and amusing, Georgina guessed, not knowing that Hugh preferred women to listen. Charles and his buxom nurse exchanged only an occasional remark, but once Georgina thought he used the name Eileen. Could he be referring to Nurse Jenkins? Charles, the tyrant invalid, who usually practised a subtle kind of sadism on his nurses?

What was in no doubt was Aunt Suzie's conversation. It boomed across the room.

"I intend going to London to see my solicitor next week. I've decided that now I've reached the age of seventy-four it's time I made my last will and testament. I mean my last, literally. So there you are, dear boy. You may have your choice."

"My choice, Highness?"

"You know exactly what I'm talking about. The Ming cabinet, or the jade carp, or the stem vases. I can see you looking at my pearls. Not them. They would be quite unsuitable, since you haven't a wife. They must go to Georgina. Even if she never wears them she may have a daughter one day." She sat back smugly. "They were a surprise, weren't they?"

"Completely. But then you have this marvellous gift for the theatre."

"I know, dear boy. I missed my vocation. Well—which is your choice?"

"You're too kind, Highness. I wouldn't dream of making a choice. It would be presumptuous. If you want to leave me a tiny tiny memento, that's your decision."

"Don't be a hypocrite. Everybody is here for the pickings. I know that well enough. But I don't mind. I'm too old to care any more about love and affection. That belongs to youth. I didn't get it then, so I'm unlikely to get it now. Actually I enjoy this game vastly more. You're all my subjects. You must please me, or out!" She swept her arms dramatically. "And lucky to keep your heads. Charles! Georgina! Where's Hugh and that girl? Spooning on the terrace? Ben is the only innocent one among you all. I may eventually decide to make him my sole heir."

"Oh, no, Aunt Suzie, you can't forget Charles," Georgina cried.

"I can fight my own battles, Georgina," came Charles' high tight voice.

"You shouldn't have to fight at all. Aunt Suzie, you ought to be ashamed of yourself."

Aunt Suzie gave her gratified chuckle, her head nodding back and forth like a clockwork mandarin. The game was being particularly enjoyable tonight. It had made her forget the annoying mystery of the similar rings. She didn't know why that had worried her so much.

On the terrace Amy said, "Do you believe in fidelity in marriage?"

"It would be the ideal situation."

"But what a magnificent ideal. Half a century of only one woman."

"You mean, how boring?"

"No, I mean how magnificent, but also how impossible."

A week ago, Hugh would have agreed with her. Life did get boring. One did feel temptations. No doubt this would happen to him again. But just now the vague small seed of distrust he had felt about Amy when he had called at her shop had grown. There was a lack of innocence about her that he found, to his surprise, he disliked in a woman. Not sexual innocence, something much more guileful. He granted her her wit and sophistication. He was sure she would be an exciting lover. But there was an underlying greedy hunger for something—men, riches, admiration, acclaim?—that he found distasteful.

Besides, his zany Georgina, masquerading with true innocence in her too sophisticated dress, was indoors, and he wanted to be with her.

"Have I shocked you?" Amy was asking in her husky voice.

"Shocked? What does that word mean?"

"Oh, yes, I know you're a hardened observer of crime."

"Who's talking about crime?"

Amy caught her lip in her teeth. For the briefest moment she seemed off balance. Hugh thought suddenly of the switched bowls in the hall. No, that was ridiculous. She would have needed to travel with one of those old Victorian carpetbags. Or a large hatbox?

"I just mean you've been trained to have a suspicious mind. I'm not planning to commit a crime. I'm only trying to seduce you."

"I'm enormously flattered."

He knew she was angry. Her chin jutted. She looked small and bony and vulnerable in the half dark.

"Who are you, Amy? Georgina and I have wondered. You can't expect us to believe you're Hal Jessel's girl friend."

"I'm his partner. I told you. He's lent me capital."

"I thought most actors were usually in financial trouble," Hugh said.

Amy, ignoring that, gave a thin laugh. "His girl friend, good God! I'd have to get past Bun—"

"Who?"

"Oh, nobody. I have a hunch it wouldn't be wise to talk about Hal's love life in this house. Why do you allow your aunt to be taken in like that?"

"Aunt Suzie taken in? You've a lot to learn about that tough old warrior. She'll play with your friend Hal just as long as it amuses her, and then out will come her sword. Georgina and I have seen them come and go."

"Who?"

"The eunuchs."

"But the last one to be around—when she dies— won't he be the lucky one?"

"Maybe. There are macabre games played in this house. I suppose one of them will become a reality. If it's only Charles slashing off his mother's head. Shall we go in? Georgina should be down."

Amy shrugged.

"What a seduction scene. Wrong night, wrong moon, wrong man."

"Wrong place," said Hugh, not wanting to appear too ungallant, but knowing suddenly that he didn't even want to touch the waif-like creature at his side. Funny. It must be the house. He always blamed the house when this odd heavy mood descended on him. For Ben it held the ghosts of children, for Georgina the sad conviction that lovely, gentle Amelia with her piratical husband had been too unhappy here. For him the atmosphere was more sinister, holding echoes of greed and violence and fear. He thought that the brief bloody war into which the family had been innocently plunged had not remained in Peking. Its aura had returned here. Which was fanciful thinking for a practical man of law.

But upstairs, alone with Georgina, the heavy mood lifted from him. Georgina had asked him about his tête-à-tête with Amy, and he had said it had been more of a sniping match.

"You were right about her in the beginning. She's an odd little nut. Secretive and uncrackable. Gives nothing away but her desire for a bit of bed."

Georgina let the black dress slide to the floor. She stood in her pale satin slip, saying she didn't think she would wear that dress again.

"It was a mistake. I'm awfully sorry, Hugh. Stupidly extravagant of me."

"Not a bit. I thought you were delicious in it."

"You didn't. You were shocked, like Ben."

"Only because other people were looking at what belongs to me."

"Really, Hugh? You mean—my back down to there?"

"I do. And if you'll only hurry up and come to bed I'll prove it."

For the first time they made love in Grandfather Nathaniel's and Grandmother Amelia's bed. Had they banished the unhappy ghosts at last? Georgina lay curled against Hugh drowsily, astonished at her happiness. More lines of poetry were drifting through her head, not Ben's little ghosts of Maytime but:

> In the month of peach-bloom and plum-bloom, in the silken-screened recess
> Love is the burden of sweet voices, and the brief night melting, and the long caress. . . .

In the morning the unseasonal heat continued. Probably because it was too hot to sleep, people were up early. Georgina lifted the curtain to look out, and saw Charles being pushed by Nurse Jenkins in her white nurse uniform, which suited her better than that vulgar floral she had worn last night. They must have been down to the riverbank to get some cool air. While she was watching she saw a flicker behind the willow tree, and Amy and Hal Jessel appeared, Amy in a cotton shirt and jeans, Hal in a very trendy brocade dressing gown, Turnbull and Ascher without a doubt.

"Hugh!" she called to the inert form in the bed. "Everybody's up except us."

"Let them be."

"And there's Aunt Suzie, and Ben, too. Good heavens, she meant what she said last night. She's wearing all that finery to play Boxers."

"Perhaps she never went to bed."

"Perhaps. She does look ridiculous in yellow satin in broad daylight. I believe she's got her pearls on, too. Hugh, do you think she meant it about leaving me those pearls?"

"I rather think she was speaking the truth, for once."

"So do I," said Georgina apprehensively. "What on

earth would I do with them? I wouldn't even want to sell them, if they belong to the Chinese government. What's the legal position?"

"I haven't an idea. Theft would have to be proved, and as it's all more than seventy years ago, I shouldn't think anyone would worry much."

Georgina shivered slightly. "They'd be unlucky. What real happiness has Aunt Suzie ever had? Or Grandfather Carrington, either? Anyway, can you see me in pearls from head to toe?"

"Not really. They're only meant for queens and prima donnas, neither of which species I care for."

"There's Smythe, too," Georgina said, still looking out of the window. "He's got his shears. He's going to work on Ben's dragon. That will please Ben. Darling, if you're not awake already you shortly will be, with the yelling. I'd better go and warn Aunt Lucy or she'll think she's back in Peking in the middle of the rebellion."

"What a mad house," Hugh muttered, burying his face in the pillow.

"You've got your new sash on, Aunt Suzie," said Ben, gratified.

"Of course I have. I'm very bloodthirsty today. I'll scare the foreigners to death."

"And your pearls."

"I promised you last night. I said Aunt Suzie would be the Empress Dowager and Prince Tuan and Jung Lu and the Boxer army all rolled into one."

"I've got my gun," said Ben.

"That ancient firearm. It'll jam when I attack the gates."

"Then I'll fight with my sword. The British soldiers are very brave."

"But they can't defeat the Boxers."

"They can when reinforcements come."

"Reinforcements haven't come though, have they?"

"Yes, they have," said Amy Russell behind them. "I'm on the side of the legations."

Aunt Suzie's long face split with delight.

"Ho, ho! That will really make a battle. Then you'd better man the walls, you foreigners, because I'm going to snipe at you from the willow tree."

"Sha, sha, sha!" The birds flew from the trees in alarm as Aunt Suzie's hoarse yells shattered the early morning peace. Presently there were the minuscule pops of Ben's toy rifle from the shrubbery.

"Charge!" he shouted in his high childish voice. "Charge, my brave men!"

"Kill! Kill!" Aunt Suzie was perched on the lower branch of the willow tree, a gigantic yellow bird hanging precariously over the steep riverbank.

Mad, thought Hugh, getting reluctantly out of bed, rubbing sleepy eyes. Certifiable, almost. He must talk to Georgina and Charles. Or one day something would happen. . . .

Not one day. Today. For before Hugh was dressed there was a louder yell, full of real terror, and a sound of splintering. Then a distant splash and Ben screaming, "Aunt Suzie! Aunt Suzie!"

Dragging on his trousers, Hugh rushed to the windows, exclaimed aloud, and made for the stairs.

Those rotten old willows, they were not sturdy like oaks, they got diseased joints, they disintegrated when subjected to too much weight. And Aunt Suzie, almost as broad as she was tall, must turn the scale at something near two hundred pounds. Especially with all her regalia on.

By the time Hugh reached the scene, she was struggling out of the river, a large sodden Ophelia, her jewelled combs lost and her dark hair streaming, her yellow dress clay-coloured with water. Amy was helping her, while Ben tugged desperately at one flopping arm, his face distraught. "Daddy, help, please! I didn't shoot her out of the tree. Truly I didn't."

Aunt Suzie, finally landed on the bank, a huge gasping goldfish, tried to say something and failed. Her face was the same muddy colour as her dress. Amy, soaked and very pale from her exertions, or fright, was saying breathlessly that she was afraid it had been her fault. She had crept up behind Aunt Suzie and given the smallest shake to the low branch on which she was perching. Not enough to push her off, but who had known that the branch would break? She had gone with this tremendous splash into the river. But thank goodness there was practically no current there, and she had never been in danger of drowning.

Nurse Jenkins was running across the lawn, her white uniform a flag of mercy. Charles, abandoned in his wheelchair, was gesticulating helplessly and calling to know what had happened. Hal lurked in the distance on the terrace. He obviously had a horror of illness or accident.

Aunt Suzie seemed to have lost consciousness. Nurse Jenkins lifted an eyelid, felt for a pulse.

"She'll come round shortly, I should think. Her pulse is quite strong. She's had a fright, of course, and she isn't young."

Georgina was coming flying across the lawn.

"What happened? I've got some brandy."

"Good thinking," said Nurse Jenkins impartially. "Just what we need. Mrs. Blenheim, can you hear me?"

Aunt Suzie stirred and gave a choked sound.

"That's right, love. Just try to swallow a little brandy."

"Who—" Aunt Suzie thrust out a pudgy suspicious arm.

"It's me, Georgina, Aunt Suzie. You'll drink the brandy for me?"

"I fell. The enemy—" Aunt Suzie swallowed and sputtered and swallowed again, with more relish. Presently she was able to sit up. She saw Ben and reached out to him. "Why are you crying, little foreign devil?"

"I didn't shoot you, Aunt Suzie."

"Couldn't hurt a bird with that ancient firearm." The basilisk eyes were now open and fully aware. "No, it was a palace plot."

"Or the wizard," said Ben. "Perhaps he shook you out of the tree."

"I'm afraid it was your weight, Mrs. Blenheim," said Amy. "The branch broke. Look, it's splintered. Lucky I was here to help you."

Hugh stooped to examine the branch and the ground beneath it.

The basilisk gaze rested on Amy.

"Did you think I wouldn't have got out of the river alive? Did you think Dragon House would be left without an Empress?"

"We must get you indoors, Mrs. Blenheim," said Nurse Jenkins briskly. "Can you walk? Mr. Morley, could you help her?"

"Coming," said Hugh. "Ben, you had better come in for breakfast. And you, Amy. You're soaked." Amy's thin face had its shut-in look.

"Lucky it's a warm day," she said. She seemed to be talking about luck a lot.

It wasn't until they had got Aunt Suzie upstairs and on to her bed, her sodden garments removed, that they discovered the pearls were missing. Obeying her distraught orders, everyone went down to the riverbank to search.

A strand about three inches long was eventually found, caught up in the broken foliage of the willow tree. The rest of the pearls, sliding off the broken string, must have fallen into the river. It wasn't much use paddling and groping in the mud. If the priceless gems were there they would be trodden deeper with every movement.

Hugh and Hal and Amy kept up the search for half an hour or so, then gave up. Georgina, meeting them as they returned to the house, seemed relieved.

"Well, that solves one problem," she said.

"The loss of a queen's ransom!" Hal exclaimed.

"My damn *fool* of a mother," said Charles bitterly. "I'll get a net and dredge up the mud."

"I doubt if you'll do any better than we did," Hugh said. "Calm down. After all, you didn't even know of the pearls' existence until yesterday."

"I expect the old Empress came to take them back," said Aunt Lucy. Everyone looked round at her. No one had heard her come in. "And a very good thing, too. They would have been very unlucky. Is Suzie going to die?"

Charles gave his thin laugh.

"Good heavens, no. It would take more than a ducking to kill my mother."

"That's nice. But I expect there will be no picnic today. No cold chicken and champagne and pug dogs and sketching material and parasols and carrying chairs. The rebellion has stopped all those frivolities. So I think I will go home before the war gets worse."

"Really, Aunt Lucy?" said Georgina. "Do you want to?"

"Yes, I do. I don't care for this house very much nowadays. It seems to be full of plotting. And people who have no right to be here come. That Angel yesterday. She was up to no good. Besides, Henrietta will be waiting for me."

Georgina gave Hugh a quick enquiring glance. He nodded, reading her thoughts as always, dear Hugh.

"Henrietta won't be there, Aunt Lucy. But Bessie will be. Hugh and Ben and I will drive you home."

Actually this was a journey Hugh wanted to make, because he was anxious to see the little red book of which

Aunt Lucy had spoken. He was convinced now that something funny was going on, although not in the realm of ghosts. In the realm of very much alive and acquisitive human beings.

After the two-hour drive across country Aunt Lucy was exhausted. Bessie, the faithful elderly housekeeper, was waiting, and nodded her head as if this was exactly what she had expected.

"I told her it would be too much for her. That sister always upsets her. Brings back her nightmares about the past. I don't believe wars are ever over, do you? They go on and on in your mind. And all those old swords and pistols and uniforms that people keep don't help."

"I'm afraid my aunt is living in the past," Georgina said.

"Yes, Miss Henrietta used to shake her out of it. Very practical, Miss Henrietta was. Wouldn't let her sister pore over her mother's letters the way she does now."

"Letters from my grandmother," Georgina exclaimed. "I didn't know there were any."

"Oh, yes. Now Miss Henrietta has gone, Miss Lucy talks to me about them. They were written after the children had been sent home from Peking and your grandparents stayed on. Your grandmother seemed very homesick then. Would you all like some tea?"

"Yes, we would. Wouldn't we, Hugh? I'll help Aunt Lucy to bed while you make it, Bessie."

"Ask her for the book," Hugh said.

"That's what I intend doing. Ben, why don't you play in the garden for a while?"

Ben sighed heavily, looking out of the window at the neat walled garden that could hold no surprises.

"There aren't any dragons or wizards here," he complained.

"And just as well, when you see the pranks they get up to."

"Mother, we never asked Aunt Suzie where she had put the horned dragon."

"Neither we did. Never mind, it will be safe somewhere."

Aunt Lucy, in her tiny low-ceilinged reassuringly English bedroom, settled back on her pillows and said she felt fine now she was home. She would take a little soup for her supper. Yes, of course Georgina could see Mamma's letters. They were in the morocco leather box in the top drawer of the bureau. It was necessary to read them in a good light as the ink was very faded.

"After all, they were written seventy-three years ago, and I don't expect Chinese ink was ever very good. Read them aloud, dear. I like to hear them."

Georgina pored over the faint writing, and began to read stumblingly.

My beloved children,

Papa and I miss you very much, I more than Papa because he is busy in the shop, and I am alone in this lonely house. I listen to the windbells, and Li's caged birds singing in the courtyard. The almond blossom is almost out which means the long winter is over. There are just the summer months (not so hot and dry as last year, I hope, when the dreadful siege was on) to live through, and then we will all be reunited.

We have heard that Miss Deacon is living with some Americans in Canton. We will probably see her before we leave China, as Papa intends going to Canton on business. I shall always owe her a great debt for nursing me safely through my illness.

As for your other friends, Ah Wan makes herself useful in the house, Cassidy is well, but looking forward to coming back to England and familiar English things as much as I am. We both feel there has been too much sorrow in this lovely city. Do you remember Mr. Fortescue? Someone has planted a willow tree on his grave, and other graves are tended carefully by both the legation staff and friendly Chinese.

I wonder if the old Empress Dowager will ever return

to her palaces? She must feel as unhappy in exile as I do.

Oh, and such a sad little story. The skeleton of a very tiny baby was found on the edge of the lily pool in the legation grounds. It must have been covered with leaves that had blown away in the winter winds. It was a girl, so I suppose it had been put out to die by some mother who couldn't feed it, and didn't want a girl. The Chinese can be very barbarous, as Aunt Lilian and poor Uncle Thomas discovered.

"Georgie cried when he heard that," Aunt Lucy suddenly interrupted.

"Because of the baby?"

"He said it was Plum Blossom. He said most absurdly that it was his and Angel's baby. That must have been why he sometimes called Suzie Plum Blossom when she was a baby. He kept remembering. As indeed we all did. Henrietta became compulsive about washing, and remained so all her life. She said we all got so dirty during the siege."

"The next letter's from Canton," Georgina said. Aunt Lucy leaned forward eagerly.

"Oh, yes, do read it. It caused us great excitement when it came because it told us about Suzie. We hadn't known there was going to be a baby."

My dearly loved children,

This is my last letter from China. Tomorrow Papa and I sail on the Orient Star, which will dock in Southampton sometime in October. The big surprise is that you have a new sister. She was born several weeks ago, and is strong and healthy with black hair and black eyes, very like Papa. She is called Suzie, and I hope you will all welcome her warmly to our home. Cassidy will take care of her on the journey as I am still not very strong. That horrid illness I had during the siege seems to have left me annoyingly weak, but the doctor assures me there is nothing wrong that English air won't cure.

Papa has some splendid treasures to bring home. He is very occupied with them. The Geneva shop will get some, and some will go to London, but he says he intends to keep the rarest of them for himself. So our home on the Thames may become a little China. It is not my taste, but as long as Papa is happy I am.

"Even then," said Georgina, "Grandfather sounded very selfish."

"He was always selfish and strong-minded and stern. Everyone thought Suzie took after him. But the odd thing was, although Mama adored Papa in spite of his sternness, she didn't really care for Suzie. She always had to pretend. Besides, Suzie had cost her her health. She was never really strong again."

"She doesn't mention Miss Deacon," Georgina said. "Although she had said they would be seeing her in Canton."

"Medora. . . . Such a pretty name. But not a pretty person. She frightened me a little. She had such a wild imagination. She was a rebel, I think. Even at that time, they had them then among the young."

"So she had to be dismissed?"

"Only because we went to school."

"Do you think that was really the reason, Aunt Lucy?"

But Aunt Lucy's brief period of clarity was blurring again. "I saw her yesterday. No, it wasn't her, it was Angel. Neither of them were up to any good."

"Why do you say that?"

"Why?" The unfocussed blue eyes looked beyond Georgina. "Because people are so greedy. Always stealing, looting, killing. Georgina! It that you? How nice of you to come and see me. Did you bring Georgie?"

"Ben, Aunt Lucy."

"Ben, of course. He's so like Georgie. You see, nothing ever ends. . . . I used to say to Henrietta that life is like a garden, the seeds you plant keep re-seeding and re-seeding. . . . "

Georgina wanted to take the letters away. There was something significant written between the lines, she was sure. Not just Grandmother Amelia's unhappiness.

Grandfather with his autocratic ways could have caused that. Something else. She wondered what Hugh had found in the shabby little red leather book.

He was quite excited.

"Look," he said. "This is a list of all Aunt Suzie's best treasures. The jade pony, the horned dragon, the Mei Ping bowl, the Ching-tê-Chen—"

"Did you say the Ching-tê-Chen?"

"That's what's written here."

"Then it could be the jar sold at Sotheby's! Aunt Suzie's umbrella stand. Hugh, it really could be!"

Hugh gave her a long thoughtful look.

"Don't let's jump to conclusions. We'll do some investigating."

"And the pearls?" Georgina asked excitedly.

"Oddly enough there's no record of any pearls."

"Perhaps because they were looted."

"I fancy some of these other things were, too. But there is a line scratched out."

"Let me see. Oh, there's no hope of reading through that smudge, is there?"

"None at all. I don't think your grandfather intended there to be."

"Could it be the pearls? And he had second thoughts and decided they were too dangerous to list? After all, he could have been shot for looting in the Imperial Palace."

"Perhaps. I doubt if we'll ever know."

Georgina nodded resignedly. "Anyway, old Father Thames has them now. I regard that as a fitting end to a rather infamous bit of behaviour on Grandfather's part. And Aunt Suzie will be a jolly sight safer without them in the house."

"Why do you say that?"

"Now she's flaunting them the word will get round among her more dubious guests."

"I imagine it already has."

"What do you mean?"

"Oh, I just have a criminal mind. I thought I saw traces of sawdust under the willow tree this morning."

"Hugh! You mean someone deliberately sawed that branch! Knowing it was the one crazy Aunt Suzie sat on."

"Maybe just loosened it slightly. I can't swear. And I don't intend to do anything about it until we've enquired about the Ching-tê-Chen jar. Must build up evidence if we're to have a case."

Georgina was rather pale.

"You mean if Aunt Suzie is to have a case. They are her possessions."

"That old woman," said Hugh, "deserves everything that might come to her. Playing this unscrupulous self-indulgent game of wills. Tantalising her deplorable retinue of eunuchs. We can't let her go on getting away with it, either for your sake or Ben's."

"I don't want that loot," Georgina said violently.

"No. But nevertheless you're married to a man who respects the law. And for that matter enjoys a damn good mystery. By the way, there's another bit of mystery here."

"What's that?"

"Something written in Chinese at the end of this book. Did your grandfather speak Manchu?"

"Yes, he did."

"Then no doubt this is his writing. It's so faint it will be difficult to decipher. I expect it's only the list of his treasures written in Chinese in case this book ever fell into Chinese hands. He seems to have been a careful man. We might take it to Ben's friends at that restaurant, and give them a real challenge."

"But there was nothing," said Georgina suddenly, half-way back to London, "to explain the two pearl rings. How both Aunt Lucy and Aunt Suzie had one. I believe that's the biggest mystery of all."

"The clue to everything?" suggested Hugh. "I wonder."

Dragon House, Peking

July, 1900

Chapter 16

Now that it was safe, with no snipers perched in trees like birds of prey, no yelling Boxers hammering on the gates, no alarm bells ringing and no cannonballs hurtling into the grounds, people streamed up the ramps on to the great wall to look over the devastated city. The ruined landscape was shocking, so were the forlorn abandoned corpses in the streets. These had a shrunken rag doll look, the soldiers in their once aggressive scarlet tiger skirts, women in crumpled bloodstained garments, the small shapes of children, and horses picked to skeletons by the roving pariah dogs. Was everyone dead? It was so uncannily still. There was the tainted smell of burnt-out fires, and corruption. And the brooding silence.

The view over the Forbidden City, on the other hand, had a look of untroubled peace, the flowering trees, the glimmer of lake water, the mellow red roofs, and the marble tigers in marble courtyards. The great gates were open, but guarded by detachments of troops. It was hopefully determined that there should be no looting in the Forbidden City and no senseless destruction, no matter how strong the desire for revenge.

Nevertheless, many of the newly arrived soldiers, speaking in a confusing babel of tongues, were impatient for loot. They had had a long exhausting dangerous march, and wanted rewards. The remaining shops in the city had already been ransacked by a few enterprising Chinese coolies who were offering their wares for sale, handcarts loaded with rolls of priceless handwoven Hanchow silks, long sable mandarin robes, jade and ivory. The foreign soldiers were buying greedily, indiscriminately and ignorantly, and stuffing their purchases into their knapsacks.

The Chinese women converts were terrified by Indian troops robbing them of their modest pieces of jewellery. The turbanned sun-blackened men from the hot Bengali plains laughed immoderately at their screams, and only ceased their persecution when two lady missionaries furiously set about them with sticks. Then they picked up their knapsacks and went off in search of richer loot that was not so hotly defended. In no time at all they were squatting on corners doing a brisk trade in silver, porcelain, silks and jade.

Their behaviour was permitted since it was comparatively harmless, a soldier's bonus, so to speak, and the Indians had a deep love of trading. But the Forbidden City was sacrosanct. Indeed, the eunuchs left behind from the Empress Dowager's flight were frightening off even the most crafty and daring of would-be looters. Their aggressive stance and fierce frowns, not to mention their curved swords, unsheathed and glittering in the sun of the quiet courtyards, were a much more successful deterrent than an officer rapping out orders.

The Carringtons had not yet emerged from the familiar shelter of the legation. Amelia was still weak from her illness, and Lilian seemed scarcely aware that the barbaric noises had stopped. Henrietta was happy because she had at last been permitted to have a real bath, in an old tin tub that Ah Wan had found, and there had even been a clean dress and pinafore ready for her. Angel and Lucy submitted less willingly to the same cleansing process. Georgie actively rebelled. All the soldiers were dirty and muddy. Wasn't Papa?

Papa, however, let Georgie down by appearing washed and shaved, with his hair glossily brushed, and wearing his good tweed jacket (which he had discarded eight weeks ago for the soon filthy shirt and trousers and bush jacket in which he had fought for the whole of the siege). He looked gaunt and hollow-cheeked, a bundle of bones, Mamma said with anxious fondness, but his eyes had a jetty brilliance. Indeed he was so noisy and lively and high-spirited that Mamma asked suspiciously if he had been welcoming the relief troops in the ruined bar of the Peking hotel.

He certainly had, he admitted frankly. M'sieu Chamot had produced his last stock of champagne, and some good French wine, even some pots of caviare. He had been hearing about the battle of Tientsin, and of the dangers of the countryside where there were still pockets of defiant Boxers. But their own safety in the city was now assured. Later he intended to see what was left of his shop. He knew it was razed to the ground, but he hoped and prayed the cellars where his stock was hidden were untouched.

"Be careful," Mamma implored. "The floor may fall in."

"Don't worry, I certainly don't mean to be buried alive after surviving all those dark nights on the wall. By the way, I believe a lot of people are now anxious to take the opportunity of exploring the Imperial Palace. But it's being guarded to prevent looting. So don't you children get any ideas about sneaking in."

His words were addressed to Georgie and Angel, but his eyes were on Miss Deacon. She opened her mouth as if to speak, then changed her mind. Nevertheless, it was as if some private message had passed between her and Papa, Georgie thought. For once Papa wasn't being cold and abrupt with her. He was too full of excitement, and so was she, by the way her eyes shone. Georgie had the funny idea that no matter what orders were being given, they both would not be able to resist taking things out of the Empress' palace if they got the chance. After all, hadn't Papa kept his and Angel's green jade pony?

Himself, he was going to sit in his favourite crooked old willow tree. Angel could come if she liked. She had said some time ago that she wanted to tidy Plum Blossom's grave, but now that Lucy was her devoted shadow she didn't seem to mind so much about Plum Blossom. You had to always make allowances for Angel, Mamma said, because she had suffered such a grievous loss. It seemed to Georgie, however, that she just grabbed on to what was alive and forgot what was dead. He would never forget Plum Blossom. In her bower of green leaves, she nestled in his heart.

He would ask Lady MacDonald if he could plant a chrysanthemum by the goldfish pool. Well, just because he wanted to, because he could sit in the willow tree and watch it grow, and watch the herons come to the pool, and listen to the thin sweet thrumming of the doves, as the whistles tied to their feet vibrated. The silence, after all the roaring and shouting and hard blaring of trumpets and crackle of guns had left him feeling dazed and sleepy. He wanted to go on being quiet now. He wanted all the rest of his life to be very quiet and very peaceful.

"It's the result of that dreadful diet," Mamma was saying to someone. "It's a wonder they have any energy at all. I believe Georgie is nodding off to sleep."

Her arms folded round him. He realised that it was a long time since he had sat in her lap, and he couldn't do so now because he would be thought a baby. But he would awfully like to.

"Our hero," said Papa jovially, ruffling his hair. "You'd have held a gun if you'd had to, wouldn't you, son? Well, I'm off to see what's going on. We'll have to trespass on Lady MacDonald's hospitality for a little longer, my love, but I'll soon have a house ready for us."

Mamma raised her large strained eyes.

"Weren't we to go home?" she asked hopefully.

"We'll see, my dear. Don't let's be too hasty. New treaties will be made with the Chinese government. After this barbarity, they'll have to be favourable to foreigners. Anyway it wouldn't be possible to get a passage on a ship for some time. Too many people will be wanting to leave. Just let's wait and see."

Mamma's eyes followed Papa as he left the room. She controlled her disappointed tears, but only because the children were watching her.

Medora ran across the courtyard after Nathaniel.

"Can I come with you, Mr. Carrington?"

"Where do you think I'm going?"

"Into the Forbidden City. I do long to see it."

"You saw it when you went to the Empress' tea party."

"Only a bit of it, and that seems so long ago."

She had tucked her arm in his. Her face was glowing with excitement. She could have sailed through the air like a dragon, or jumped over the white Chinese moon. That was how her euphoria affected her. It was the most wonderful brilliant feeling, coming too seldom, but when it did, washing away all past depression and discontent.

Nathaniel smiled at her, humouring her.

"You've been awfully curt with me lately, Mr. Carrington."

"Have I? I'm sorry for that. It's been a bad time. But now, thank God, it's over. And I'll always be in your debt for getting my wife through her illness."

"Pay some of it off now," said Medora slyly. "Take me with you."

Nathaniel looked down at her.

"Then behave yourself. Don't leave my side. We'll have to talk our way past the guards and those damned eunuchs."

"I want to see where the Empress Dowager slept," Medora said happily. "I'll bet it's the most opulent place you ever saw."

Actually the bedroom, when they discovered it, after a search hindered by watchful eunuchs, was far from opulent. Medora simply couldn't believe that she was standing in the room where that formidable old woman, the Empress of China, became a simple person in need of refreshment and rest. Her brick bed, under which a fire could be lit in the winter, looked hard and uncomfortable. The hangings were of modest white crepe and apricot silk, and there was a homely perfume of dried rose petals coming from the scented pillows. For the rest, there were some lacquered pieces of furniture, a bronze basin and towels, probably left accidentally after the Empress' hasty preparations for departure, incongruously a photograph of Queen Victoria on a table by the bed, one powerful queen regarding another, and several rare and exquisite enamelled clocks about the room, ticking busily, as if the Empress had been obsessively conscious of time.

Inquisitively Medora opened drawers. The Empress' silk pyjamas and wraps, bottles and jars of makeup preparations, fingernail shields, amethyst and gold hairpins and combs, the square-toed slippers that disguised her unbound feet. In the wardrobes rows of stiffly embroidered tunics and dresses and elaborate head decorations. And in the secret drawer of a lacquered cabinet (Nathaniel was familiar with pieces of furniture like this), jewellery that had not yet had time to be buried in a secret place, as the Empress had commanded.

An enormous eunuch, scowling ferociously, stood in the doorway. He knew that he was in danger of being thrashed to death if his mistress' orders were not carried out. With an imperative movement of his hand he indicated that Medora and Nathaniel must go. Nathaniel said something in Manchu. His knowledge of the language had been instrumental in his getting this far in the palace.

But the eunuch was obviously outraged at the white foreigners' presumption in entering his mistress' most private apartments. His dismissal was angry and urgent.

"Better go," Nathaniel said, his hand on Medora's arm. "Mustn't press our luck too far. It only needs one drunken soldier to do something reckless and the bloodshed will start all over again."

"But it was wonderful," Medora said as they went back through the long series of colourful rooms, and across little sunlit courtyards alive with the crooning of doves. "I'd never have believed I could get to see so much. Honestly, it's worth all we've been through."

"We're the lucky ones. We're still alive."

"I know."

"Now I want to discover what's left of my shop."

"May I come?"

He gave her a sideways look as he nodded assent. He was still gripping her arm hard, his eyes glittering with intense excitement. She realised that he was sharing her mood exactly, acquisitive, lustful, bemused.

The shop in the ruined street was a drunken collection of wood and plaster, the sign JAMES CARRINGTON & SONS hanging upside down, the front door fallen in.

They stepped warily over shattered glass and rubble. It was just possible to creep into the dark interior. Nathaniel began throwing away debris to clear the floor over the trapdoor. He scrabbled through the thick layer of sand and finally was able to haul up the door.

It was pitch-dark in the cellar, but he had brought

candles, and in any case he knew every inch of the way. Down the ladder, among the carefully stowed cases, telling Medora to wait a few minutes until the air had cleared. It was pretty foul after eight weeks of the room being sealed up like a tomb. But everything was intact, he announced joyfully. He knew that before he had even lit a candle. His desk was exactly as he had left it, the crated treasures were undisturbed. There was dust everywhere, of course. But good lord, the decanter of Spanish sherry left standing on the desk hadn't even toppled over. It was perfectly drinkable.

"Come on down," he called to Medora.

He had lit two candles and stuck them in a celadon bowl where they leaned drunkenly, dripping grease, and casting an eerie light on the dusty surroundings. They also lit up Nathaniel's face so that Medora could see its look of blazing excitement. The man was a fanatic about his possessions. She believed he would commit murder for them. He had looked profoundly relieved when he had been told that his wife was not going to die, but his face had not been alive with this look of triumph. Was it caused by the safety of his treasures, or by her being there? She longed to think the latter. Her heart was thudding as she came down the ladder into the strange atmosphere of half daylight, half candlelight, and a lurking dusty darkness. She stumbled on a rug, stooped to straighten it and shake off the accumulated dust.

"That's right," said Nathaniel softly.

"It's a pity. Is it spoiled?"

"No, it won't be spoiled. Look what I have." He had taken a chunky object out of his pocket and was holding it under the candlelight. It was a small gilt bronze horned dragon, its paws splayed aggressively, its mouth open in a defiant baby roar. It was an enchanting piece of sculpting, humorous and brilliant. And a very short time ago Medora had seen it on a table beside the Empress Dowager's throne.

"You stole it!" she gasped.

Nathaniel began to laugh softly.

"Yes, I stole it. Right under the nose of those eunuchs."

"But there was to be no looting, you said."

"I decided I was a fool not to get some rewards. Those yellow devils could pay something back for what we went through, my wife nearly dying, my children beginning to starve, and scared out of their wits, all that bloody fighting I went through. I needed some revenge. Besides I've seldom seen anything I wanted as much as this." He rocked the absurd little creature with its air of infantile ferocity on the palm of his hand. "Isn't it perfect? From the six dynasties, I would guess. About the third century A.D."

"You take what you want, don't you?"

"Yes. I do. My wife must never know, of course. I have something else, as well."

"No!"

He looked with amusement at her appalled face as he held up the long string of dark-coloured beads. No, not beads. Fabulous smoky black pearls.

"The Empress'!" Medora whispered.

"I did a little sleight of hand in her bedroom." With a careless gesture he flung the pearls round her neck.

She fingered them incredulously. "The Empress of China's black pearls!"

"You like that, don't you? It gives you delusions of grandeur."

"Not delusions. This is the real thing. Oh, my! What are you going to do with them?"

"Hide them, in the meantime. My wife would certainly never wear them, even if they had been honestly acquired. She wouldn't look well in them. They're your sort of thing, aren't they?" His voice had gone deeper. "Sultry. Sinister." Medora giggled.

"Me, sultry and sinister!"

"You look it just now." He drew her towards him.

"Mr. Carrington"—her legs were trembling, her breath gone—"you're dangerous."

"Take off your blouse and skirt." His fingers were running up and down her spine, caressing her as a moment ago he had caressed the little dragon. Things he wanted. "What did you shake the rug clean for?" he asked.

Angel had got tired of being down at the goldfish pool. It had become a dull place now that they could wander so much farther afield. She was also tired of Georgie mooning in the willow tree. She shook the branch on which he sat, violently, and, taken unawares, he tumbled to the ground like a ripe apple.

"Why did you do that?" he asked angrily. "I nearly fell on Plum Blossom's grave."

"Because you're being boring. Let's go somewhere. Let's go into the Forbidden City."

"You know we can't do that. The soldiers will stop us."

"Then let's go on the wall."

"We've been on the wall. There's nothing to see now the Boxers have gone."

"Then let's go and see if your father's shop is all right. He'll be pleased if we tell him it is."

"That's too far," said Georgie doubtfully.

"It's only down Legation Street. You're not scared, are you?"

"No, I am not."

"You sound as if you are. This war's made you scared."

"I never were," Georgie said indignantly. "And the war's over."

"Then come *on!*"

Angel was in her most belligerent mood, and it was wise to give in to her. After all the fighting and people killing each other, Georgie thought he would give in for the rest of his life, for the sake of peace.

Nobody stopped them. The soldiers seemed tired after their long march. There were groups of them lounging in the shade of the wall, exhibiting treasures among themselves. One had a gold belt buckle and a pretty Louis XV painted watch, another was trying to stuff a large porcelain bowl into a feed bag. In a few days the city was going to be picked clean of treasures, just as the bodies of horses and worse, dead Chinese, were picked clean by the scavenger dogs. An old Chinese was moving up and down, humbly offering a tray of sticky sweet cakes. He had a thin grey beard and slitted black eyes that held no expression when the soldiers refused his wares. The roofs of the Imperial Palace glowed orange vermilion in the hot sun. There were bad smells and dust and slinking dogs and one fast-moving ghost of a cat. All the paper lanterns and the colourful decorations of a Chinese street had gone. It was funny and creepy, and a long trudge to Papa's shop. Georgie soon regretted the journey. What was there to see, for the whole street was in ruins? Papa's shop couldn't possibly have escaped, and he didn't want to see it a heap of rubble with all the things Papa cared about lost.

Angel, however, was tireless, like that ghost cat, her thin body with its angular shoulders slipping along. It was she who exclaimed suddenly, "Here it is. Look, there's the sign."

"It's all broken down," Georgie said. "I told you it would be."

"Yes, but perhaps there are still some treasures. Look, the trapdoor's open. Let's go down."

"Should we?" Georgie said uneasily. "There might be—"

"Might be what?"

"A dead Boxer."

"You've seen dead Boxers before. I told you you were scared."

"I am not."

Both children were whispering, however. They stepped carefully through the rubble and peered down the square hole leading to the cellar.

"Candles burning!" Georgie hissed. "Someone—" He paused, staring. "Someone's there. It looks like—"

Angel stared, too.

"Miss Deacon!"

"Papa!" Georgie gripped Angel's hand, dragging her back. When he could get his breath again he whispered, "What are they doing?"

Angel's face had narrowed and taken on an infinitely cynical adult look.

"Making a baby."

"A baby!" Georgie said incredulously.

It was Angel's turn to pull him away and onto the road.

"We have to go."

"Why?"

"Grown-ups can get mad."

"About making a baby?"

"About you seeing them do it."

Georgie had completely lost his lethargy. He was extremely embarrassed (Papa without his trousers!) but also intensely curious.

"Angel, how do you know?"

"Know what?"

"That that's what they're doing."

"Because that's how it's done, you ignorant little boy. But don't you dare say a word."

"Why?"

"Because people don't like being told on."

Georgie understood that. He had been brought up not to tell tales. All the same—

"Angel?"

"What is it? Come on, you're so slow."

"Shouldn't it be Mamma that Papa makes a baby with?"

"I expect your papa's gone a bit Chinese and wants several wives."

"I don't actually think Mamma would care for that."

"That's why you're never to tell."

Georgie nodded. He knew he never would tell because Mamma would be deeply hurt if she were only one of several wives. He still felt shocked, but under the shock he felt a curious throb of pleasure and excitement.

"Angel."

"Yes, you silly little boy."

"I did know that's how babies are made."

"Liar! I've seen peasants in the paddy fields. You haven't."

"I just know," said Georgie.

A week later Papa announced two important things. He had found a house for them to move into. It had five courtyards, and there was still furniture in it, beds, sofas, chairs, crockery and kitchen utensils. He had found some good trustworthy Chinese boys to clean it up, and had also managed to acquire a small stock of food, flour, rice, eggs, melons and potatoes. They would move the next day.

The other thing he had to tell them was that Miss Deacon had decided to go away. She wanted to go to Canton. After all she had come to China to see the country, and one couldn't blame her for being weary of Peking. There was an American exporter of Cantonese ware in Canton who would look after her. She would leave Peking as soon as trains were running again.

Rather than have a governess the children could go to the English school. They would find playmates there. They needed more company, especially Lucy, who was far too shy and timid. And now that Lilian had decided to go back to Shansi—oh yes, that was some more news—they would be losing Angel.

Soon after the siege had lifted Lilian had begun to

throw off her listless despair. Her sombre eyes still held visions of horrors, but now she talked and sometimes smiled.

Amelia warmly greeted her return to life.

"You couldn't go on grieving forever, my darling. You're too young and Angel needs you."

"Has she been naughty?"

"Well, just a little. She and Georgie are fine when they're apart, but together they're complete imps. Oh, I'm not complaining. They've helped each other get through this awful time, and they've come to no harm."

"She's a strong-willed child, just like her father. That's why I must see that her energies are directed in the way he would have wished. She'll make a splendid helper in the mission."

"Lilian, she's only eight."

"No one is ever too young to begin, Thomas used to say. He would have expected us to carry on his work. That's why we must go back."

In this new starkly determined mood Lilian was almost as unreachable as she had been in her despair. Amelia, privately relieved that this problem was solving itself, could only say, "Georgie will miss Angel. But I must tell you that he had always expected her to have wings, so now perhaps he can comfort himself that she is growing them."

As for Miss Deacon leaving Canton, no one seemed particularly upset about that. Georgie was intensely disappointed that she didn't have a baby in her arms, and decided that Angel had been telling lies. You had to like someone to make a baby with them, and Papa looked at poor Miss Deacon as if he hated her. Now that they were living in their own house again he never even came to the schoolroom to give them a motto for the day. It was as if he didn't want to be near Miss Deacon. Perhaps it was because she hadn't made the baby for him. She herself had got to be a bit like Aunt Lilian, very quiet and brooding, although occasionally her eyes flared with anger and she said she couldn't wait to go to Canton. She never liked staying long in one place. "I was never meant to teach children, anyway," she said cruelly. "It was only fun for a while."

"Don't you care for us at all?" Henrietta asked.

"Oh, yes, I think you're all sweet. But I'm a terribly restless creature. When I've had an experience"—she shrugged in a worldly-wise way—"I want to move on." She really didn't care about any of them, Georgie decided. No wonder Papa would hardly speak to her, and enquired daily about the progress being made on repairing the railroad.

Many other people wanted to leave Peking. Some had already gone, by Peking cart or mule, preferring the long arduous journey through still dangerous country to staying in the devastated disease-ridden city. But the ones who were staying were determinedly making the best of things. The Congers had moved back to the American legation, finding that it was still habitable, although the dining room had been used as a laundry for the hospital, American marines had been using other rooms for sleeping, and the kitchen had been their mess room. Parts of the building were completely destroyed.

Lady Comerford had accepted Lady MacDonald's invitation to stay on in the British legation, since tragically her own house and all her possessions had been destroyed by fire. She moved to a larger room, and one of her servants came looking for her. This cheered her. God had apparently forgotten her, or he would have taken her during the siege. But Ching Mee with her bland yellow face had a better memory. One must appreciate small blessings.

Colonel Manners, too, continued to take refuge in the legation. Since the fighting had stopped he had discontinued his instructions to his very youthful army—for one thing most of his recruits had dispersed—but had found a use for his services in the hospital where many wounded still lay on the straw mattresses on the floor. The sandbags had been removed from the windows, and the appalling noise had stopped. But there was still a shortage of mosquito nets so the flies remained a torment. The more helpless patients were glad of someone to pull the punkah or brush away the beastly buzzing flies, or just to talk to them. Colonel Manners had a fund of stories about the Opium War which were immensely popular. He was getting back his resilience. If he lived another ten years he would boast also about the part he had played in this minuscule but fierce and bloody war.

Life really was getting back to normal when Sir Claude and Lady MacDonald announced their intention to give a dinner party. They were being recalled to England. It was both their farewell to special friends, and a celebration that the siege was over.

Chapter 17

The table looked remarkably festive considering that supplies of fresh food were still limited. The silver and crystal had been brought out, and there was a centrepiece of chrysanthemums, perfect curling blooms grown as only the Chinese gardeners knew how. Everyone had dressed up, the men in white dinner jackets, the ladies in evening gowns that had survived fire, or being cut up to make sandbags.

Amelia wore her beige lace, her long rope of creamy pearls, her elbow length satin gloves, freshly laundered by Cassidy. She was slowly recovering from the deadly tiredness that had followed her illness, and had put on a little weight, although Cassidy thought her still distressingly thin. None of the women looked her best. The poor diet had left their faces pale, their hair dull. But compared to what they had been a few weeks ago they considered themselves at the peak of beauty. It was so civilised to be dressed for a party and to be exchanging courtesies and small talk again.

Amelia's eyes kept going to Nathaniel, who also had lost weight. His face was gaunt, his fine tall body so sparsely fleshed that his dinner jacket hung loosely. He was not a soldier, and being so suddenly plunged into bloody fighting had left its mark on him. He was irritable, jumpy and barely approachable. But time would take care of this. The horrible experience would fade from all their minds.

There was, however, another small episode that Amelia knew would not fade from her mind, although she would do her utmost to minimise its significance. One night recently someone had tapped at Nathaniel's bedroom door, and when the door failed to open (had he locked it?) there had been the sound of stifled sobbing. Fortunately for Amelia's peace of mind this did not last long. The nocturnal visitor soon went away.

It was the morning after this incident that Nathaniel announced Miss Deacon's intended departure. The girl herself showed no sign of midnight tears. Indeed, she had a hardy aggressive look, as if the proposed change of scene were completely to her liking.

"Green fields and pastures new," she said flippantly. "That's me, Mrs. Carrington." It was Nathaniel then who looked put out, as if Miss Deacon's enthusiasm surprised and affronted him.

Amelia knew the pattern all too well. Nathaniel had been tempted by this strange unpredictable young woman and was sensibly getting her out of his sight. One should be grateful and appreciative for his action, not heartsick because he was so vulnerable. Who could blame a peaceful man, loving and seeking only beautiful things, and plunged into terrible violence, for having private temptations? He would inevitably want to seek escape in healthy passions, and she herself was debilitated from her illness. So Miss Deacon out of the way was the happiest solution.

Indeed, at the dinner party, everyone was looking to the future. The men were talking about the new golf course they were planning, one and a half miles long and with splendid natural hazards. The racecourse grandstand was going to be rebuilt immediately. Nathaniel said that he had found a very promising pony which he intended racing. It was also quiet enough for the children to ride.

"So fortunate all your children survived," Lady Comerford said to Amelia.

"Yes, isn't it? Lucy gave us a fright when she got ill, but luckily she recovered very quickly. I only hope they don't remember those dreadful weeks too vividly."

"They won't do that," Colonel Manners assured her. "They're much too young. I'll make a bet they've practically forgotten the whole thing already. Or what they remember will be the fun, the Boxers' red sashes and the Bannermen's tiger skirts, and the trumpets and all the paraphernalia."

"I'm sure Henrietta will remember not having a bath," Amelia said. "She's an obsessively fastidious child."

"I hear you're losing your governess," Lady Comerford said.

"Miss Deacon? Yes. She seems to be a confirmed wanderer."

"Just as well she's moving on," said Nathaniel. "She's a little too erratic to be a good governess."

"But I'll never forget how good she was to me when I was ill," Amelia said. "She really saved my life. We'll always be in her debt for that, won't we, Nathaniel?"

She hoped no one else noticed the way his face tightened.

"Naturally. I'm seeing that she'll be taken care of in Canton. After that, I hope she'll go back home. She's really too young and irresponsible to be wandering about the world alone."

"A curious personality," Lady Comerford said. "Half angel, half devil, I've always thought."

"Oh, come, she's only a child," said Colonel Manners vigorously. "I didn't see any of the devil in her. Thought she was singularly unattractive. Too thin and long-legged. Like a migrating stork. Without the function of storks, however, I hope."

He laughed loudly at his witticism, and Amelia wondered why her heart gave such an uncomfortable bump. Surely—no, she had never thought of that!

"Well, her good side took care of me," she said gently. "But I never did pretend to understand her."

Nathaniel was behind her, draping the lacy shawl over her shoulders.

"Mustn't get a chill, dearest." His voice was solicitous, his eyes full of an absolute tenderness. "The evenings are drawing in, as we'd say in England. I suppose we'll soon be in for more of those unpleasant sandstorms from the Gobi. I've persuaded Amelia to put up with another winter here. She'll like it when everything gets back to normal."

What was normal? Amelia wondered. Pretending to be unaware of her husband's straying passions? Being humbly glad for this quite genuine care and tenderness? What other way was there? She intended to begin reading Chinese poetry again, and to take lessons in painting on silk although she could never hope to equal the exquisitely fine brushwork of the native artists. She might also learn to speak enough Manchu so that she could understand her servants. The winter would pass.

"There'll be no more receptions in the Imperial Palace," Lady Comerford observed. "We'll have to make our own amusements. I wonder if the Empress will ever dare to show her face in Peking again."

"Oh, she will," came Sir Claude MacDonald's voice.

"We hear she's holding court in Shensi. I predict she'll make a triumphal return in a year or two. But do business while you can, Carrington. Who knows what edicts will be issued in the future? The Chinese will drive the foreigners out in the end."

Nathaniel gave a small private smile. "I'll heed your advice, sir. But I've not done too badly so far."

Late that night, after their return from the MacDonalds' rather sober and sad dinner party (too many faces had been missing, too many graves had been dug), he wrote in his little leather-bound book:

1 green jade Mongolian pony—Ming
1 bronze horned dragon—Six dynasties (as far as I know, only one other like it in existence)
1 string finest black pearls, previously in the possession of the Dowager Empress Tz'u-Hsi

None of the objects entered in this private book was intended for sale. They were to form the nucleus of his own collection which he intended eventually to be the finest in England. He was a man to whom possessions mattered even more than his family, certainly infinitely more than that strange wild young woman with whom he had committed a monumental lunacy. Now that aberration, caused by the heady excitement of the day, had passed, he wanted her out of his sight as soon as possible. Amelia, his children, his possessions—none of these was to be endangered by that very young and amoral adventuress. Even if he had to give in to her extremely unreasonable demand and let her have the Empress' black pearls for her own. She could then, she said, her face taking on its lambent look, imagine she was the great Chinese queen herself, she could fly on dragons, she could hold court and be committed to no one.

She was a little mad, Nathaniel realised uneasily. But she had agreed to go away peaceably as soon as the trains were running again. That should be any day now. The whistle would sound, the smoke would billow over the dun brown landscape, the telegraph wires would hum, the peasants in the fields would turn their inscrutable gaze to the flying monster, accepting at last that it was here to stay. The chilly winter winds would begin to blow, the willows would drop their leaves, the bare trees would be infested with crows, like clusters of grapes, the last camel trains would come in from Mongolia. One might get in another visit to the Great Wall, and the Ming tombs (alas, without young Rupert Fortescue) before the winter really set in.

Nathaniel shook himself out of his dream, sighed, and scratched out the entry, "1 string black pearls previously in the possession of the Dowager Empress Tz'u-Hsi." He supposed giving them to Medora was inevitable. Although he grudged parting with such marvellous treasure, he felt pleased about the gesture. How many men would have been so magnanimous?

Dragon House, England
June, 1975

Chapter 18

Ever since she had returned from Dragon House on Sunday evening Amy had been waiting for the telephone call. Usually possessing a cool intelligence and a single-minded determination to get what she wanted, she found herself confused, nervously apprehensive and in a state of angry frustration. The fury of a woman scorned? Hardly. Hugh Morley wasn't that devastating. But it infuriated her that he should be so much under the influence of his dowdy and naïve wife. He should have been a pushover. He was good-looking, too, and quite amusing. They could have had fun. She felt deprived and rejected, a state of mind she thought she had overcome years ago. Its return made her vindictive and reckless.

She wasn't at all nervous about Bunny's anticipated telephone call. As she had said to Hal (who was remarkably gutless), she refused to be intimidated by that odd little rabbit of a man. That was all he was, a rabbit with dark glasses and a deliberately deep and ominous voice who played at being sinister. Admittedly, he had a lot of useful talent. But she had talent, too. She was of as much value to him as he was to her. So why should she be intimidated?

Nevertheless, when the telephone did ring late at night, startling her out of a light sleep, she had some trouble in keeping her voice laconic.

"Yes, Mr. Beaumont. It is Mr. Beaumont, isn't it?"

"Don't do that again, Miss Russell."

"Do what?" In spite of her determination to remain calm, the gravelly voice sent tingles over her.

"Assume that your caller is me, and use my name."

"But—"

"Supposing it had been your friend, Mr. Hugh Morley. I've been making enquiries about him. He has quite a reputation as a rising young barrister."

"Him!" said Amy scornfully. "Why does it matter if he hears your name?"

"It matters. But I didn't ring you to scold. I'm a kind man. I merely wanted to invite you to tea tomorrow. I hope you can come."

To tea. Where did he live? This was a new intimacy. Hitherto they had met only in the anonymity of the Hôtel Richmonde.

"In Cheyne Walk," he said, as if hearing her thoughts. "I have a very modest flat. About five? Ring the doorbell twice so I'll know who it is."

"You don't like surprises?" Amy was striving for non-chalance.

"Only fools do, don't you agree?"

The telephone clicked. Mr. Bunny Beaumont intended to have the last word, as no doubt he usually did. And Amy was furious with herself for trembling. She had to get up and drink a wine glass of brandy before she got rid of her ridiculous attack of jitters.

She was glad the summons had come so soon. And it was a pity Bunny Beaumont didn't like surprises because he was going to get one. She didn't think he would object to it. She thought he might even call her a clever girl.

The Ching-tê-Chen wine jar, the young man at Sotheby's said, had been sold to a Texan millionaire. The seller's name had appeared in the catalogue as Mr. Vincent Beaumont whose address was the Hôtel Richmonde in Geneva.

"A Swiss bank, of course," Hugh said. "Elementary. Thank you very much."

"I hope there's no fraud—"

"There well may be, but that's nothing to do with your firm. I congratulate your experts on correctly identifying such a valuable umbrella stand."

There had also been another expert involved, Hugh surmised. Someone who had cleverly spotted the jar in Aunt Suzie's house. Someone with more than a passing knowledge of Chinese antiquities.

He had made the visit to Sotheby's in his lunch hour. He had to be back in court in the afternoon. The comparatively dull and undemanding case being heard gave him opportunities to mull over what he had learned. It was Georgina's suggestion, that evening, that they immediately telephone the Hôtel Richmonde and ask to speak to Mr. Vincent Beaumont. Indeed, she was all for flying over and coming face to face with that mysterious gentleman. That, said Hugh, would not only be impetuous but rash. It was perfectly possible that there was more than one Ching-tê-Chen wine jar in existence. Aunt Suzie's may be somewhere else altogether. One couldn't go about making wild accusations of fraud or theft.

"Then why has Aunt Suzie's jar disappeared?" Georgina asked logically. "It's that Amy Russell, I'm certain.

She has a foxy face. And remember, we didn't find the horned dragon either. That's a delectable rarity that is all too easily removable. I don't know, Hugh. I have a feeling a lot of things are going to walk out of Dragon House. The pearls, too."

"We know where they are. If Charles hasn't dredged them up by now. But let's take this a step at a time. We'll try to find out more about Mr. Vincent Beaumont."

The Hôtel Richmonde was helpful, but disappointing. Indeed, Mr. Vincent Beaumont had stayed there. He was a fairly regular visitor. But unfortunately for Mr. Morley he had left several days ago. Ah, his permanent address was not the sort of information the hotel divulged.

"It's in England?"

"Sorry, sir."

"London," Hugh persisted.

"I am not permitted—"

"What a pity." Hugh hazarded a quick guess. "Mr. Beaumont collects Oriental porcelain and I believe he has a piece I'm interested in."

"Then I suggest you contact the Far Eastern Art Galleries, sir. I believe Mr. Beaumont is a customer of theirs."

"In Geneva?"

"A well-known shop. Very long established. It used to have an English owner, James Carrington. I'm sure you must have heard of it if you're a collector."

Hugh put the telephone down, and smacked his palms together.

"What do you know, Georgina! Your grandfather's shop. And I'll bet Amy Russell knows more about the firm of James Carrington than you do. These convenient interior decorating jobs in Geneva. Utter rubbish. She's been keeping out of the way until after the Sotheby sale."

"I told you she was up to something," said Georgina calmly. "What will you do?"

"Go and see her. I think she's quite a little ferret. Don't you?"

"I thought you liked her."

"She intrigued me. I admit it. She intrigues me even more now. But not in the same way."

"What has she got to do with Mr. Vincent Beaumont, I wonder?"

"I suspect he's the master mind."

"Prince Tuan," Georgina murmured.

"What?"

"Aunt Suzie, the Empress Dowager, must have a Prince Tuan plotting against her. Should we tell her?"

"I don't think we should alarm her."

"Aunt Suzie! Alarmed! She'll be delighted. You know how she revels in having enemies."

"Have you talked to her today?"

"Yes, I rang to see how she was. She sounded angry and bored. Said that bossy Nurse Jenkins was keeping her in bed in case of delayed shock. The pugs hadn't had their morning walk and Charles was getting neurotic about his garden. He had spent the morning digging holes with his long-handled trowel and planting things although the weather was much too hot and dry. And Nurse Jenkins moved things to dust them and never put them back in the right place."

"Nurse Jenkins dusting! I thought she'd consider herself above such menial work."

"I expect Aunt Suzie ordered her to. You know how she can't keep housemaids. It really serves her right if she can't find things. I wonder if that's how the little dragon disappeared."

"It'll turn up. But probably not in Dragon House."

"Now, Hugh, you're getting too suspicious."

"I'll certainly be suspicious if one like it comes up in a sale. But we'll have cracked this puzzle before that has time to happen. First priority is to call on Amy."

"Aren't you going to telephone first?"

"No chance. I prefer the element of surprise. But before I go there I thought you and I and Ben might have a meal at Ho Ming's. Ben would like that."

"And get Grandfather's little red book translated?"

"That was my idea."

"Yes," said Georgina slowly. "Let's do that. Hugh?" she added.

"Yes, love?"

"I'm so glad you've decided you don't like Amy after all."

"That happened," Hugh said laconically. "Actually it happened before I suspected she was up to something devious." He pinched Georgina's cheek. "But you wouldn't want me to be a chap who doesn't notice women, would you?"

"Other women," said Georgina. "Yes, I would."

By midday that day the sky had clouded, and it looked as if the drought might be about to break at last. Although the heat lingered, Amy found herself giving intermittent shivers of pure tension. It wasn't only the thought of the tête-à-tête tea she was to have with Bunny Beaumont. It was the surprise she had for him.

She mustn't be intimidated. She mustn't lose her nerve. She must make her demand and stick to it.

She had decided that the hard work and the competitive struggle of being an interior decorator was not for her. The prim Victorian pictures, the chintzes and wallpapers, the button-backed chairs and sofas, were all totally boring. She wanted to get back into the rarefied world of priceless antiques, and this time not as a shop assistant, no matter how knowledgeable, but as owner of her own business. It hadn't seemed possible that this could happen, that she could bid in the great auction rooms in London, New York and Geneva.

After last weekend, she could see the way.

Just after she had set out for Chelsea it began to rain.

The air acquired an instantaneous freshness, smelling of newly washed leaves and grass. A thin chilly breeze sprang up. The long unseasonal drought was over. People's footsteps became brisker, umbrellas appeared. Amy stood at the bus stop, her narrow shoulders hunched, a scarf tied round her head. She had come without raincoat or umbrella. If she went back for them she would be late. She preferred to arrive soaked rather than unpunctual. It was vital that Bunny should be in the best of moods.

The rain, in a strange way, dampened not only her clothing but her exuberance. She felt more apprehension than excitement as she pressed the buzzer outside Bunny's block of flats and waited for the gravelly voice. Would he be annoyed because she had acted individually and excluded Hal from this little coup? Would he demand the lion's share of what he called the spoils of war? If he became nasty would she be able to stand up to him?

Her chin jutted. Of course she would. The blood of martyrs and the wildly foolishly courageous ran in her veins. That was what stood the test.

All the same, as she established her identity and was bidden to come in, her private piece of loot weighed like a rock in her handbag.

Should she have tried to dispose of it without Bunny's help? No, she hadn't a hope. But she must make him promise not to tell Hal who, like a great many of his kind, had a vicious bitchy temper when aroused. He'd do a thing like breaking up her shop. Start a small war of his own.

"Come in, angel. Oh, dear, you're very damp. How disagreeable."

"I know. I'd forgotten it could rain in England."

"It can and it does. The bathroom is through there if you want to tidy yourself. Don't be long. I have tea ready."

The curtains were drawn—permanently, Amy suspected, since Bunny Beaumont was another of Hal's night people. At first she could scarcely see the figure tucked deep in an armchair beside the tea table. But when she came back from the bathroom, her hair smoothed and her face shiny from its towelling, her eyes had become accustomed to the gloom, and she could see the man more clearly than she had ever seen him.

It was because he was not wearing his dark glasses. The eyes revealed were curiously light-coloured and red-rimmed. With his crumpled pink cheeks and white hair he really was ridiculously like a rabbit. One could see where he had got his nickname. It was inevitable. He was an albino.

. He obviously played up to his name with neurotic relish, for he wore a bow tie, a brocade waistcoat buttoned strenuously over his plump stomach, and a checked jacket. He looked quite bizarre, the white rabbit from *Alice in Wonderland*. What was more, the shelf behind his chair held a variety of toy rabbits, some worn and threadbare, some new and fluffy.

"You're looking at my collection, I see," he said in his deep rasping voice. "My friends pander to my whims and give me dear little bunnies for Christmas and birthday presents. There's something very reassuring about soft woollen rabbits, although I know some people prefer teddy bears. No doubt I suffered some kind of trauma when I was very young. I don't remember what it was. But does it matter? I'm not in the least embarrassed about my hobby. Although it's a far cry from Chinese antiquities. I see that thought in your clever eyes. What is your weakness, my angel? Apart from money. Men?"

"I like men," said Amy levelly. "But I wouldn't call them a weakness. I wouldn't allow them to be that."

Hugh, she thought. Pity about Hugh, who could have been fun. He shouldn't have slighted her. She put her handbag on the floor where she could feel it reassuringly against her ankles.

"No? You terrify me. So self-sufficient. Did you inherit that stony little heart?"

"Perhaps. But you know my background, don't you?" Suddenly she was nervous about opening her handbag, and became garrulous. "My mother always said I was my grandmother over again. When she—my grandmother—was only eight she saw her father beheaded by a mad Boxer. It did something traumatic to her, and I guess that was passed on to my mother and then to me. At least, that's what I was always told when I was being a difficult child. And then history was repeated when my parents were caught in China during the people's revolution. And killed, I guess, because I never heard from them again. I was at school in England. From then on I've been mostly alone."

"You're quite a study, aren't you?" said Bunny. "I'd say it was your missionary great-grandfather, the one who was beheaded, who is responsible for your genes. Intolerant. Bible-ranting. Pretending to be God. Didn't they know the damage they did? It's my belief that that small infinitely unimportant war wouldn't have started had it not been for the missionaries."

"It wasn't an unimportant war."

"Not to those who inherited it, no. Like you. Like that old woman living in her house on the Thames with her ill-gotten treasures. The long shadow of the past. Do you like being melodramatic? I do. It's one of my pastimes."

"Don't you want to know what happened at the weekend?" Amy asked edgily.

"Indeed, I do. But shall we have tea before business? Milk or lemon? And do be greedy with the muffins. I always am. I hope our mutual friend Hal had a pleasant weekend. How was the old lady? Amenable?"

"She did promise to go to London this week to sign her new will."

"Oh, splendid. No doubt that means extra pickings

for Hal. But with wills there's many a slip, so our way is better. Quietly and discreetly."

"But I doubt if she'll be going to London now," Amy interrupted.

The light eyes flew open.

"Why not? What happened?"

"She had an accident. She fell in the river, and could easily have drowned. She didn't because I was there."

"You saved her? Quite a heroine, aren't you?"

Amy stared at her host, meeting that strange light gaze levelly.

"I made the branch of the willow tree she was sitting on break and tip her in, and then I saved her."

"Good gracious. You surprise me more and more. Why did you save her? Did you have instant regrets?"

"Oh, I didn't intend to kill her. I only wanted the opportunity of getting something for myself. For myself," she repeated firmly. "And I did."

"So!" said Bunny softly. "You've been getting ideas. I suspected this was a risk I would have to take with you. You're a very enterprising and ambitious young lady. But, having acquired this thing for yourself, why are you telling me?"

"Because I need your help in selling the—the object, the loot."

"You, with your knowledge? I thought you cut your teeth on Chinese ivories."

"This is neither ivories nor porcelain nor jade. Look."

Amy opened her handbag and took out the bulging leather pouch. She tipped it up and spilled the pearls on to the table. They lay in a dark glistening pool. Bunny drew in his breath audibly.

"Black pearls. Once belonging to the throne of China. Am I right?"

"Yes."

"But where has the old devil—I mean, why weren't

they known about? A treasure like this. Why didn't she want to show them off?"

"She did, on her birthday last weekend. She scarcely ever had before."

"A king's ransom," Bunny murmured in a hypnotised voice.

"A queen's," said Amy in her tight voice. "Mine."

Bunny's finger poked among the pearls, a slow thoughtful movement.

"Thunderclouds and lightning," he said. "Smoke and fire."

"They make me poetic, too."

"So you pushed the old lady into the river to get them?"

Amy nodded.

"I knew she was going to be playing this daft game of Boxers, wearing the pearls." She gave a faint giggle. "Everyone thinks they're still buried in the mud. Poor Charles will be fishing for weeks."

Bunny leaned back.

"Does Hal know?"

"No. I told you, these are mine."

"They were not in your contract, my dear. Not a reward like this."

"I'm prepared to give you twenty percent. The rest is mine!"

"And I'm to find a buyer?"

"Why else would I have told you? You'd never have known about them. The old woman only took them out of her bank on Saturday. For the sole purpose of dazzling us. She's a ridiculous vain old monster."

"And I imagine she did dazzle you." Bunny rolled half a dozen pearls in his palm. "Such famous gems. This won't be easy."

"Don't be silly. They can be made into necklets. Earrings. Who's to know they were ever the Empress of China's black pearls?"

"Fortunately. Otherwise some people might be wary of them, thinking them bloodstained."

"Everything in that weird house is bloodstained."

"And what do you think they're worth?" Bunny asked reflectively.

"I don't know. Thirty thousand. Forty thousand."

"More than that if they could be sold as a complete string. But not in driblets. Not by the back door."

"Then how much?"

"What a greedy little girl you are. Perhaps half the sum you mentioned. I know a man in Amsterdam who owes me a favour." Bunny's eyes were on Amy's face, cunningly. "Half and half," he said.

"No, that's not fair. You got the wine jar. These are mine."

"Half and half," said Bunny. "Take it or leave it. Come to think of it, I might have pearl waistcoat buttons made. Rather regal, don't you think? I enjoy feeling regal. Quite like a Prince of the Manchu Empire myself. Come, my dear little girl, don't sulk. You've done splendidly so far. But do remember that this is my operation. Without me you'd have known nothing about it."

"It was Hal who met Mrs. Blenheim," Amy said stubbornly.

"I don't deny it. But dear Hal's brains inside that beautiful head are no larger than a sparrow's. He's thinking purely in terms of T'ang horses, or a nice piece of jade. You and I have the larger vision. You want to be rich. I want to be rich. Have some more tea."

"No, thank you."

"We're forced to trust each other," Bunny went on rumblingly. "I believe I can trust you. But you must go on pleasing me. That's the single most important thing I expect of my friends. Hal knows. Others know."

Facing that white stare, Amy found herself without words. It was silly to feel afraid now that the interview was over, but she was suddenly remembering Hal's words about not underestimating this bland man. All her brave intentions to stand her ground vanished. How could she be so intimidated by Bunny Beaumont who had no blood in his veins, only cotton-wool stuffing, like a toy rabbit?

Yet she was, and she knew she would agree to his terms. In a few days she would obey his summons once more, and go to collect her share of the sale of the pearls. Then she would leave London, disappear, get out of his orbit. She would pray never to see him again.

But it wasn't fair, because now she would never get the jade pony which really was honestly rightfully hers. Her grandmother had told her so. To the end of her life Grandmother had related the story of the hot day in Peking when she and her cousin Georgie had found the beautiful green jade pony, like cool water, in the deserted palace of Prince Su. It had been a bitter grievance that her Uncle Nathaniel had confiscated it and never given it back. Dishonest actions bred dishonest actions, Amy thought, just as wars bred wars. She had no feeling of guilt whatever for planning to get her share of the Carrington fortune.

behave yourself. Don't leave my side. We'll
lk our way past the guards and those damned

Chapter 19

Amy had been expecting a visit from Hal and was surprised that he didn't come until ten o'clock that evening. He seemed excited and restless. He kept prowling about the room picking up and putting down things, muttering, "Junk. Once one's handled the real thing—as you know only too well—"

"Get yourself a drink and sit down," Amy said. Her own nerves had remained uncomfortably stretched ever since her visit to Bunny. "I don't know what you're so uptight about."

"I have a new part. In a twenty-six-episode serial. A whole year's work. Security at last. Isn't that marvellous?"

"So no more visits to Dragon House?" Amy said sharply.

"Thank God, no. I'm settling for the rewards I already have."

"Is that wise? Wouldn't it be better to fade out slowly?"

"When the famous will is signed and revoked and signed again and again. The cliff-hanging drama of it all. The gloating and the power and those revolting fingernails that make me feel physically ill." Hal gave a shudder that was not exaggerated. "The silly old fool thought the will her supreme weapon. I'd like her to know I'm throwing it in her face."

"I thought you hankered for a T'ang horse or two."

"I admit I wouldn't have said no if they'd happened along. But this part coming up has changed my plans. I'm not taking any more risks. You and Bunny will have to carry on without me. You can court poor Charles like mad, can't you?"

"Supposing I don't want to go down there again either?"

"But you're the expert. I was only the guide. Bunny won't allow you out. Not after the triumph of the wine jar. He was cock-a-hoop about that. Did he tell you so?"

"Does he ever?"

"Well, he doesn't have a way with women. I could put it like that. But he's pleased with you and he won't let you go, you know."

"Of course he will. I'm free. I can leave London tomorrow if I want to."

"To do what?"

"Start my own business. Maybe in Paris or Rome."

"And you think Bunny won't stretch out his long paws to scoop you back?"

You must go on pleasing me. Hal knows. Others know. . . . The rumbling voice echoed in her ears.

"Why should he do that?" she asked uneasily.

"Because you're useful to him. I was, too, when I discovered Dragon House and its treasures, and that terrible latter-day queen. But now I've been patted on the head for being a good boy, and told I may be excused. Oh, believe me, while there's still gold in the mine Bunny won't let you escape. Especially"—Hal's summery blue eyes looked admiringly at Amy—"after the coup of the pearls."

"He told you!"

"I saw them. He had them in a dish. Like a sort of monstrous caviare."

"The fool! Why doesn't he hide them?"

"Even super rabbits have weaknesses. Bunny's is that he can't resist gloating."

"He won't show them to anyone else?"

"Who knows? He has some odd friends in the dark burrows of his life. I say, that's good, isn't it? I might begin writing. I've always wanted to. I'm an artist, really, not someone with iron nerves like you. Imagine pushing Her Royal Highness into the river, but cleverly not letting her drown. Didn't you nearly strangle her when you broke the pearls?"

"No," said Amy shortly.

"You were lucky."

The doorbell rang, a long imperative peal demanding an answer.

Amy jumped convulsively. Hal's head shot up.

"Who's that? Are you expecting someone?"

"At eleven o'clock at night?"

Hal stood up, the slightest cringe to his posture.

"Wouldn't be the police?"

"Why should it be?"

"You don't think the old lady has died?"

"Oh, shut up!" As the doorbell rang again, Amy went purposefully through the shop. "Who is it?" she called through the closed door.

"Hugh Morley."

"Oh, for goodness sake!" She tugged irritably at the locks. Was he planning an affair, after all? A kind of warmed-over passion? He had a hope!

"What are you doing here at this time of night?"

"I wondered if you could help Georgina and me clear up a mystery. And no, it can't wait till morning if that's what you're about to say. Oh, I see Hal's here. That's providential."

"Why is it providential? Really, Hugh, you do sound pompous at times."

"Do I? Then this couldn't be a more suitable time for a little pomposity. Or a little truth." Hugh had come into the living room and stood easily against the fireplace, the calm sunlit Victorian scene behind his head.

"Will you have a drink? Something to eat?" Amy was prevaricating, and knew that that showed weakness. She couldn't help it. She was beginning to feel afraid.

"No, thank you. Georgina and Ben and I have just eaten a large Chinese meal."

"Really? Then clearing up this mystery isn't so urgent?"

"Actually Georgina and I were clearing up another part of it. We imagine the whole thing is going to fit together when we've discovered the whereabouts of Mr. Vincent Beaumont."

"Who?" Amy's voice came out, tense and sharp.

Hal said nothing.

"Mr. Vincent Beaumont. The man who disposed of that famous Ching-tê-Chen wine jar, after you had removed it from Aunt Suzie's house, Miss Russell. You don't deny doing that, do you?"

"I honestly don't know what you're talking about."

"Oh, come. I wouldn't have thought such an original girl as you would have to resort to clichés. You know exactly what I'm talking about. You identified the Ching-tê-Chen, replaced it with a cheap, vaguely similar jar, and removed it to Sotheby's via Mr. Vincent Beaumont. I rather urgently want to see that gentleman since he has one hundred thousand pounds that belongs to my wife's family."

"What an *extraordinary* story!" Amy breathed. "Really,

anyone who visits that ridiculous house seems to get more than a bit touched by it. All that yelling and playing war games. It's not far off being a lunatic asylum. Hal, what do you say? Do you know what Hugh is getting at?"

"Not a clue," said Hal. "Actually, as far as I'm concerned, Dragon House and I have said a fond farewell. I've got a marvellous new part, and—"

Hugh interrupted crisply, "And you won't be playing it if you don't tell me about Mr. Vincent Beaumont. Where he is, who he is?"

Hal's face had gone very pale. Coward, thought Amy. But her own skin was beginning to feel damp.

"Now, look here, that's pretty high-handed. If I don't want to talk about Bun—"

Amy's thin body went rigid, as she suppressed a tremor of anger with Hal for his stupidity.

"Bunny," she said. "Hugh doesn't know who you're talking about, Hal."

"On the contrary, I think I do," said Hugh. "I heard you use that name yourself at the weekend. Bun. Mr. Bunny Beaumont?"

"That's it," said Amy carelessly. "Harmless and innocent, isn't it? Not a crook's name. And what is it you propose to do if Hal and I refuse to talk about friends?"

"Begin a police investigation regarding the disappearance of certain valuable objects from Dragon House, and their illegal sale. And don't think I don't know what I'm talking about. I'm a criminal lawyer, remember?"

"One would never doubt it," Amy murmured.

"It's also extremely likely that there'll be a charge of attempted murder."

"Oh, no. I hadn't the faintest intention of killing her," Amy exclaimed, the words flying out of her mouth before she could prevent them. Then she stood silent, in rigid horror at what she had done. But murder! Never murder! She had heard enough about dead bodies and violence all her life.

"Sit down," said Hugh kindly. "Do you want a drink?"

She shook her head. She couldn't meet his eyes or Hal's. It was that word murder. She might be dishonest, but she wasn't a killer.

"I saved her," she whispered.

"And the pearls?" said Hugh. "But never mind the pearls. Georgina and I know about them, and don't particularly want to see them again. I fancy they're extremely unlucky. Now—Mr. Bunny Beaumont?"

It was strange, but Hugh's hostile stare made Amy feel that she was in a trance.

She began to talk fast, with the hint of a whine in her voice. She was what she had never stopped being in spite of her determined façade, the deprived child, the one left out from good fortune, the one always on the outside.

"My grandmother, Angel, was jealous of the Carrington children all her life. Henrietta and Lucy and George. She said they had everything. Handsome parents, loving care, treasure. Whereas the only treasure she had ever had, her Uncle Nathaniel had snatched from her. And she was taken back to the wretched poverty of Shansi, where she had to pretend to be religious because that was what her mother, and her dead father, expected. But she never was, although she married a missionary. She was bitter all her life. My mother inherited her bitterness. She hated China, too, and died there. Killed in another war. And I was always the poorest girl. I simply had to get rich; and I'd do it the way Great-Uncle Nathaniel Carrington had done. By skill and dedication and dishonesty. I really had a flying start because I genuinely love Chinese things. I have a second sense about them, just as Great-Uncle Nathaniel had. They were very pleased with me when they had given me a job in the Far Eastern Art Galleries. They said I was a chip off the old block, my Great-Uncle Nathaniel. That was where Bunny found me," she added.

"Amy, shut up!" Hal implored.

"I can't now," said Amy, beginning to cry. "I can only tell you that it all began with the Boxer Rebellion, when my great-grandfather had his head cut off. That damn war just goes on and on in our family, and I suppose it will until all the ill-gotten loot has disappeared. Bunny Beaumont lives in Cheyne Walk. I've got the number of his flat written down somewhere."

"Amy!" exclaimed Hal, appalled.

Amy stood at her desk, jostling papers. From the back view, she looked thin, hunched, waif-like, eternally deprived, and scarcely more than eight years old. A replica of her grandmother? The figure Aunt Lucy had seen on the stairs?

Hugh didn't know. He told himself that this, too, was probably acting, and he mustn't allow himself to weaken.

He crossed the room and took Amy's arm.

"Have you got the number? Good? We'll all go."

"Not me——" Hal began.

"Oh, yes, you, too. Otherwise I might be obliged to call the police."

Actually, forty-five minutes later, he did have to call the police. From Mr. Bunny Beaumont's flat, using the telephone in Bunny's bizarre blue satin bedroom with the wide bed on which its owner would never lie again.

For that gentleman was tossed across the back of the deep low armchair in the sitting room, his body as limp and flaccid as one of his macabre stuffed rabbits. There were five or six glimmering black globes on the carpet, the pearls that had escaped the thief. The Lalique dish in which Hal had seen them displayed earlier was upside down beneath the table. That was the only sign that Bunny had put up any fight at all.

"He would have been afraid to," Hal said in a suffocating voice. "One or two of his friends were strong—well, sort of sailor types—you know. Out for what they could get. As you said, Mr. Morley"—his lips were so stiff with shock, he could scarcely get the words out—"the Empress' pearls aren't the luckiest gems in the world."

He looked about to faint. Amy, who might have fainted, didn't. She straightened herself and looked three inches taller. She held her head very high as she walked out of the room. Adversity was so familiar, it was like being home again. She would never let it defeat her. She hadn't been made for a soft life, any more than her great-grandfather, Thomas Beddow, had.

Chapter 20

On the drive down to Dragon House on this fine late May morning, the hedges and fields a soft living green after the rain, Ben said, "She was awfully good at playing Boxers."

"Who?" Georgina asked.

"Miss Russell. I wish she'd be there again."

"She won't be," said Hugh. "All your life, old chap, you'll meet people who come and go. It's written, as they say."

"Where's it written? In the little book Ho Ming read to you last night?"

"Some of it."

"Is that why you didn't go to the office today, and why I'm not at school?"

"Partly."

"Is it written in Manchu?"

"Yes, it is. A language your grandfather was familiar with."

"Aunt Suzie isn't. She couldn't read what was written on her banner."

"And there'll be no Boxer games today," Georgina said.

"Oh, Mother, it's such a fine day. I'm sure Aunt Suzie—"

"Aunt Suzie is still recovering from her fall in the river."

"That was that old magician in the willow tree," Ben said fiercely.

"Ben!" Georgina's face was earnest. "There isn't a magician. That's just your imagination. And you're getting too big for make-believe games."

"Aunt Suzie isn't too big for them, and she's far bigger than me."

"Actually, she won't be playing games any more, either. I'm sorry, Ben. But people have to grow up. Aunt Suzie has taken longer than most."

"The children didn't grow up," Ben muttered.

"Henrietta and Lucy and Georgie? But of course they did."

"No, they didn't. They're always children. I hear them."

"Actually he may be right," Hugh murmured to Georgina. "None of them did grow up in a normal way, not even your charming dreamy father. Neither did Angel, apparently. The trauma of the siege must have stayed with them all. Ben's caught something of this. But not to worry." His voice dropped lower. "Today it ends."

Ben leaned back in his seat, letting the soft air through the open window flow over his face. He was thinking of peach blossom and plum blossom, doves cooing and a heron in a lake, and hot sun dazzling his eyelids.

And in my dreams I see
The little ghosts of Maytime waving farewell to me. . . .

Aunt Suzie opened her eyes in the darkened room. In spite of her doze she was still feeling extraordinarily tired. That know-all nurse of Charles' said that that was natural. She was suffering from delayed shock. It would be advisable to keep to her room for another day or so.

But the pugs were whining to go out, and she hated being shut up here alone. She kept thinking she heard shuffling noises, as though someone were searching for something. This was an absurd fancy, and merely a memory of the days when Papa had used to roam about the house checking on his treasures. He had lived here alone, except for a housekeeper and a gardener, during the last years of his life. He must have been very lonely, remembering Mamma with her famous beauty, and the children when they had been young and dependent on him.

In later life, he had become obsessed by his collection probably because it was permanent and unchangeable and a constant comfort to him. Suzie had at last found her way into his good graces when, at the age of twelve or thirteen, she had shown a genuine interest in the beautiful objects. But although Papa had welcomed her company there had always been a reserve in his eyes when he looked at her. It had been because she was a gauche plump schoolgirl. He was still remembering Mamma's affront that they had had such a plain child, such an ugly duckling who was never going to grow into a swan.

Her looks hadn't been her fault. She had developed a deep gnawing bitterness that had never left her although it had found a certain alleviation when, on Papa's death, she had acquired possession of Dragon House and its treasures.

But in her dim bedroom on this warm summery day, she finally admitted to herself that she had never been happy in Dragon House, even during the last thirty years as its mistress and owner. It was haunted for her by small slights and cruelties, Henrietta in her bossy voice telling Lucy to shut the schoolroom door. "We don't want Suzie up here, she's such a baby, she spoils our games." Georgie, with completely innocent perplexity, saying that, with her black hair and eyes she looked like a Chinese devil. She surely didn't belong to their family, did she? And Mamma not denying that remark. Which was the ultimate cruelty.

So if she looked like a Chinese devil why shouldn't she behave like one? She had done so through a turbulent childhood and a painful adolescence. And afterwards, because by then tantrums and tempers and an iron will had become a habit, they went on through her two marriages, and her inauspicious attempt at motherhood.

She had become completely egocentric and domineering. But not happy in this dark haunted house. Still lonely, in spite of her pugs and her wardrobe of heavily embroidered silk and satin robes, and her succession of handsome servile young men, and her fantasies.

No one shut her out now, as Henrietta and Lucy had done in the past. No one challenged her reign. And her son had become her reluctant prisoner so that she was never alone. Yet here she was, perplexed and discontented and weighed down by the past, both remembered and unremembered.

Suffering from shock, Nurse Jenkins said. Yes, that must be what it was.

However, it only required Georgina's telephone call to rejuvenate her. Georgina and Hugh and Ben were driving down to see her. They had something to tell her. What could it be?

No matter. She would rouse herself and put on Ben's favourite robe, the one with the dragon spreading fiery red claws. Ben—even more than Hal—was her favourite person. Hal, when he got his reward, would disappear. She knew that well enough. She was amused and diverted by him, but not fooled. Hence, the reward would be delayed for some time yet. She had changed her mind about going to London to remake her will. The shock of her fall into the river had left niggling doubts.

But Ben was purely innocent. Her eyes held a brief rare tenderness as she thought of him. She knew what she would do. Today she would give him the jade pony.

It was when she was looking for it that she noticed the twin carp, in rare white jade, were not in their usual place on the sofa table in the drawing room. Now where had they been moved to? Goodness, the horned dragon had gone too. What were those stupid servants up to, moving her treasures. They knew the rules. Nothing was to be moved, ever.

Or had there been a thief?

"Charles!" she called, in panic. "Charles!"

Then she remembered that Charles was in his garden, no doubt with the faithful Nurse Jenkins in attendance. So she went hurrying out of the house, a purely Chinese figure in her stiff embroidered robe, with her high-set hair comb bobbing, her slanted eyes narrowed against the bright sunlight.

Her square feet clattered on the steps down to the pergola, and beyond it to Charles' sheltered garden. The pugs snuffled and wheezed behind her. Over the terrace the wind-bells tinkled with a ghostly sound, like a half-remembered dream.

"Mother!" Charles frowned up at her. "Should you be running in this heat?"

"She should not," said Nurse Jenkins. "Whatever is the matter, Mrs. Blenheim?"

"My things are disappearing! The carp, the dragon, goodness knows what else."

Charles scratched at the earth with his long-handled trowel.

"I expect you've just moved them somewhere. Anyway, with the strange people you bring into the house, what can you expect? I sometimes think they ought to be accompanied by a Scotland Yard detective."

"Charles, how dare you!"

"Well, through their antics you've lost your pearls. By the way, I've arranged for a complete search to be made in the river tomorrow. And I wouldn't worry about the other things. I daresay they'll turn up. Aren't you going to admire my garden? Look at the peonies."

Aunt Suzie gave a fleeting sour glance at the lush drooping heads of the red and white peonies. Her eyes fixed on a piece of bare earth.

"What's in there? You said you'd been planting seeds. Why hasn't the rain made them sprout?"

Charles shot a quick glance at Nurse Jenkins, and she, surprisingly, made a strangled sound, like a suppressed hoot of laughter. The impudence of her, Aunt Suzie thought furiously. These two were hand in glove over something.

"What are you both up to? I must say, nurse, you allow your patient to do some strange things."

To her further fury she saw Nurse Jenkins' plump hand come to rest, with a curiously intimate movement, on Charles' shoulder. And he had the indecency to hold it there as if he liked the physical contact. Charles, her eunuch son!

"Mother, Eileen and I have a surprise for you. We're going to be married."

"Eileen? Who's Eileen?" she cried hysterically.

"This is Eileen, Mother. We've been sleeping together for the last three months. I'm not as damaged as I thought I was. I hope that news doesn't disappoint you."

"You're making it up. You're pretending. You're living in a fantasy. Isn't he, nurse? Or are you encouraging him?"

"If you mean, Mother, did Eileen help me to become normal again, yes, she did, and that's why I love her."

"You can't walk!"

"No, I can't walk. And we both know there's no hope of that. But there are compensations. Aren't there, Eileen? One is that we'll be leaving Dragon House as soon as we've found a place of our own."

"And what do you propose living on? Your wife's earnings?"

"Not on you, Mother. That's for certain."

"But I'll be left alone!" Aunt Suzie raged. "I'm an old woman. You might have the patience to wait until I die. I could even promise—"

"Not to change the famous will again! Oh, God, no. Eileen and I don't intend to play that game. We'll manage very well."

Aunt Suzie suddenly put her arm across her eyes. The house, dark and towering behind the trees, seemed to be waiting for her like a prison, its rooms full of half-heard sounds, of ghosts.

She felt dizzy and ill. She sat down on a garden seat, reminding herself that Charles had always told lies. This wishful thinking that he was a normal virile man. It was cruel of Nurse Jenkins to encourage him. What could she give that brash buxom creature to make her go away? One could only bribe an enemy if one couldn't kill him.

Sha, sha, sha, kill, kill, kill. . . .

"Aunt Suzie! Are you asleep?" came Ben's clear voice.

"Are you all right, Aunt Suzie?" said Georgina, bending over her anxiously. "You look awfully pale. Charles, what's wrong with her?"

"She's still suffering from shock," Charles said. "Isn't she, nurse?"

"She should have stayed in her room," said Nurse Jenkins.

"We've just arrived, Aunt Suzie. Hugh, come and help her indoors."

"To give me more shocks?" Aunt Suzie enquired, the strength coming back to her voice.

"I'm afraid so," said Hugh reluctantly. "But after you've had a little brandy."

"I'm perfectly all right," said Aunt Suzie, halfway to the house. "I've only just been told that my son means to marry his nurse. I shall have to bribe the creature to make her go away. What have I got to bribe her with?"

"Nothing," said Hugh.

"What do you mean? With a house full of treasures that no doubt that woman has had her eyes on—"

"But none of them yours, Aunt Suzie."

"Hugh," Georgina said. "Not yet. Get her inside first. Ben, why don't you go and see how Smythe's dragon is getting on."

In the drawing room Aunt Suzie sat squarely on the couch as if she were sitting on the Dragon Throne. She refused brandy, and characteristically went straight to the point.

"When my father died he left his estate equally among his children. I chose to take the Chinese things, the other three preferred cash. They were squeamish about looted treasure, ill-gotten gains, all that nonsense. Their loss proved to be my gain. Not that any of us knew, in 1930, how Oriental art would rise in value, and not that Henrietta or Lucy or your father, Georgina, complained when it did. They were a singularly unmercenary lot. And so was I. I only wanted to enjoy the beauty of the treasures, and the importance of owning them. As I have done all these years. But now, Hugh, you make this extraordinary statement that none of these things are mine."

"I'm afraid that's true, Aunt Suzie. It's a legal point."

"Was I disinherited?" she demanded in a deep, offended voice.

"No, you weren't disinherited. You simply never should have inherited in the first place."

Aunt Suzie's face settled into deep lines.

"Why? Was I so disliked?"

"No, no, it's not that, Aunt Suzie," Georgina said. "But your mother—Amelia—Hugh, you tell her."

"Georgina is trying to say, Aunt Suzie, that you were not Amelia's child. You were illegitimate. And according to the law at the time of your father's death, illegitimate children didn't inherit unless specifically directed. Your father's will simply left his estate to his children, which meant in law Henrietta, Lucy and Georgie."

"Not Suzie!" The outraged cry came from the old lady, as if she were deeply affronted on someone else's behalf, the ghost of the plain graceless child who had always been unwelcome. "Didn't Papa care at all about Suzie?"

"He was probably mistaken about the law," Georgina said soothingly. "I've no doubt he meant you to have your share, and didn't realise your illegitimacy mattered."

"Yet he did make a specific note in the little book in which he recorded his treasures," Hugh said. "He left that in Henrietta's keeping, probably because he thought she would be a wise guardian, and go into the matter if she saw fit."

"Then why didn't she go into the matter?" Aunt Suzie demanded.

"Because it was written in Chinese, and she never bothered to have it translated. She probably thought it unimportant, and only to do with the treasures. Indeed, your birth would have been quite difficult to prove since you were born in Canton where I doubt if records were kept."

"It was entered in the family Bible."

"A long time afterwards, I believe. On your—on Amelia's death."

Aunt Suzie clasped her hands together and sat very still.

"Who was my mother?" she asked at last.

"Can't you guess?"

"No, I can't. Some little tramp my father picked up during the siege? Someone who made him forget to be frightened for an hour or two? A Chinese prostitute from the Willow Lanes?"

"Oh, Aunt Suzie, you're not fair to Grandfather," Georgina exclaimed.

"Fair to him! That ruthless man. Took all he wanted in all directions and never paid, and got away with it, the rogue."

"No, Aunt Suzie." Georgina took one of the clenched hands in her own. "'He suffered in his way. I think he wanted her terribly. Medora Deacon, the children's governess. But I think he might have overcome his feelings if it hadn't been for the stress of the siege. Everyone's nerves must have been in shreds, and his particularly because Amelia had nearly died of typhoid. Medora had nursed her and saved her life. Medora herself was an odd passionate creature, a fly-by-night, living for the moment. Don't you think so, Hugh? I don't think Grandfather stood much chance in the end. She was determined to have him."

"And how do you know that, my clever niece? Have you proof or are you just using the famous intuition of a sensitive woman? Which my own mother obviously wouldn't have possessed."

"She possessed something," said Hugh. "Even if it was just a desire for revenge. I think, in modern terms, she was a schizophrenic. They wouldn't have understood that then. The letter—her letter to your father—is carefully copied into the back of this notebook."

"Let me see!" The long-nailed hands snatched for the book.

"You wouldn't understand it, because your father took the precaution of translating it into Chinese. Georgina and I had it interpreted for us last night. Shall I read it aloud?"

"Please."

"It begins:

"My dear Mr. Carrington,
 Our baby was born seven days ago, here in Canton. She is a girl, and if you don't come and claim her I will have to make a journey into the country and follow the old Chinese custom of leaving her by the roadside, which, as you know, will cause no flurry at all in this barbaric country. I don't know what you will decide to do with her, but do remember that your wife owes her life to me. This may persuade her to be a little forgiving. I will leave the baby's dowry with her. I would like her called Tz'u-Hsi, after the Empress Dowager whom I have always admired enormously. For myself, I have to be free. I just have to. It's my nature."

As Hugh stopped reading, Aunt Suzie nodded twice, slowly. Georgina thought it was in understanding of Medora's insistence on being free. She was that sort of person herself.

Then she asked, "What was the dowry?"

"The black pearls. Your father must have given them to Medora after—afterwards. The other thing was the Empress' ring. That explains the two rings, Lucy's and yours. Your mother must have been at the tea party when all the foreign white ladies received rings."

"Then the pearls at least are mine, if they can be recovered."

"If they can be. But don't build hopes on that."

Aunt Suzie missed the significance in Hugh's voice. She was looking into the distance, her eyes slitted beneath the hooded lids.

"I don't think I want them. I think I only care for the last part of the dowry which my father granted me. The name of an empress." She added, almost flippantly, waving her hands in the direction of the lacquered tables and screens and porcelain vases, "Who do all these things belong to now?"

"Strictly speaking, to your sister Lucy and Georgina," Hugh answered. "But we'll never dispute ownership. When you die Georgina and I have both decided that they must go to a museum. We only must ask you, Aunt Suzie, not to put them as bequests in your will, not to have these greedy dishonest young men hanging around. In other words, not to play power games as the Empress Dowager did, because they are dangerous. You nearly lost your life and someone else has lost his, very unpleasantly."

Aunt Suzie, however, showed no interest in that revelation. She was lost in her own thoughts.

"They should have told me who I was long ago. Long ago. I've been so hurt always. It made me a bitch. Even to my own son. Oh, by the way, I think Charles has planted one or two treasures in his garden. The little horned dragon, perhaps. You see, the habit of looting goes on. But I'd like—I'd prefer you to say nothing. It won't deprive Ben much. I had intended to give him the jade pony today, anyway, and I believe that was all he wanted."

"Aunt Suzie!" Georgina cried emotionally.

"No, Georgina, don't look at me like that. Seventy-four is too late to learn how to cry. Now"—she suddenly stripped off the long turquoise nail protectors—"can someone find me a pair of scissors. I must trim my nails before I go."

"What do you mean?" Hugh asked in surprise. "You don't mean to leave here. This house is yours. You bought it."

"And I no longer want it. I believe I never did. I shall go and live abroad."

"Where?" Georgina asked.

"Somewhere in the sun. I'll begin with Saint-Tropez. I had a pleasant holiday there once. Will someone help me to pack?"

"Now?"

"Why wait? Tell Smythe to get out the car. Hugh, you might find out about flights."

Hugh looked bemused.

"What about accommodation?"

"Oh, I'll just arrive," Aunt Suzie said regally. "Everyone will remember me."

"She's mad," Hugh muttered, as Aunt Suzie went out of the room, her square feet landing firmly on the parquet floor, her head held high.

"She's rather wonderful, Hugh. You must admit it. The other three Carrington children may have been saner, but she's the one with the panache, the all-banners-flying look."

"She's a superb actress. Don't be taken in by her."

All the same, Georgina, and Ben, too, shed tears when, two hours later, Aunt Suzie, erect and regal in the back of the Daimler, drove away from the haunted house, the crooked willow, the flawed dream, to the exile that was never going to end.

It was all over, Ben thought sadly, with a feeling of immense loss. The guns had ceased firing. Now the garden would be quiet.

Here is romantic suspense at its best—in the
beguiling story of a young woman's unexpected legacy and a bewildering impersonation
that threatens her future.

THE HOUSE ON HAY HILL
by Dorothy Eden
X2839 $1.75

One of today's outstanding novelists writes tales about love,
intrigue, wealth, power—and, of course, romance. *THE HOUSE
ON HAY HILL* will keep the reader's dreams intact and keep
the reader turning pages deep into the night.

"Dorothy Eden is a talented storyteller with an engaging style
and a wry sense of humor."—*Minneapolis Tribune*

"When Dorothy Eden brings out a new book, it's news, for she's
an author with incredible talent."—*Novel Reflections*

Fawcett Crest Books
by
DOROTHY EDEN

AN AFTERNOON WALK	Q2739	$1.50
DARKWATER	Q2679	$1.50
THE HOUSE ON HAY HILL	X2839	$1.75
LADY OF MALLOW	Q2796	$1.50
THE MARRIAGE CHEST	2-2032-5	$1.50
MELBURY SQUARE	2-2973-4	$1.75
THE MILLIONAIRE'S DAUGHTER	Q2446	$1.50
NEVER CALL IT LOVING	X2872	$1.75
RAVENSCROFT	2-2998-X	$1.50
THE SHADOW WIFE	Q2802	$1.50
SIEGE IN THE SUN	Q2736	$1.50
SLEEP IN THE WOODS	Q2571	$1.50
SPEAK TO ME OF LOVE	X2735	$1.75
THE VINES OF YARRABEE	X2806	$1.75
WAITING FOR WILLA	P2622	$1.25
WINTERWOOD	Q2619	$1.50